ODDS AGAINST SURVIVAL

For one brief moment Zach thought he would actually make it.

Then he heard the *crack!* of a rifle, saw out of the corner of his eyes the powder flash not twenty paces to his left.

His pony died in midstride. As it collapsed, Zach went flying. He lay stunned, fighting for air. He tried to get up, couldn't. He heard a shout, managed to lift his head. He wanted to see death when it came for him. He had made his bid for freedom and come up short. He wasn't afraid. Again he thought of Morning Sky, of little Jacob. He wondered what day it was. He saw, through a haze, the face of a Blackfoot warrior, features twisted with hate, brandishing a war-club. Zach watched the club descend. An explosion of white pain was the last thing he knew.

It should have been the end—but it wasn't. Instead it was the beginning of the grittiest and greatest battle a mountain man ever waged for his life, pride, honor, and all he loved. . . .

GREEN RIVER RENDEZVOUS

Green River Rendezvous

High Country, Volume 2

by

Jason Manning

A SIGNET BOOK

SIGNET
Published by the Penguin Group
Penguin Books USA Inc., 375 Hudson Street,
New York, New York 10014, U.S.A.
Penguin Books Ltd, 27 Wrights Lane,
London W8 5TZ, England
Penguin Books Australia Ltd, Ringwood,
Victoria, Australia
Penguin Books Canada Ltd, 10 Alcorn Avenue,
Toronto, Ontario, Canada M4V 3B2
Penguin Books (N.Z.) Ltd, 182–190 Wairau Road,
Auckland 10, New Zealand

Penguin Books Ltd, Registered Offices:
Harmondsworth, Middlesex, England

First published by Signet,
an imprint of Dutton Signet,
a division of Penguin Books USA Inc.

First Printing, November, 1993
10 9 8 7 6 5 4 3 2 1

Copyright © Jason Manning, 1993
All rights reserved

Cover art by Robert Hunt

 REGISTERED TRADEMARK—MARCA REGISTRADA

Printed in the United States of America

Chapter 1

The Brigade

I

The black-tail buck broke cover and ventured to the water's edge.

The creek was frozen clear across. Last night's snowfall was white dusting on the blue-sheened glaze of ice. It was iced from bank to bank, but not to the bottom, and the deer knew this. It knew also where to find the thinnest ice—it had come here before, as had other deer. A distinctive trail hidden beneath the snow testified to that.

This trail had brought Zach Hannah within shooting range.

Of course, the trail was covered with snow, but Zach had seen the old scars on the trees along the trail—scars made by bucks rubbing the velvet off their racks. And so he had ventured to remain for hours in the vicinity, hoping for the best. There were no guarantees that a deer would use the trail today.

But game had been scarce all winter in this remote high valley deep in the Wind River Range, and Zach had spent yesterday on a fruitless hunt.

The buck was a fine specimen. Zach could see it clearly from his vantage point, thirty yards downstream and on the opposite bank. He had crossed by means of a log which had been felled last year by beaver and which now formed a natural bridge completely across the stream.

He had selected his spot with care, in a stand of aspen. With his back to the trunk of a young tree, he had shaken the aspen to bring the snow down off the leafless branches. The fallen snow cloaked his broad shoulders and wolfskin headgear. And there he had remained standing for hours, motionless, patient beyond measure. Only the vapor of his exhaled breath in the frosty air betrayed him. It was not betrayal enough to save the buck.

Zach did not move when the black-tail appeared. Had he done so, the deer would have bolted. He knew the buck would check its surroundings before taking a drink. The black-tail looked in Zach's direction but did not see the hunter. The winter world was a world of white and gray and shadings of brown, with the occasional patch of verdure provided by evergreens. Zach's snow-bedecked buckskins were dun-colored. His face was bronzed from exposure to the elements. The fur he wore was timber wolf, gray and white. He blended perfectly with his surroundings. And he did not have a scent that might alert the deer. Before going out on the hunt, he had smoked his clothing in a cedar fire.

Satisfied that no danger lurked nearby, the canny buck pawed at the thin crust of ice where the game trail met the creek. A spur of the bank jutted into the stream here, and on the upper flank of the spur the quickening of the current had kept the ice thinner than elsewhere. The buck's cloven hoof struck the ice once, twice. The creature paused to look around again, in case the sharp click of bone against ice had alerted a predator.

Still Zach had not moved.

The buck continued to strike at the ice until it broke, then dipped its head to drink.

Slowly, Zach raised his rifle.

The rifle was a Hawken. Its barrel was thirty-four inches long, octagonal, and light, at less than nine pounds. The half-stock was curly maple, as was the butt-stock, with a crescent-shaped brass butt-plate. The set-trigger's guard was compact. The barrel sights were low. The percussion lock boasted a peculiar steel basket called a "snail" which enclosed the nipple. The ramrod was hickory, held by brass rings beneath a metal rib. It was a strong yet graceful weapon, this "plains rifle," as folks had taken to calling it, weighing not over twelve pounds total. A .53 caliber, its half-ounce round ball, preferably of Galena lead, motivated by good powder, preferably Dupont, could stop a full-grown bull bison in its tracks.

Zach had done so on several occasions. He respected the power of the Hawken, relied on its accuracy and dependability. There were those who still swore by the flintlock; Zach's good friend, the old leatherstocking Shadmore, was one of them.

"That thar Hawken is a handsome fire-stick, shore nuff." This concession always preceded Shadmore's frequent dissertation comparing the caplock to the flintlock. "But once you run out of caps you are gone beaver, scout. Now, with an ol' Kaintuck rifle like mine, long as you kin find a rock you kin make a flint."

But Zach stuck with the Hawken. While the requirement of a percussion cap might be a legitimate shortcoming, he had never suffered on account of it, and the range and stopping power of the rifle more than made up for it in his mind. He believed the caplock more certain in wet weather and high wind—the latter could blow a flintlock's priming right out of the pan.

He could still remember, vivid as yesterday, the pride and excitement he had felt buying the rifle from the Hawken brothers in St. Louis. That had been seven years ago, just before he signed up with the Rocky Mountain Fur Company and ventured west for the first time, drawn by the mysterious allure of the legendary Shining Mountains.

Much water had passed under the bridge since that day, and to a large degree Zach Hannah was not the same man who had prowled the bustling streets of St. Louis in that summer of 1823. No one back in Copper Creek, Tennessee, would have recognized him now. Probably not even his ol' Uncle Simon, his only kin. Zach had endured much hardship and danger and loneliness, and these things had left indelible marks on him.

In many respects he was a hard man, though not hard-hearted. Never had been, and hoped never to be. For that reason, as he raised the Hawken, slowly and surely, he experienced a twinge of regret at having to take the life of such a splendid creature as that black-tail. The buck was one of God's creations, and Zach had come to feel a bond of kinship which he could not fully explain with every critter in this high country. But he had a job to do, a duty to fulfill—and he took responsibilities seriously. He had a wife and a boy to feed. They relied on him, and he would not fail them.

So he brought rifle to shoulder and drew a bead on the unsuspecting deer. His finger brushed the trigger. For a fleeting moment he thought of Blackfeet. Every white man in the mountains thought of those rascals before he did anything that would give his presence away. The Blackfeet were implacable enemies to every "hair-face" in the country. But Zach did not let this sobering thought deter him. He had seen no Blackfoot sign—or the sign of any other Indian, for that matter—in this valley for months. Besides, it was winter—a fact that reduced (though did not eliminate) the possibility that a Blackfoot war party might be on the rampage.

Regardless of the risks, big or small, he had to shoot.

He squeezed the trigger.

The Hawken kicked against his shoulder. Through white powder-smoke he saw the buck jump sideways. Then, as the sound of the gunshot bounced off the bleak gray peaks looming on all sides, the blacktail fell dead, its neck broken by the bullet.

II

Zach reloaded before moving from the spot. Powder, ball, percussion cap. He worked quickly, and his gray eyes ceaselessly scanned the woods as he did so. When done, he left the aspen and crossed the creek, running surefooted across the log bridge to the other side. In a moment he was kneeling beside the dead buck. As he did so, a sound broke the wintry stillness—the distant howl of a timber wolf. Zach's head snapped up. He listened with bated breath. The sound was not repeated.

The call was genuine. Zach knew it was wolf, and not some sly redskin. There were wolves in the valley. A pack of them. He had seen them on occasion, always at a distance. The winter had to be hard on them. Prey was scarce. Zach did not mind sharing the valley with them. They had never tampered with him or his. In fact, according to his wife, Morning Sky, the wolf was his totem.

Years ago, when, one might say, he and Sky were newlyweds, he had left her—the first time he had been required to do so—on business for the Rocky

Mountain Fur Company. That time, he recalled, had been in the dead of a winter every bit as severe as this one. And on that occasion, mishap had befallen him. His horse had lost its footing on ice and fallen. In the fall, Zach had broken a leg.

On that very day, by everyone's best reckoning, a hundred miles or more from where Zach lay busted up in the snow, a wolf had visited Morning Sky.

She believed it had been a spirit-wolf. In retrospect, she further believed it had come to tell her, in some unspecified spirit-wolf way, that her husband was in danger but would survive to return to her.

Fortunately for Zach, he had not been alone. Sean Michael Devlin had been with him. Devlin, whom he had once called friend, had stuck with him that time. Zach's broken bone had not been their sole misfortune. Caught in a blizzard, they had lost their way. One of their horses had run off. The other had been killed by wolves. Horsemeat had sustained them for days. And when once again starvation was imminent, the wolves had come again, and Devlin had killed one, and, after that, wolf meat had kept them going long enough to reach the company outpost. In Zach's opinion, wolves had saved his life and Devlin's.

There was a spirit here in the high country, thought Zach. If pressed to do so he could not have defined it, but it was there, and it moved through the wolves and the black-tail and all living creatures, as well as through the trees and the rocks and the streams. It moved, too, in Zach's soul. That spirit bound them all together in some inexplicable but, for Zach at least, very profound way. It had been the key to his survival that long-ago winter, and to the spirit-wolf's visit to Morning Sky. It explained many things, even though it could scarcely be explained.

Zach laid a hand on the carcass of the black-tail. His apology was silent—thought, not spoken—and heartfelt. Then he plugged the bullet hole with mud; he would leave no blood trail. Leaning the Hawken against a tree, he bent and picked the black-tail up, draping the carcass over a shoulder. He retrieved his rifle and left the creek.

A half-mile from the site of the kill he stopped, lowered the buck to the ground, and prepared to butcher it out. The job was better done before the carcass froze clean through, which would not take long. But it was work he did not care to do at the kill-site. One reason was the off-chance that there might indeed be hostiles in the valley. If so, they would be drawn to the site by the gunshot, like beaver drawn by the scent of castoreum. Another reason was that he did not want to drive other game away from the watering place. Dressing out the buck on the spot would leave a spoor from which other animals would shy.

Zach carried a length of braided rawhide; this he tied around the buck's back legs, and he threw the other end over the stout, low-hanging branch of a tree. In a moment the buck was strung up. He worked swiftly, and with skill. One quick slash of a keen-edged hunting knife opened up the black-tail's jugular. The carcass was cooling, but the blood had not yet coagulated. After the buck had been bled, he eviscerated the animal, removing the internal organs as well as the leg glands, which would taint the meat. Heart, liver, and kidneys he retained. Bladder, intestines, and glands he discarded. Wiping the knife clean, he began to dress the black-tail out.

He first skinned the buck from throat to rump, taking the hide off completely and laying it out on the ground. At the second rib, he cut through the backbone on each side, using his hatchet now. He left nothing. Brisket, loin, rump, shoulder, shank, and all the other cuts he deposited on the skin. This done, he let the carcass down and used the rawhide to tie the skin up in a compact bundle, hair side out. In this way he carried the meat and was on his way within the half-hour.

He stuck close to the creek, heading downstream. The brigade's winter camp had been of his choosing, and he had chosen well. The site was on a high, rocky bench, on the southern flank of a mountain, and so sheltered as much as possible from the harsh blast of the blue norther, and close enough to the creek so that fetching water—or ice that could be melted—would not be a difficult enterprise.

Choosing the site for winter camp was Zach's responsibility. He was the brigade's booshway. The others had selected him to lead them by a unanimous vote. Though only Jubal Wilkes was younger than he, Zach Hannah was already something of a legend among the mountain men. He had lived alone in the mountains for years, and he knew the high country better than most white men. In the three seasons he had served as booshway he had never led the brigade astray. He had unfailingly guided them to prime beaver country every season. He had been instrumental in the brigade's enviable success in eluding the predatory Blackfeet. Not many trapping brigades could say the same.

They all relied on him—Fletcher, Montez, Wilkes, Baptiste, the Scotsman MacGregor, even Shadmore, who had taken it upon himself to teach Zach the fundamentals of survival on the western frontier back in '23. It was a case now of the student having surpassed the teacher. That didn't bother Shadmore. He was proud of Zach. As far as Shad was concerned, Zach was as close to the son he had never had as was likely to come down the pike.

Zach had chosen this remote valley because in his wanderings he had seldom seen Indian sign within its borders. Last year had witnessed severe Blackfoot depredations from the Absarokas to the Great Basin. At the previous summer's rendezvous, most of the brigades had brought news of Indian mayhem. A dozen mountain men affiliated with the Rocky Mountain Fur Company had "gone under"; their topknots now decorated Blackfoot shield or scalp-pole.

But Zach Hannah's brigade had not been with the Blackfoot plague all last season. It was a fine record, and Zach wanted to get through the winter at least with that record intact.

So it was with chagrin that, on his way back to the

winter camp, he came across entirely unexpected Blackfoot sign.

III

The winter camp consisted of four "half-faced" cabins—chinked logs on three sides and the fourth side draped with buckskin or buffalo hide. Every cabin sported a fireplace on the back wall, constructed of what Baptiste called *bousillage:* mud, twigs, shale, and small stones, which hardened into a substance as fireproof and durable, said the Spaniard Montez, as adobe. The cabin roofing was split logs laid side by side, atop which was placed a thick layer of sod.

The half-faced cabins were cramped but provided good shelter from wind and snow and sleet. Shadmore and Wilkes shared one. Fletcher, Montez, and MacGregor shared another. Baptiste rated one of his own, because two summers ago he had squawed up with a Shoshone woman he called his little *fleur-de-lis,* whom everyone else referred to as Flower. Zach, Morning Sky, and their three-year-old son, Jacob, occupied the fourth cabin.

The horses were kept in a pole corral, nestled against a rock face with an overhang which provided the animals with some protection from the elements. But all their mounts were sturdy stock, mountain mustangs, shaggy now with their winter coats. No thoroughbreds in the cavallard, that was true

enough. But the mustang was durable—a character-
istic which mitigated against its appearance and its
unruly disposition.

When Zach arrived in camp, he found Baptiste
and MacGregor and Shadmore around an outside
cookfire made with the smokeless wood of the quaking aspen. Flower was tending to dough-cakes cooking on hot flat stones around the fire. The cakes
were made from camas-root flour. Combined with
her jam made from wild currants or huckleberries,
depending on what was available, the cakes were
considered a treat by every member of the brigade.

Flower was broad of beam and moon-faced.
Though a notorious scold, she was brave and strong
and resilient, and devoted to Baptiste. The burly
French-Canadian pretended he could take her or
leave her, but this facade fooled no one, especially
not Flower. When he was gruff, she ignored him.
She knew a man had to act like he was independent
for the benefit of his friends, and for his own benefit, sometimes. This was particularly true of a mountain man. No hivernan worth his salt wanted to be
known as a feller tied down to his squaw. Oh, he
decked her out with fofarraw purchased with hairy
bank notes at the annual rendezvous, and treated her
in a decent Christian manner most of the time, but
he wasn't supposed to depend on her, because a
mountain man didn't depend on anybody. He was
entirely self-sufficient, his own boss. It was all right
for Baptiste to like having Flower around to warm his

blankets and mend his garments, but he wasn't supposed to need her in an emotional sense.

Of course, Baptiste was emotionally attached to his Shoshone squaw, and the other men knew it, and they joshed him about it in a good-natured way—all except Zach. In fact, Zach rarely joshed about anything these days.

After three years with the brigade, Zach was still standoffish. That observation was foremost in Shadmore's mind as he watched Zach come into camp. The grizzled old leatherstocking was puffing on a pipe with a reed stem, its clay bowl filled with tobacco cut with willow bark, diced up fine. Honest-to-God tobacco was a precious commodity in the mountains, and it would be at next summer's rendezvous in the Green River valley before more could be obtained, so Shadmore blended his diminishing supply with willow. Puffing on this heady mixture, he noted that Zach's expression seemed even more stern than usual.

It bothered Shadmore that Zach was so remote. He hadn't been that way when first they had met, back in '23, on a Rocky Mountain Fur Company keelboat heading up the Old Miss from St. Louis. Zach had been a kid then, eager to learn, wide-eyed and bushy-tailed about everything, as full up with energy as a cat in a room filled with rocking chairs.

But then Zach had made the acquaintance of Morning Sky, and women, in Shadmore's studied opinion, were bad medicine. Not that they didn't have their uses. And certainly not that Morning Sky wasn't a pure-dee punkin'. Shadmore liked the dickens out of her. But the fact of the matter was this: Women played havoc with a man's peace of mind. And Morning Sky had been the catalyst of the big change in Zach Hannah—a change which Shadmore did not believe was for the best.

Because the day Coyote—Sean Michael Devlin—had made off with Sky, the cheerful, enthusiastic boy in Zach Hannah perished. Sure, it hadn't been Sky's fault. Devlin had deceived her, had told her he was taking her to her beloved Zach. In truth, he had taken her for himself. Stolen her. But there had been no way for Zach to know the truth of it at the time. He had built his whole world around Sky—like Baptiste was doing with his Shoshone squaw—and when it appeared that Sky had left him on her own free will and accord, Zach's world had shattered like thin ice. He had gone off into the mountains alone, embittered, forsaking all further contact with other humans.

Shadmore had never expected to see Zach Hannah again after that dark day. To say that running across him again, years later, had been a pleasant surprise was classic understatement.

Zach had saved Shadmore and the brigade from a Blackfoot death trap, and he'd stuck with them ever since. Reluctantly, at first. Later, they had found Morning Sky. Learning the truth behind her disappearance, Zach had taken her back. He had even taken in Devlin's child, little Jacob, without a negative word about it. As far as the boy was concerned,

Zach Hannah was his father. Jacob did not know any better, and that was the way Zach intended to keep it. Shadmore reckoned Zach would kill anybody who was foolish enough to say otherwise.

But in spite of all this reuniting—in spite of the fact that for all intents and purposes Zach's world had been put back together again, piece by piece, the experiences had changed him, and he kept his distance. Not so much physically, though he did spend a lot of time off on his own, scouting and hunting and such, but emotionally. He was closer to Shadmore than the others. But it was like he was afraid to get too close to people, for fear they would betray him. At least, that was the way Shadmore saw it. As a consequence, the others in the brigade respected, even admired, him. But they were not his friends, and that state of affairs was Zach's doing, not theirs. One might even venture to say it was Zach's preference.

He was closest of all to Sky and the boy, and it was to the half-faced cabin where he expected them to be that Zach headed, with only a civil nod at Flower and the three mountain men congregated around the open fire.

"What'd you find out thar, hoss?" queried Shadmore.

"Black-tail," replied Zach, walking on.

"Sumpin' else, I warrant," said the old leatherstocking.

Zach Hannah stopped and turned. He looked impassively at Shadmore. Then at MacGregor and

Baptiste. They were watching him like a trio of hawks.

"Blackfoot sign," he said, with no more emotion than if he had been commenting on the weather.

It was all he offered, and he continued on his way.

At the word "Blackfoot," MacGregor and Baptiste stood up quick, grabbing rifles that were never far from them. It was a reaction as involuntary as sneezing.

"Smooth down yore hackles," said Shadmore, chuckling. He alone of the three had not moved. Had not so much as twitched. "Iffen them rascals war in the neighborhood he would've tole us so."

"That Zach, he is a cold one," said Baptiste, and it wasn't meant to be a compliment.

"Aye," agreed the Scotsman, "but there's no better booshway, in my book."

"Go find the Spaniard," Shadmore told MacGregor. "I reckon most of us will be on the trail purty soon."

MacGregor left the fire to do Shadmore's bidding, and the old mountain man watched him go with a keen, appraising eye.

The Scotsman had been with the brigade for several seasons now, and had never done anything to warrant less than full acceptance by the others—all of whom had been together for much longer than that. But MacGregor had been an employee of the Rocky Mountain Fur Company's old rival, the Hudson Bay Company, before joining the brigade.

In Shadmore's opinion, MacGregor was a strange

bird. He wore a kilt over his leggins, for one thing. For another, he liked to play his bagpipes, which Shadmore compared, in a highly unfavorable light, to the screeching of a hundred riled-up squaws mingled with the squawking of a thousand carrion crows. But, apart from appearance and habit which Shadmore found curious and annoying, MacGregor had betrayed the Hudson Bay Company on account of Morning Sky. Because of this, Shadmore wasn't too sure about the man. He wasn't convinced that MacGregor was wholly reliable, and he acknowledged to himself that he probably never would be, even if the Scotsman never did anything to warrant such suspicion. Fact remained, what a man did once he could do again, and MacGregor was still in love with Morning Sky.

It had happened this way: After stealing Morning Sky away, Devlin had fled north to Blackfoot country. For most white men that would have been foolishness tantamount to suicide, but Devlin—Coyote, as Shadmore preferred to call him—had killed a Crow warrior named Rides A Dark Horse, an act which had endeared him to the Blackfeet, who hated the Crows something fierce.

The Hudson Bay Company had been doing business with the Blackfeet for years, trading them guns and ammunition, among other things, in exchange for furs, and MacGregor had run a trading post north of the Missouri, as the Hudson Bay's representative with that tribe. He had hobnobbed with the Blackfeet, in other words, giving them weapons with which they had killed other white men, and some of those dead men had been Shadmore's acquaintances. So that was one mark against MacGregor in Shadmore's book, and accounted as well for the reserve of others in the brigade. Ironically, Zach alone did not seem to care what MacGregor had done in the past.

MacGregor had taken Sean "Coyote" Devlin in as a partner in his trading venture, but in time had fallen out with Devlin, while falling in love with Morning Sky. When Devlin had discovered that Sky was carrying his child, he had become irate and abusive. So said MacGregor, and Shadmore figured that was pretty close to the truth of the matter, considering what he knew about Devlin's character—or lack of it. So MacGregor had quit the Hudson Bay Company and slipped away with Sky. He further claimed to have consigned a great many rifles, the property of the Hudson Bay Company, to the bottom of the Missouri River, declaring that the trade with the rampaging Blackfeet had always bothered his conscience. That part of the story Shadmore wasn't certain he could buy.

Now, Sky had told MacGregor from the first that her heart belonged to a man named Zach Hannah, and the Scotsman had agreed to help her find her true husband. Sacrificing his own happiness for the happiness of the woman he loved was a fine and noble act, surely. This part of the story Shad had acquired from Sky herself, rather than from MacGregor. Shadmore was the first to admit of his skeptical nature, and he was dubious of MacGregor and the man's ulterior motives, but Sky seemed convinced he was a genuine friend.

Finding Sky and MacGregor gone, Devlin had taken off in pursuit and met up with a Blackfoot war party. But a man named Eli Simpson had caught up with Sky and the Scotsman first.

Simpson had been a Rocky Mountain Fur Company man. One day, while out trapping with Devlin and a feller named Cooper, Eli had run afoul of a grizzly bear, which had maimed him badly. Devlin and Cooper had left him for dead, a cowardly act that violated the code of the mountain man. Precious few were the laws by which a mountain man consented to live, but sticking by his partner through thick and thin, even if it spelled certain death, was one of them.

Somehow, against all odds, Eli had survived. But the experience had changed him—entirely for the worse. He had become consumed by revenge, obsessed with finding Devlin and Cooper and making them pay for abandoning him in the wilderness. Cooper had paid his price—a terrible death down in Arapaho country, and then Simpson had set out to track Coyote down.

Finding Morning Sky, whom he knew to associate with Devlin, Simpson had taken her away from MacGregor by force, leaving the Scotsman for dead. By then, Zach and Shadmore and the rest of the brigade had been on Eli's trail, because the crazy ol' sonuvabitch had killed one of their own—a trapper named Cleeson—when he had tried to get information regarding Devlin's whereabouts.

MacGregor had recovered. Shadmore considered that a certified miracle, because the Scotsman's head had been bashed in. He had lingered at death's door for days and taken quite a while longer than that to recover fully, but recover he had, and Zach had taken him into the brigade with no questions asked. Zach knew how he felt about Morning Sky, and how Sky counted MacGregor a good friend, but he had never appeared the least bit jealous, which was surprising, thought Shadmore, considering what had happened before. For his part, MacGregor had never said a bad word about Zach and seemed grateful to Hannah for taking him in, but Shadmore firmly believed the whole business had all the ingredients for big trouble somewhere down the line.

So Zach had been reunited with Sky, and Simpson had died at the hands of the Blackfeet, and Devlin—well, nobody knew for sure what had become of Coyote. He had simply vanished. Shadmore could only hope he had met a bad end, but he had a feeling the man would turn up again at the worst possible moment.

The end result of it all was that MacGregor worried Shadmore. Maybe because the Scotsman was a daily living reminder of a past that still persisted in coloring the lives of the two people Shad held dearest: Zach Hannah and Morning Sky. Devlin and little Jacob and the Scotsman were all threads in a tapestry of tragedy which had changed Zach, and

Shadmore had a hunch the final act of that tragedy had not yet been played.

IV

When Zach approached the half-faced cabin he shared with his wife and son, Morning Sky came running out to greet him. He smiled at the sight of her. She was a vision, true enough. Childbearing had not robbed her of one ounce of beauty or vitality. She was just as she had been when first he had laid eyes on her. No, maybe even prettier. Like wine, she seemed to improve with age. Whatever her secret was, she was the only person who walked the earth possessed of the ability to bring a genuine smile of pleasure on his lips.

Morning Sky's father had been a French-Canadian. As a result, she was not as dark of complexion as full-blooded Indians, and her features were more aquiline. Whereas most other Indian women tended to have rather coarse, copper-hued skin, Sky's was honey-and-cream. Her eyes were a deep, spectacular violet-blue. She was tall and willowy, and her black hair shone like polished obsidian—so black that it had blue highlights when the sun struck it just right. She and Flower were as different as day and night in appearance. In attitude there were differences, as well. While Flower could be a strident nag when she wished to be, Sky never lost her temper, with Zach or anyone else, never raised her voice, and never belabored a point. She never had to with Zach; he was always attentive, always sensitive to her feelings.

She threw herself into his arms, and he dropped his burden of black-tail and embraced her. She always greeted him like this, whether he was gone for an hour or for a week. He speculated that it had something to do with the long separation they had endured. In the years that she had spent, reluctantly, with Devlin, not knowing where or how to find Zach and thinking that Zach would not want her back anyway. Those same years Zach had spent in self-imposed exile from the human race up in these lonesome mountains. Because of all that had occurred, she did not take his presence, or their present happiness, for granted.

They kissed. It was a lingering, passionate kiss. His passion for her never seemed to diminish, and he knew it never would. He loved her as he loved the high country, with equal intensity. Once she had been his whole world. Nothing else had mattered. Now, though, she had to share his love with the mountains. That was the way it had to be. Zach had learned that in human relationships, nothing lasted forever. Tomorrow could see it gone. That it would end someday was as certain as the fact that the mountains would stand forever. Because this was so, he could not allow her to become his whole world again, not this go-round. He knew a man could invest in happiness by giving his love to a woman, but in so doing he agreed to pay a terrible price in the long run. A price paid in grief. On the other hand, when a man loved the high country he could love it with a whole heart, without reservation, because it would always be there.

Oddly enough, this did not diminish his love for Morning Sky. If anything, it intensified it. Like her, he lived day to day, taking nothing about the situation for granted.

At length he said, "There are Blackfeet in the valley."

The news made her afraid. Not for herself. Though half-Blackfoot, she could expect only death from them. She had been captured by the Absaroka Crows as a child; she had been raised by these enemies of the Blackfeet. She had married a Crow warrior, Tall Wolf, and though she had not borne him children before his untimely death, that would make no difference to a Blackfoot executioner. Now she was the woman of one of the mountain men—a man the Blackfeet feared and respected and hated all at the same time. For all these reasons she was persona non grata as far as the Blackfeet were concerned.

But Morning Sky was the not the kind who worried about her own well-being. She was concerned only for her child, and Zach. Her husband's scalp was greatly sought after by the Blackfeet. He had outfoxed them time and again, having been forced to kill a half-dozen of their finest warriors. Morning Sky could only hope that Zach would find a way to outfox them again.

Still, she could not help but worry. She had lost

him once. And if she lost him again, she would die inside and never love again or take another man. This she had resolved. But she could not die, though she might wish to, because of Jacob. She would live for her son.

"War party?" she asked.

"No." Zach looked positively grim, and that only intensified her anxiety. "That's the puzzlement, Sky. There are women. A couple of travois. What are they doing on the trail in the dead of winter? They should have been settled down into a nice cozy winter camp long ago. I don't understand it."

She nodded. It was strange. And it was small comfort that it wasn't a war party. The Blackfeet would still fight, even if they weren't on the warpath looking for trouble. They would still try to take white scalps if they learned of the brigade's presence in the valley.

"What will you do?" she asked.

"I hope they're just passin' through. But we have to make sure."

"And if they are not?"

Zach shrugged. If the Blackfeet decided to settle in this valley, then before winter was out there would be a fight. It would be better to get it over with now. But there were a couple of problems with that, too. One, the brigade was outnumbered. Two, there were women and, by his reckoning, at least two children with the band—this much a study of the tracks had told him. Zach did not cotton to the idea of making war on women and children. Blackfoot women would fight—a few, he had heard, had become full-fledged warriors and were celebrated for their ferocity and daring. Still, a woman was a woman.

Morning Sky glanced at the skin full of venison. "You fired a shot," she said.

Zach smiled. "You're as smart as you are pretty."

She blushed, pleased. His compliments still had that effect on her.

"Don't know if they heard it or not," he admitted. " 'Course, I didn't come across their sign until after. Bad luck."

He hadn't mentioned this to Shadmore or the others, and he was a little disappointed that they hadn't figured it out for themselves, first thing, seeing him come into camp with the deer meat. They would, in time. But he was right proud of Sky for having done so.

"Where is little Jacob?" he asked.

"He went down to the creek with Montez, to get some ice."

Zach nodded. For water, they had to resort to chopping out chunks of ice and melting them in a pan over a fire. Jacob was not permitted to leave the camp on his own, but he was an inquisitive and energetic child, and it was virtually impossible to keep him bottled up. Too much could befall a youngster, even one as dauntless and precocious as little Jacob, in a high country winter, so the only recourse was to assign someone as his guardian.

Montez was the perfect choice.

Next to Zach and Sky, the Spaniard was little Jacob's favorite adult in the whole world. This had surprised Zach at first. Montez was a rather grim and taciturn character. His scarred and swarthy visage always wore a scowl—except when Jacob was around. The boy seemed to bring out something in Montez that nobody and nothing else could, something cheerful and animated and full of life. Zach had heard that young children were infallible judges of human nature; if this was so, Jacob had discerned hidden virtues in the Spaniard which no one else had seen.

Zach knew next to nothing about Montez's past. Nobody did. The man didn't talk about himself, or what he had done in his life, or even where he came from. But Zach and Sky had learned to trust Montez to look after Jacob. The Spaniard would die before letting anything happen to the boy.

"I must go," said Zach.

"I know."

"Montez will stay here."

She merely nodded, trying to put on a brave face.

"When Fletch and young Wilkes get back, tell them what happened. Tell them I said they should stay here and guard the camp."

"I will tell them. But they will want to follow you when they learn what has happened."

Zach smiled faintly. "Neither one wants to miss a good fight."

He caught a glimpse of anxiety flitting across Sky's features, and put a comforting arm around her shoulders.

"I don't expect there will be one," he added.

She smiled back at him—a feeble attempt to fool him into thinking his words had reassured her. But he could see that they had not.

Shadmore and Baptiste were walking over. They were ready for the trail. Harvesting a quick kiss from Sky, Zach went to meet them.

"Sent the Scotsman out to fetch Montez," Shadmore told him. "Shore wish Fletch and Jubal was back from huntin'. Hope they don't run into them red rascals."

"Nous avons eu bonne chance," said Baptiste. "But no one can be lucky forever." The French-Canadian punctuated his pessimistic observation with a very Gallic shrug.

"More'n luck's kept us clear of them Blackfoot all this time," declared Shadmore, as always unswervingly loyal to Zach Hannah.

"Well," said Zach, "with any luck at all, they'll just pass right on through."

Yet for some reason he didn't think it would be that easy.

V

Zach led his "moccasin posse" to the place where he had first discovered the sign of the Blackfeet, about two miles due west of the winter camp. The tracks were easy to read in the snow.

"Leastways they ain't headin' straight fer camp," said Shadmore.

"At least they weren't when they passed this way," said MacGregor.

The Scotsman had been the first among the trappers to comprehend the significance of the sequence of events—Zach's shot which had killed the blacktail and his subsequent discovery of the Indian trail.

"The flamin' scoundrels might've turned back," he added.

Shadmore knelt to take a closer look at the tracks. Blackfoot, of course—just like Zach had said. Every tribe made its moccasins a little differently. Sometimes the differences were unappreciable, but reading Indian sign had been one of the first frontier lessons Shadmore had taught Zach, and Zach had learned it well.

The Blackfoot moccasin could scarcely be distinguished from the Flathead. Both sewed their footwear on the right side of the sole, as opposed to the Crows, who made their moccasins of one piece sewn at the heel, or the Gros Ventres of the Prairie, who sewed on an extra rawhide sole. The Blackfeet adorned their moccasins with an anklet and a long tongue. Often the anklets were of colored cloth. Blue or red cloth, edged with beads or dyed horsehair, usually decorated the tongue. Three prongs of beads or horsehair woven into the hide ran from the top of the tongue fanning out to the toe. These three prongs represented the three tribal clans: the Blackfeet, the Bloods, and the Piegans. In the deep snow

it was easy for men well versed in such studies to realize that these moccasins were not only sewn on the
right side of the sole but also adorned with anklets
and bead-decorated tongues. All four trappers knew
that a Flathead moccasin was singularly plain—
devoid of any decoration whatsoever, in keeping with
the very sober and practical nature of that tribe.

Zach, too, paid close attention to the tracks. While
he and Shadmore studied the ground, moving back
and forth along the Blackfoot trail for about thirty
paces, being careful not to disturb the sign, the other
mountain men waited and scanned the surrounding
forest. It wasn't that they weren't accomplished
trackers in their own right. But they were willing to
leave it to two of the best in the business, while
keeping a wary eye peeled for Indian ambuscade.

For his part, Zach had made a rough estimate of
the size of the Blackfoot party earlier that morning,
but moved by a sense of urgency to warn the brigade
of the hostile presence in the valley, he had not
spent all the time he would have liked studying the
sign on the first go-round.

Now, he put all his hard-earned experience and
powers of keen observation to the task. To the eye of
an amateur the trail was nothing more than churned
snow—the passage of horses and several travois as
well as the Indians seemingly made the "message"
the tracks might have conveyed impossibly garbled.
But after ten minutes of study, Zach and Shadmore
came together to consult.

"Twenty-five on foot, by my reckonin'," said

Shadmore. "Seven horses, and four of 'em mounted. T'other three are pullin' travois."

Zach nodded. "Seventeen braves, seven women on foot. Of the four ridden horses, three carry children. One carries a woman. She is either ailin' or hurt. One of the travois carries a wounded man. He still bleeds now and again. The rough trail keeps opening up his wound, I reckon. Won't last long. One of the women afoot carries an infant on her back. The horses are in a bad way. Weak, underfed. It's been a long trail, with little rest for them. With only two travois for their possibles, the band is mighty poor. If they had a winter camp, they left it in a big hurry, and most all they possessed was abandoned in their haste."

Shadmore's eyes were bright with pride. He had not read half of what Zach had derived from a careful examination of the trail. Some of it Shadmore could scarcely believe a man could garner from ordinary sign, but he did not question Zach's deductions. He knew they would be close to the mark, no matter how extraordinary it all seemed.

"So what d'you reckon they're doin' out hyar this time of year?" asked the old leatherstocking.

Zach shrugged. "They're in a desperate way, that's certain. But I'd be guessin' if I said more."

"Don't let me stop you. Go ahead and guess."

Zach's narrowed gray eyes ceaselessly scanned the forest as he spoke.

"I figure they wintered over in Gros Ventre country, south of here. The Big Bellies and the Blackfoot have been revivin' an old friendship the past three, four years, ever since the Big Bellies got thrown out of their southern stomping grounds by the Arapahoes. But this bunch got into a scrape, maybe with their Gros Ventre cousins."

"Yeah," said Shadmore. "A family squabble. Wouldn't surprise me one bit. Injuns quarrel over the silliest things. The Absaroka Crows split with the Gros Ventres generations ago in a dustup over who got the choice cut of a fresh-killed buffalo. The two tribes still won't have nothin' to do one with the other."

"So this bunch might be trying to work its way back to their own country, or at least put some ground between themselves and the Big Bellies before settlin' down to wait out the winter. But they'll have a hard time of it. They left most if not all of their skin lodges behind."

"One thing's sartin . . . they won't be in too good a mood."

Zach smiled. "Is a Blackfoot ever in a good mood?"

"Point taken. What do you aim to do?"

"Follow 'em."

"How fur?"

"We got to make sure they leave the valley."

"Reckon that's right. Just so's we kin sleep sound at night. What if they don't leave?"

"Can't cross a bridge till you come to it."

Zach gestured for MacGregor and Baptiste to close up, then moved on.

VI

Before long they had stopped again, to grimly study the tracks of four Blackfoot braves who had branched off from the main group.

"Looks like they heard yore shot, after all," said Shadmore.

"If they find your trail it will lead them straight back to the winter camp," worried MacGregor.

"Reckon we'd best hie on back," said Shadmore.

"Aye," seconded the Scotsman. "No way to know when Jubal and Fletcher will return from their hunt. That could mean Montez alone against four bucks."

They all looked to Zach for the word. There did not seem to be any alternative to hastening back to the winter camp. Of course, there was the chance that the four Blackfoot scouts would fail to cut Zach's trail and, hence, might fail to locate the camp. But none wished to take that chance. Baptiste had Flower to worry about. MacGregor had his unrequited love for Morning Sky to motivate him. As for Shadmore, he cared for them all. Zach had as much to lose as the rest of them. So his hesitation to give the word struck them all as peculiar under the circumstances.

Yet for a moment Zach did not speak. He stood there, looking at the tracks in the snow, and his head was slightly tilted to one side. Shadmore thought he looked like a man who was listening to something. In fact he was.

"Hear it?" he asked them, at length.

"Hear what?" asked Shad.

"I canna hear a flamin' thing," confessed the Scotsman.

"Wait," said Zach.

None of them felt like waiting—all were anxious to return to the camp—but they did as he told them, and listened as hard as they could.

"Aye," said MacGregor, in a whisper. "I hear it now. But what is it? I canna tell, for the life of me."

Shadmore wore an expression of pure disgust.

"Wagh! I must be gettin' old. I cain't hear a dang-blasted thing."

"Come on," said Zach.

He broke into a loping run.

The other three hesitated, for the direction Zach was taking was not the direction their hearts bade them go. He was following the Blackfoot trail still, and that drew them further away from the winter camp now imperiled by the four Blackfoot braves doubling back into the heart of the valley to investigate a gunshot.

But in the end they followed him. They had done so, without question, for years now, and not once had they been sorry for the faith they put in him. This was not the time to change.

They ran for a quarter of a mile through pine and aspen and spruce—the valley was thickly wooded virtually from one end to the other. Beaver had created meadows and marshes down near the creek, but the Blackfoot trail led further and further away from the stream.

A quarter-mile run was no strain for any of them, least of all Shadmore, who, despite his many winters, was as spry as a mountain goat. So no one was winded when Zach, still ahead of the rest, stopped suddenly and darted to the right, dropping behind a log.

Ahead lay a small clearing, and the other three mountain men caught a glimpse of the solitary Blackfoot standing there aiming a rifle at them.

"Mon Dieu!" gasped Baptiste, diving for the ground.

Shadmore and MacGregor didn't waste their breath as they scattered for cover.

The Blackfoot squeezed his smoothbore's trigger.

The hammer fell, but the powder charge failed to ignite.

With an exclamation of anger, the warrior hurled the rifle away and brandished his tomahawk. He screamed a defiant taunt.

All four men were acquainted with the Blackfoot tongue. Shadmore and Morning Sky had taught Zach. MacGregor had spent his Hudson Bay years trading with the tribe. Of them all, Baptiste knew the least. But even he could tell that the lone Blackfoot was challenging them to come and kill him. To get up off the ground and fight like men.

The French-Canadian smiled grimly. On one knee, he raised rifle to shoulder.

"I weel oblige," he said.

Zach appeared suddenly beside him and struck the barrel aside before Baptiste pulled the trigger.

VII

Baptiste flared. No mountain man worth his salt cared to be interfered with. But before he could re-act with anything more than an expression of out-rage, Zach spoke.

"No shooting."

It was all he needed to say by way of explaining his actions. It made eminent sense. The valley was swarming with Blackfeet, and there was no way of knowing how many were within earshot of a rifle's report. If the lone warrior's smoothbore had dis-charged properly it would have been a different story altogether, but it hadn't, and there was still at least a chance of dealing with him in a relatively quiet, dis-creet manner. Baptiste was a man of typical Gallic moods—his anger was quick to flash but just as quick to subside.

So he nodded, to indicate he understood, and that was all Zach was waiting for. The latter stood and ad-vanced dauntlessly into the clearing.

Seeing Zach approach so calmly infuriated the Blackfoot brave. He raised the tomahawk high and charged with a shrieking war cry. Zach brought his Hawken rifle up and blocked the down-swept hatchet. At the same time he drove a knee into the warrior's groin. The Blackfoot doubled over, and Zach dropped him by laying the butt of the Hawken hard across the back of his neck. The brave sprawled in the snow and lay motionless.

The other trappers ventured into the clearing to

stand around the fallen brave. Zach, meanwhile, knelt to turn the unconscious Indian onto his back and feel at the side of the neck for a pulse.

"Gone under?" inquired Shadmore.

"Alive," replied Zach.

Baptiste drew his knife.

"I have a remedy for that," said the French-Canadian.

"No," said Zach.

Baptiste scowled. "He is Blackfoot. He must die."

And so it stood—the law of the wilderness had no rules attached to it save that one: Kill or be killed. The Blackfeet showed no mercy, the white man didn't either. The enemy you killed today could not kill you, or one of your colleagues, tomorrow. In the longer term, he could not sire more enemies. Killing this warrior would mean he could not father future Blackfoot braves bent on taking white scalps. For there was this about the Blackfeet which seemed innate: They would fight until the end. There would be no surrender, no rapprochement. It was a struggle to the death with them. The mountain men realized this and accepted the challenge. There was nothing particularly bloodthirsty about Baptiste's solution. It was merely the way of things.

"No," repeated Zach.

"He would kill us," said Baptiste.

Ignoring him, Zach turned to MacGregor. "Do you know him?"

The Scotsman took a long look. His years among

the Blackfeet had left him acquainted with many of them, but at length he shook his head.

"I canna remember ever seeing him before. But why did they leave him behind, I'm wondering?"

"There's a good reason," said Zach. "Look yonder."

He pointed, and for the first time the other three saw the buffalo-hide bundle on the edge of the clearing, at the base of a tree.

The belligerent Blackfoot had been the focus of their attention up to that moment. The realization that the brave was not alone was a credit to Zach Hannah's ability to keep a clear head in moments of high danger, which allowed him to see all things at all times. This was an essential ingredient to his success in surviving and in keeping the brigade out of the kind of trouble which had plagued other high country trappers in recent years.

"Watch him," Zach told MacGregor, indicating the unconscious warrior. Then, with Shadmore and Baptiste, he approached the bundle cautiously.

Using the barrel of his rifle, he lifted the edge of the buffalo robe.

Beneath it they found a woman. At first glance she appeared to them to be sleeping. But of course no one could have slept through the altercation which had just occurred. Zach hunkered down and took a closer look. She was unconscious. The reason: a grievous wound in her side. A poultice of mud and moss had been applied. Her doeskins were dark with dried blood.

"Bullet hole," said Zach. "Couple days old. She's in a bad way."

"Yep," agreed Shadmore, having noticed the woman's unhealthy pallor and ragged breathing. "She's not long fer this world, I reckon."

Rising, Zach looked solemnly at the old leatherstocking. "Can't save her?"

No one knew more about frontier medicine than Shadmore, and all who knew him turned to him in such matters. He made a closer examination of the wound beneath the poultice. It was not a pleasant sight.

"Bullet's still in her," he said. "The lead's pizened the wound. She's goin' 'crost the river, Zach, and ain't a thing I kin do about it."

Zach glanced across the clearing at the unconscious warrior, guarded by the kilt-garbed Scotsman.

"That explains him. She must be his squaw, or some relation."

Shadmore nodded. Even the Blackfeet stuck with a wounded member of their tribe through thick and thin, but only as long as there was a chance for the person's recovery—regardless of whether this loyalty slowed the group down, as in this case. But once it was clear that death was the only solution, the well-being of the group became the first priority, and the mortally wounded member would be abandoned. It was Indian custom, and so beyond reproach. Often the person abandoned to his or her fate would be the first to suggest that course of action.

The brave that Zach had dealt with so effectively,

whether husband or brother, would then be free to follow his conscience, and this warrior had chosen to stay behind, willing to die, if need be, to protect the woman so long as she drew breath. It mattered not to him that she was doomed. Such sacrifice was an issue of honor, and Zach admired the brave for it. He had sung the death chant that Zach had been the first among the mountain men to hear. The chant drew the attention of the spirits to the fact that a soul would soon need guidance to the next world.

"So what do we do?" asked Shadmore.

Zach was frowning. The situation posed several problems for him. They had to return to the winter camp with all possible haste. The logical action would be to leave the woman to die, as she was bound eventually to do, cut the warrior's throat, and start back.

Yet Zach was loathe to leave the woman, just as the warrior had been, while she lived. There were wolves in the valley, for one thing. And, as hard a man as he had become, he did not relish the thought of killing the defenseless brave, Blackfoot or not. Especially one with such honor and courage. It would be downright murder in his book.

They could not take the woman with them. Not only would she slow them down but the attempt would probably hasten her end. No, someone would have to stay, to replace the Blackfoot warrior in his deathbed vigil.

He looked at his companions. Could he make them understand his point of view? Shadmore, possibly. Maybe even the Scotsman. But Baptiste? Certainly not. To the French-Canadian, as to most mountain men, Blackfeet—women as well as men, and even children, for that matter—were not worth an ounce of compassion. This was war, and all was fair in its prosecution.

But Zach did not view this mountain war as his war. He had never wanted to be a part of it, and had tried, prior to joining the brigade, to remain remote from it. During his solitary years in the high country he had resented both antagonists bringing their blood feud into the mountains. Even now, with a booshway's responsibilities, he preferred to avoid trouble. Sometimes, though, that was simply impossible.

"One of us must stay," he said.

"*Pourquoi?*" exclaimed Baptiste.

As far as the French-Canadian was concerned, the solution was simple and perfectly understandable. The risks in staying were too obvious to need enumeration. Let one die, slay the other, and leave with a clear conscience.

The query irritated Zach. It wasn't that he expected the others to obey him without question. In any brigade, as in any Indian group, the man who led the way did so only as long as he demonstrated the ability to lead to the satisfaction of those who consented to follow him. An Indian brave would not obey his chief if to do so made no sense to him, and neither would a mountain man obey his booshway if he did not think it was in his best interests to do so.

Baptiste was not being insubordinate. He was just exercising his rights. But Zach was aggravated, nonetheless, because time was of the essence, and he wasn't sure he could explain the reasons for his decision no matter how much time he took.

"I'll stay, then," he said. "You all get back to the winter camp."

"*C'est folle*," declared Baptiste. "Your woman, your son are . . ."

"I said I'd stay," snapped Zach. "You don't need to remind me about Sky and little Jacob."

"No," said Shadmore. "I'll stay."

The offer surprised Zach. Grateful, he laid a hand on the old hivernan's bony shoulder.

"Thank you. But it's a risky proposition. I have no right . . ."

"I reckon I unnerstand the risks," said Shadmore. "And you feel strong about it—'cause I know how much you're frettin' over Sky and the younker. Don't worry yoreself about me. I've outfoxed these red rascals many a year now, and I kin still do it. I'll stay till she's gone under, in case wolves or such happen by and git a notion. But what d'you want done with the buck yonder?"

"Hold him here until I return," replied Zach. "We need to know what has occurred to bring this band into our valley."

"You reckon he'll tell you all about it, hoss? He might not be too fond of you oncet he comes to, seein' as how you put a knot on his head."

"You never know if you'll get an answer unless you ask the question."

"Huh," grunted Shadmore. "I cain't hardly argue with that purty piece of logic, now kin I?"

"I say we all go," persisted Baptiste. "We are out-numbered as it is. Now we separate? It makes no sense to me."

"Hell, Frenchie," chuckled Shadmore. "Thar's only four of them Injuns unaccounted fer. You could clean their plows all by yore little lonesome. You don't need a creaky ol' fool like me. I'm too old and slow. I'd just hold you-all back, and then I'd just git in the way once the ruckus got started."

Zach smiled. "There's no better man in a fight than you, Shad, and we all know that to be the gospel. Take care, old friend, and run no risks you can rightly avoid. I'll be back before the day is done."

"I kin take care of my own topknot. You just hie on back to Morning Sky and that young'un, scout, and be quick about it."

VIII

There were two ways to go about it. They could go straight back to the winter camp, or they could follow the four Blackfeet who had split off from the main group.

Baptiste was all for the second course. It would be fairly easy to track the Indians in the snow. If their trail led to the winter camp, well and good. If it did not, they could still probably catch up with the warriors and kill them. Would the main party turn back and search for the four scouts if they failed to return? Baptiste didn't think so. The band was obviously in a desperate retreat. They had suffered some sort of calamity. There had been violence, some of them had been hurt, and now they were leaving their wounded behind on the trail. They were traveling fast and light and it didn't seem likely they would retrace their steps to locate a few missing scouts.

But Zach decided against this course. They would reach the winter camp sooner if they backtracked themselves rather than trail the four Blackfeet. And if it happened that the warriors were not a threat to the camp, he saw no need in fighting them. He and the French-Canadian were clearly of different opinions concerning the practice of killing Blackfeet for no other reason than that they were Blackfeet.

So it was that Zach, MacGregor, and Baptiste hastened back to the winter camp. They ran most of the way. As it turned out, that was the right decision. Because the four warriors *had* found Zach's trail and *had* followed it to the camp, and the fight was already in progress.

When they heard the shooting they were alarmed, but took heart from the knowledge that the gunfire meant the fight was not lost—at least they were not too late. Had Fletcher and Wilkes returned from their hunt in time to aid Montez? Or was the Spaniard holding out somehow all by himself?

Either way, there was not a second to waste. The

sense of urgency, however, did not cause them to throw caution to the wind. They did not charge blindly into the thick of the fray. Dead, they could help no one. It was necessary to learn as much as possible about the situation before playing a part in the drama.

To accomplish this, they sought the vantage point of high ground. The winter camp was located on a bench jutting from the shoulder of a mountain, and they ascended the slope to a place in the woods a hundred yards above the camp, where they could see everything from the cover of the fir and lodgepole pine.

It was immediately obvious to them that Wilkes and Fletcher had not returned. Montez, Flower, Morning Sky, and little Jacob were on their own.

The Spaniard had apparently led the others to the corral. Zach surmised that he had somehow known the Blackfeet were closing in and had hoped to reach the horses and make a getaway. The half-faced cabins were particularly ill-suited for defense. Lacking one wall, they could become a death trap. Montez had realized this. He'd been in his share of scrapes, and he knew his business, and had opted for a mounted flight.

But the Blackfeet had struck before escape could be accomplished. Two horses were down beneath the ledge. Montez and the others had taken cover behind the carcasses, their backs to the rock face. The rest of the horses milled in the corral, highly agitated by the shooting and the smell of their own kind's blood.

Three of the warriors were closing in on the corral from three different directions, trading lead with Montez. But the Spaniard had two rifles; Flower was reloading for him, and she was very good at the task. Morning Sky was wielding the flintlock pistol Zach had given her long ago. She was a better-than-average shot with it. He had seen to that. Sky had never much cared for shooting, but he had insisted on constant practice. The dividend of this persistence, not to mention the expenditure of quite a lot of powder and shot, was her proficiency.

Montez and Sky on the one hand, and the three warriors on the other, were doing a lot of shooting, and all participants were trying to avoid hitting the horses between them. The Blackfeet realized that the brigade's cavallard would be a tremendous boon to their group.

But it was the fourth Blackfoot who posed the greatest threat. He was skulking along the ledge above Montez and Sky and the others—and they had no idea he was there.

It required no wild conjecture to gauge his intentions. Once directly above his prey, he would leap down into their midst, wielding tomahawk and knife. When he did, the others would rush forward. They were keeping Montez and Sky occupied now. Once their brother made his move they would move also, desiring to share in the terrible glory of the kill.

Zach and his companions ascertained all this in a

glance, and in the next heartbeat Zach and Baptiste both had raised their rifles, drawn a bead, and fired.

Their rifles discharged almost simultaneously. Both bullets struck the Indian on the ledge. He tottered on the brink for an instant before pinwheeling down into the corral.

For one bewildered moment Montez and Sky and other three Blackfeet stopped shooting. All were trying to figure out what had happened. And into that lull burst Zach and Baptiste and MacGregor, charging down the slope, weaving through the trees. Both Zach and the French-Canadian reloaded as they ran. At least two of the Blackfeet switched their fire to this new threat. Zach flinched as a bullet struck a tree trunk in a spray of wood splinters when he raced by.

It was not the Indian way to stand and fight, especially against superior numbers. Of a sudden they were outnumbered, and they knew it. So one gave a signal which sounded uncannily like the bark of a coyote, and in an instant they were scattering.

"They must not escape!" yelled Zach.

He did not need to tell the others why the three Blackfeet had to die. They could not permit word to get back to the rest of the Blackfoot band that a party of white trappers had wintered in the valley.

MacGregor stopped, steadied himself, and fired. One of the warriors stumbled and fell. An instant later he was back on his feet and running again, wounded but not mortally. Zach stopped him for good with his second shot. He did not relish shooting a man in the back, but in this case he had no choice. Seconds after he had fired, Baptiste pulled up, drew a bead, and put another warrior down.

That left one, and he was swift of foot and soon out of sight down in the shinnery along the creek, seeming to vanish into the tangle of bare brown branches draped with snow.

Zach and his two companions reached the ledge and wasted no time leaping into the corral below. All three landed with an agile grace, befitting mountain men. Slow, clumsy, and out-of-condition individuals did not long survive in the high country.

"I weel get the devil!" cried Baptiste.

He lunged at the nearest horse. The mustang shied away, snorting, but the French-Canadian latched onto the animal's mane and vaulted aboard. He was gone in an instant, kicking the horse into a jump that cleared the top pole of the corral fence.

"I'll go with him," MacGregor told Zach. "See to your family."

"Don't let him get away."

The Scotsman grinned. "He canna get away, Zach."

He did not waste his time trying to catch up another horse. Baptiste had been lucky. There was no time for testing his own luck. So he vaulted the corral pole and sprinted for the creek in the mounted French-Canadian's wake.

Zach turned and hurried to the two dead horses, behind which Sky and the others had forted up. Montez was leaning against one of the carcasses, and

Flower was beside him, using a knife to cut blood-stained buckskin away from his shoulder.

"How bad are you hit?" asked Zach.

The Spaniard's face, drenched with cold sweat, had an unhealthy pallor, but he managed a taut, pain-wracked smile.

"I have lived through worse."

Zach looked across at Morning Sky, who stood with little Jacob by her side, an arm around the boy's shoulders. Both were unharmed, and he experienced such a flood of relief that he had to swallow hard against the sudden lump in his throat.

"You did well," he told Montez. "I owe you."

"*De nada,*" said Montez, dismissing it. "I had to kill two horses. We hoped to escape, but the Indians, they were too quick, so I cut the throats of these *caballos*—there was no cover here."

Zach nodded. He had already noted that the throats of the dead mustangs had been cut and had surmised that it was the Spaniard's handiwork.

"Doesn't matter," he replied. "It was the only thing you could do."

He went to Sky then, putting the Hawken down and wrapping an arm around her while running his hand through Jacob's tousled black hair.

"Thank God you are both safe."

"I wasn't afraid," declared Jacob, looking earnestly up at Zach, a very serious expression on his face.

"I knew you wouldn't be," said Zach, repressing a smile.

From some distance down the creek came a single rifle report.

A few minutes later Baptiste and MacGregor returned, the former still mounted, with the corpse of the fourth warrior draped over the mustang in front of him.

IX

Reaching the corral, Baptiste grabbed the dead warrior by the hair and lifted him off the horse to hang him over the uppermost corral pole. He did this with remarkable ease, being a man possessed of incredible physical strength.

"Like I said," crowed the French-Canadian proudly. "I get the devil. Flower, *mon petite cheri*, I bring heem for you."

The Shoshone woman left Montez and approached the corpse. She moved as one entranced. She, too, grabbed the dead Blackfoot, lifting the hair to study the features. Then she spat in the corpse's face. She still carried the knife with which she had been cutting the buckskin away from Montez's wound, and now she raised the blade as though bent on taking the Indian's scalp.

"No!" snapped Zach, stepping forward quickly.

He spoke so forcefully that Flower jumped back. Her expression was inscrutable, but her black eyes gleamed with ferocity.

Baptiste chuckled.

"She don't care for Blackfeet," he said. "Eet is a fine gift I bring her—a Blackfoot scalp."

"I don't cotton to scalp-taking."

"I keel him. His scalp is mine to do with as I weel."

"Not in front of my boy."

"A boy is never too young to learn. It is your Blackfoot woman, I think, you worry about. These four were her blood brothers."

"They are not my brothers," said Sky firmly. "If they knew of me they would not hesitate to kill me."

"If you want the scalp so bad," said Zach, "take him down into the bushes before you do your dirty work." He looked at Flower. "The deed won't be done here."

Baptiste opened his mouth to make further protest, but Flower spoke sharply to him in her native tongue. The French-Canadian lapsed into a sullen silence, and Flower returned to Montez without another glance at Zach. She hid her feelings well, and Zach hadn't a clue as to her true sentiment concerning his skirmish with Baptiste.

The bullet was lodged in the Spaniard's shoulder, and while he bit down hard on a Galena "lead pill," Flower began to probe the wound with the tip of the knife. Zach took Sky and little Jacob back to their half-faced cabin, though the boy was inclined to stay with Montez.

"Where is Shadmore?" asked Sky.

"He is safe. But I must get back to him."

She nodded, asking for no elaboration.

"Is Montez going to die, Father?" asked Jacob, very solemn.

"No, boy. He'll pull through and be right as rain in no time. You'll see."

"I hate the Blackfeet."

Zach glanced at Sky. Her smile was wistful.

"You have Blackfoot blood in your veins, Jacob," she said.

"I don't want it." He looked gravely up at Zach. "Why do they hate everybody, Father? Why do they want to kill Montez?"

"They don't much like us being here in these mountains, Jacob. They figure this is their country, and that we're trespassers."

"Is it their country?"

Little Jacob never ceased to amaze Zach. The boy was sharp as a tack for one so young, with a quick and inquisitive mind.

"It doesn't belong to anybody," he replied. "Except God." He kissed Sky. "I've got to be going."

"Be safe."

He nodded and walked away. MacGregor caught up with him before he had gotten out of the winter camp.

"Want some company?" asked the Scotsman.

"Stay here. Look after things."

"I thought there for a minute you and Baptiste were going to have a dustup. One day he might get it in his head to try for your scalp."

Zach made no reply and walked on.

Leaving the winter camp, he wondered if Mac-

Gregor would be all that dismayed if the French-Canadian did indeed decide someday to try to kill him. He didn't need telling to know how the Scotsman felt about Morning Sky. Not that this colored Zach's judgment of the ex–Hudson Bay man. He did not believe MacGregor would ever try to steal Sky away, as Devlin had done. He might desire her, but not on those terms. But he would be there for her and little Jacob, ready and able to take Zach's place as protector and provider. In a way, that was comforting to know. The events of the day had left Zach disturbed. He saw them as a portent of things to come. The brigade had managed for years to avoid serious trouble with the Blackfeet, but Zach had a hunch that their streak of luck was about to end.

X

Shadmore was right where Zach had left him.

The Blackfoot warrior had regained consciousness, and the old leatherstocking had his rifle trained on the brave. But the Blackfoot did not appear to have a thought for making more trouble or trying to escape. He was on his knees beside the wounded woman, and he was chanting the death song. The sound sent a chill down Zach's spine.

"Sky and the boy all right?" asked Shad, without taking his eyes off his prisoner.

"They're fine. We had a ruckus."

That news drew a quick, surprised glance from Shadmore.

"Them four braves?"

"Yep." Zach told him all about the fight, using as few words as possible. He omitted the confrontation with Baptiste over the taking of scalps. "What about her?" He nodded at the woman bundled up in the buffalo robe.

"She's a fighter. I'll give her that."

"Gotten anything out of him?"

"Nary a kind word. 'Course, iffen looks could kill, I'd be gone beaver. What exactly you aimin' to do with this rascal, anyroad?"

"Any ideas?"

"Well, we could kill him and be done with it."

"That sounds like Baptiste talking."

"Iffen it'll make you feel better about it, give him a weapon and fight it out, fair and square. One thing's sartin. You let him go, he'll tell them others we're here, and we won't have no peace in this hyar valley atall."

Zach handed his Hawken over to Shadmore. "Think I'll try to palaver with him."

"Good luck."

Zach crossed the clearing, hunkered down on the other side of the dying woman from the warrior. The latter stopped chanting and glowered at him.

"How are you called?" asked Zach in the Blackfoot tongue.

His fluency with the language startled the warrior.

"I am called Long Runner."

"She is your woman?"

Long Runner's face was an impassive bronze mask. He nodded once, curtly.

"My heart is sad."

Long Runner's chin rose a defiant inch. "I go with her."

"Not by my hand."

"I go with her," said the warrior, adamant. He looked at Shadmore, standing off about twenty paces, and at the rifle in the old mountain man's grasp, and Zach had a feeling that Long Runner was contemplating what would amount to suicide: making a belligerent move in hopes that Shadmore would shoot. Zach figured it would work, so he decided he might ought to distract the Blackfoot.

"Why have you come to our valley?" he asked.

"These are not your valleys, or your mountains," said Long Runner, indignant.

"We wish only to be left in peace."

Long Runner's grunt expressed nothing if not rank skepticism.

"You kill Blackfoot."

"We did not kill your woman."

The Blackfoot's expression darkened. "No. The Big Bellies." He spat, as though the name left a sour taste in his mouth.

Now, thought Zach, they were starting to make some progress.

He glanced at Shadmore, an eyebrow raised. Shadmore nodded. So the Gros Ventres and the

Blackfeet had had a falling-out. That was no surprise.

"But the Gros Ventres are your brothers," said
Zach, agitating for more information.

"They are snakes in the grass."

The woman beneath the buffalo robe moaned and
moved. Zach bent closer, heard the death rattle, unmistakable, in her throat. Her body went rigid
momentarily—then suddenly went limp.

She was gone.

Zach felt sorry for her—and for Long Runner. He
knew what the warrior was going through, though his
Indian stoicism forbade him to express it. Zach had
lost loved ones. His parents had perished in a cholera epidemic over ten years ago in Copper Creek,
Tennessee. And about six years ago he had lost
Morning Sky—forever, he had thought at the time.

"She has no more pain," he said, and covered her
face with the buffalo robe.

Long Runner's shriek froze the blood in Zach's
veins. The Blackfoot lunged across the woman's body
at Zach. From the corner of his eye, Zach saw
Shadmore hoist rifle to shoulder.

"Don't shoot!" shouted Zach.

Long Runner tackled him. They fought a brief and
fierce tussle in the snow. The Blackfoot managed to
get Zach's knife. He wanted to die, but he wasn't opposed to taking at least one white man with him, in
good old Blackfoot fashion. His plan was to kill Zach
and then make a move at the old hunter, figuring the
latter's rifle would reunite him with the woman he

loved, whose spirit was crossing over to the other side.

All things being even, Long Runner would have been a match for Zach. But all things were not even. The warrior had suffered a long winter trail and was still feeling the effects of his previous scuffle with Zach. As a result, Zach managed to wrest the knife out of his grasp. And once Zach had the knife, Long Runner stopped fighting. He tore at his buckskin jerkin, exposing his chest—he was asking Zach to plunge the knife into his heart, expecting it.

Zach didn't oblige him. He stood up, returning the knife to its sheath.

"Well," said Zach, "whatever else can be said about you Blackfeet, you're no cowards. That's certain. Go back to your people, Long Runner. Live." He nodded at the dead woman. "It is what she would want, I reckon."

And he turned his back on the warrior, rejoining Shadmore.

The old leatherstocking was shaking his head ruefully.

"You beat all I ever seen, Zach Hannah."

"Let's go."

"What about this plunder?" Shadmore indicated the rifle, powder horn, shot pouch, tomahawk, and knife lying in the snow at his feet—these were Long Runner's belongings.

"You wouldn't leave a man unarmed in this country, would you?"

"Oh, heck no. Not even a rascally Blackfoot. What would he have to kill us with tomorrow iffen we took all this gear today?"

Zach smiled tolerantly. "Can you kill him, Shad? Can you shoot him down in cold blood?"

"It's what he wants, ain't it?"

"Do it, if you can."

"I reckon he'd do the same fer us."

Zach shrugged. He was no longer smiling.

"I wouldn't fer myself, you unnerstand," snapped Shadmore, irritated. "I'm thinkin' more of Sky and little Jacob. Don't you figger this feller will tell his cahoots we're here? Don't you 'spect we'll have Blackfoot guests fer dinner tonight?"

Zach glanced at Long Runner.

The warrior was on his feet, standing next to his woman's body, watching the two mountain men with a fierce, dark scowl on his face.

"Can't cross a bridge before you come to it," said Zach.

Shadmore made a face. "Dang it all, Zach Hannah. You always say such."

"It's true, isn't it?"

"True or not, I wish you'd stop sayin' it. You been giving me that line for years now, and it's got to the point where I feel like I ain't never gonna git to that danged bridge."

"We'll get to it soon," was Zach's enigmatic reply. "Sooner than we want."

He turned and walked away.

Shadmore shook his head, stared at Long Runner.

"Reckon I'll see you later," he muttered, and followed Zach out of the clearing, on the path back to the brigade's winter camp.

Chapter 2

The Rendezvous

I

Rendezvous that summer was held in the Green River country. To reach it, Zach Hannah's brigade headed down the upper canyons, past the lakes, and to the broad lower valley where the river departed the mountains.

The upper valley, squeezed between steep rocky slopes, was marshy. The river itself wandered serpentine through a waist-high carpet of luxurious sedge, browned by the summer sun. The trappers were hauling heavy packs of fur, so they avoided the wetlands and kept instead to the stony flanks of the mountains, moving through thick stands of lodgepole pine and Douglas fir.

Near the Green River Lakes they came upon a boneyard—a band of elks had apparently foundered in the snow here last winter, and all had perished. The bones were scattered, picked clean by coyote and carrion crow. It was a reminder to all of them of the previous winter's severity, though none cared to be reminded.

Contrary to Shadmore's apprehensions, they had seen no more of the Blackfeet. The day after the fight at the winter camp, Zach had tracked the band and returned to report that, though Long Runner had rejoined his people, the whole bunch had departed the valley.

Shadmore couldn't figure that one out. Either Long Runner hadn't told his brothers about the trappers, or the news just hadn't impressed them sufficiently to cause them to alter their course through the valley. Apparently, neither had the fact that the four warriors dispatched to investigate Zach's gunshot failed to rejoin the band.

It didn't make any sense. A band chased out of their own winter camp, suffering the travail of a difficult trek through the high country in a season that by no stretch of the imagination was conducive to such travel, short on food and in desperate need of shelter, with the wounded and the young suffering most of all from exposure—why hadn't they jumped at the chance to kill a small party of trappers and thereby secure food and shelter, not to mention scalps?

Shadmore did not think for a minute that Long Runner had kept what he knew a secret. Though Zach had spared his life, the warrior would not feel obliged to return the favor with his silence. Especially since he had not wished his life spared. Not that Indians were without honor. Shadmore knew better. He had tremendous respect for their ways, regardless of the fact that he consistently referred to them as "red rascals" and "scoundrelous savages." But their ideas about honorable behavior differed markedly from those a white man would hold dear. The honorable thing for Long Runner would have been to inform his brethren that there were mountain men in the valley who needed killing. To keep silent would have been to betray his own people.

So why hadn't the Blackfeet turned back and taken issue with the brigade?

The only thing Shadmore could figure was that they feared for their women and children. This had not been a war party, after all.

Whatever the truth of the matter—and Shadmore didn't think he'd ever know for sure—Zach's gamble in letting Long Runner go free had paid off. And the brigade had come through with only two horses dead and Montez wounded and some hard feelings between Zach and Baptiste regarding the taking of scalps. Their luck had not deserted them.

As for the quarrel between Zach and the French-Canadian, the former seemed willing to forget the whole affair, and indeed he seemed to have put it entirely behind him. But Baptiste was broody for days after, and watched the booshway with sullen eyes. It was just like a damned *mangeur de lard* to harbor a grudge, thought Shadmore. The old leatherstocking calculated that they had not heard the last of it. Baptiste would bide his time and then strike back in some typically underhanded way. Or, at the very least—and Shadmore hoped this would be the case—he would sign on with another brigade at rendezvous. Shadmore figured that if this happened he would miss Flower's delicious dough-cakes, but there was precious little about the French-Canadian that he would miss.

Nearing the rendezvous site, though, all thoughts of Baptiste and Blackfeet flew from Shadmore's mind. He relished seeing old friends again, and getting a strong dose of honest-to-God liquor—not to mention stocking up on bona fide tobacco. He was right tired of smoking willow bark.

Seven years ago, Major Henry and William Ashley had led the Rocky Mountain Fur Company up the wide Missouri in search of a fortune in "brown gold"—beaver fur. Backed by the funding of wealthy speculators, and with some of the best frontiersmen to be had in its ranks, the company had seemed to have a bright future indeed back in '23.

Yet one disaster after another had plagued the Rocky Mountain boys. The Missouri had claimed one of their keelboats and many of their provisions. Indians had made off with their horse herd. That first winter they had forted up at the mouth of the Yellowstone, far short of the Shining Mountains which had been their destination. Ashley had returned to St. Louis to acquire more keelboats, more supplies, and more horses.

In the spring of '24 Ashley had embarked from St.

Louis a second time, heading for the fort where Henry and most of the frontiersmen waited. But the Arikaras, whose villages were located at the juncture of the Missouri and the Grand Rivers, had declared all-out war against the white man because some trappers had allied themselves with the Sioux, enemies of the Arikara Nation. The Rees had attacked Ashley's expedition, killing some of the Rocky Mountain men with guns Ashley had foolishly give them as gifts of appeasement.

Major Henry and eighty of his trappers—Zach Hannah among them—had hurried down the Missouri in hastily constructed Mackinaw boats to rescue Ashley. Allied with the Sioux and elements of the United States Army under the command of the pompous Colonel Leavenworth, they had managed to drive the Rees out of their fortified riverside towns. It was a hollow victory. The Arikaras returned the next year, still hostile, and resumed their war, rendering the Missouri, the main road west, effectively useless.

These setbacks had soured Major Henry and Ashley on the enterprise, and they altered their plans. The company was divided into brigades. Usually with from half a dozen to a score of trappers each, these brigades were allowed to choose their own leaders, or booshways. The groups scattered into the mountains, left to fend for themselves and to trap what they could while keeping a wary eye peeled for rampaging Blackfeet. They agreed to meet at rendezvous each summer and trade their furs to

Ashley, who took it upon himself every year to transport supplies to the appointed meeting place. This suited the trappers just fine. They preferred going on their own stick. They had little faith in Ashley's leadership ability, and Major Henry was too strict on the subject of discipline to suit their wild, free natures. They could go where they wanted and do what they pleased and the only restriction was a "gentleman's agreement" to sell their furs to the company at fair prices.

This arrangement proved highly lucrative for Ashley and his backers. The trappers usually turned right around and spent their profits on much-needed provisions which Ashley bought at cut-rate bulk prices in St. Louis. He profited once there, because he sold these goods at inflated "mountain prices," and a second time when he carried the furs back east and sold them on the flourishing open market. From 1824 to 1827, Ashley brought $180,000 worth of furs back from rendezvous. Finally, in '27, having made his money, and tired of the game, Ashley sold out to Jedediah Smith, William Sublette, and David Jackson. These mountain men, booshways all, became the new captains of the Rocky Mountain Fur Company.

It was business as before, with one difference which proved to be of paramount importance: The Rocky Mountain brigades were all loyal to Smith, Sublette, and Jackson. Unlike Ashley, these men were their own kind—mountain men like themselves, who understood them better and treated them more fairly than Ashley ever had.

Success breeds imitation. The Rocky Mountain Fur Company soon found itself in competition with other organizations. For the past few years, these rival companies had sent representatives to rendezvous, trying to make off with some of the Rocky Mountain's business.

Hundreds of Indians attended rendezvous— Crows, Flatheads, Shoshones, Nez Percé, and others. They had discovered how profitable trapping and trading could be. Bound to no company, they traded with anyone, and the rival companies could prosper as a result of their patronage, even though most of the white trappers remained loyal to Smith, Sublette, and Jackson.

This competition, and the cutthroat practices engaged in by the rival companies, led naturally to hard feelings. But as long as the men who had originally come west with the Rocky Mountain Fur Company abided by that tacit understanding that they would "float their stick" with Sublette and his partners, they held the advantage. In all there were some thirty brigades of Rocky Mountain alumni, about four hundred men total. No other company could match them.

Rendezvous, then, was the biggest event of the year for the six hundred or so white trappers who plied their trade and lived the free life in the high country which they were handmade by God to lead, and twice that number of friendly Indians attended the Green River rendezvous. It was a wild, wide-open fortnight of devilment and debauchery. Fighting, drinking, gambling, feasting, and of course trading, took place.

As Zach and his brigade emerged from the confines of the upper river canyons into the broad and verdant valley of the Green's lower reaches, they could tell the rendezvous was going full blast, even from several miles' distance. A haze of dust marked the site, and there was so much shooting one might have thought a full-scale battle was being waged.

In fact, a lot of shooting always accompanied a rendezvous. There were shooting matches, most accompanied by high wagers. And there was seldom a shortage of drunks inclined to shoot at the sky. Aside from this, it was customary to greet an incoming party with a fusillade, the mountain man version of the naval tradition of a twenty-one-gun salute.

Occasionally, too, there would be shooting in anger. No rendezvous had yet come and gone without at least one killing. You couldn't throw six hundred frontiersmen and hundreds more Indians together without a dozen quarrels erupting each day. Sometimes the fight was over a woman's favors. Sometimes thievery, of which there was plenty, was the cause. Sometimes an imagined slight was the reason for the ruckus.

There were any number of good reasons for a quarrel and no machinery in place to settle disputes in a peaceful fashion. Mountain-man temperament did not lend itself to the establishment of a frontier court, no matter how rough-hewn. Disputes were settled with fists or knives or guns, and the strongest survived.

So Zach's brigade heard the shooting miles away, and saw the dust, and everyone's spirits rose and blood quickened in anticipation. With one exception.

It was fiesta for Montez, carnival for Baptiste, and hoedown-time for Shadmore and Wilkes and Fletcher and MacGregor. But Zach did not share their enthusiasm.

He did not relish the idea of socializing with his peers. He was a loner at heart, even though he had taken up again with Shadmore and the others. Every year he looked forward to the summer rendezvous with about as much pleasure as he would anticipate a tooth-pulling.

But he had to attend. As booshway, he had certain duties to perform in connection with the rendezvous. And he needed more powder and shot, and this year he hoped to get his hands on a book or two—even though reading material was not in great demand among frontiersmen and so usually in short supply. He figured it was about time to get little Jacob started on his learning. The boy was smart, and eager to learn, and Zach figured he would do a far sight better than young Zach Hannah had done in that schoolhouse back in Copper Creek, Tennessee.

If he had known what awaited him at the Green River rendezvous, though, Zach would have turned right around and hightailed it back into the mountains with Sky and little Jacob.

II

They were yet a quarter-mile shy of the edge of the rendezvous encampment when a lone man rode out from the hodgepodge of tepees and tents and lean-tos to intercept them. The encampment extended more than a mile along the river, and scattered across the grassy bottom of the valley were herds of horses and mules—Zach calculated a couple thousand at least.

The rider proved to be Joseph Meek, a member of Jim Bridger's brigade. They knew him from the previous summer's rendezvous. Last year Meek had accompanied William Sublette from St. Louis when Sublette freighted supplies and trade goods out to the Powder River site.

Meek was a big, bearded fellow with a cheerful disposition and a fine sense of humor. He was well liked by just about everyone. But his forehead was creased with worry as he galloped up.

"Howdy, Zach, Shad, boys." Meek's blue eyes, usually twinkling with merriment, but now dark and solemn, scanned the packs of fur belonging to the brigade. "Ya'll had a good season, I see."

"We fared well," said Zach.

"Any Injun trouble?"

"Not much."

"Lucky."

"How about you?"

Meek grinned, shaking his head. "Jim got it in his head to lead us up into Blackfoot country. We started out on the Tongue River. Found some beaver, but quick trapped 'em out. Next we tried the Bighorn, all the way up to Bovey's Fork."

"Wagh!" exclaimed Shadmore. "That neck of the woods is allus swarmin' with them red rascals."

"Plenty of beaver, though."

"That's beggin' for trouble. So you had Blackfeet on yore backsides all season, I warrant."

"Well, it weren't Blackfoot gave us the most trouble. First off, we got caught in a snowstorm. Heavy snow up thataway late in the winter. Then a bunch of warm days, and the snow was quick to melt and the rivers rose. Lost thirty horses and a couple hundred traps tryin' to get across Bovey's Fork."

"You didn't turn back?" queried Shadmore.

"With Jim Bridger for booshway? What do you think, hoss? We kept on, right through Pryor's Gap, to the Rosebud and thence to the Yellowstone. Now fellers, thar's a place where that river makes a big bend, with plenty of grass in the bottoms, and plenty cottonwood, too. Prime fixin's for a rendezvous."

"Shore," said Shadmore wryly, "iffen the Blackfeet'll just oblige us and move on up into Canada."

"We had us a scrape or two, but they never did find out where our main camp was. We crossed the Yellowstone in bullboats and set up on the Judith

River. Never seen so much beaver. Problem was, there was this godawful-big Blackfoot village on the Judith. We stuck it out for a while, and made a nice haul, but after a spell we figured it was pressin' our luck and headed back down the Yellowstone."

"Well, you could kick me to death with grasshopper legs," said Shadmore in admiration. "You fellers trapped beaver right under Blackfoot noses!"

"Tell the truth," chuckled Meek, "It was bears rather than Blackfoot what nearly done me in this year. Me and Hawkins was amblin' along the Yellowstone one mornin' when we seen this bear on the other side. We shot acrost and he dropped, and we thought we had kilt the critter. So we tied up our hosses, stripped down, and swum over to skin it. Left our guns on the other side. All we had was our knives in our teeth. Well, wouldn't you know it, that ol' bear warn't dead at all. Just playin' possum. And no sooner did we come out of the river than he jumped up and took out after us. We lit out, with that bear on our heels. Jumped into the river with it right behind us.

"Now Hawkins, he didn't fight the current. It was plenty strong, and it swept us all three downriver purty quick. The bear was going downstream backwards, and I ended up above him, and he saw me and tried to swim agin the current to get me, so I was obliged to swim agin the current, too.

"Hawkins, he managed to get ashore, and commenced to whoopin' and hollerin' and carryin' on like nobody's business. The bear heard all this commotion, like Hawkins wanted, and it forgot about me and decided it was time to get ashore too. Lucky for us, it picked the wrong side of the river. So I swum over to join Hawkins and we spent a while cussin' 'crost the river at that bear, and it growled back at us, and we all carried on like that till Hawkins and me realized we was stark naked. So we figured to go on upstream and find our plunder, and it was then that we realized we was on the wrong side of the river.

"Warn't nothin' fer it but to go on upstream and swim back acrost. Thing is, that damfool bear kept right on going along with us on the other side. We tried doubling back, and it doubled back with us. I swear, we marched up and down that stretch of river fer a good long while, gettin' madder and madder.

"Finally, we went downstream and then left the river, circlin' round at least a mile, and when we got back to the bank we was right acrost from where our clothes and rifles was, and we figured we'd lost that bear finally. Imagine our surprise when we seen that bear sitting right acrost the river, not a stone's throw from our plunder, like he'd been awaitin' there all along fer us to show back up!

"By this time it was gettin' on to sundown, so we just plumb give up and headed back to camp, naked as a pair of jaybirds, with just our knives fer weapons. And you kin figure out for yerselves the kind of reception we got from the rest of the brigade, showin' up in such condition. Them's the *bare* facts, boys."

But while the others were laughing at this tale,

Meek got to looking solemn all over again. He glanced over his shoulder at the encampment, and Zach could sense his apprehension. In fact, Zach had wondered all along if Meek had told his bear story just to put off telling them what he had rushed out to tell them. Something was amiss, and Meek had come to warn them—of that much Zach was certain.

"We've got us some competition. Thar's a new bunch out hyar now. Call themselves the American Fur Company. Run by a Major Vanderburg and a feller name Drips. Big money behind them—John Jacob Astor himself."

The others exchanged surprised looks. All of them had heard of Astor. His was an American success story. Born in Germany, he had arrived penniless in Baltimore. He had started in business with a small fur shop in New York and being a shrewd and ambitious man, soon parlayed himself into one of the country's leading merchants. He had become involved in the China trade. Back during the second war with England, when President Jefferson had put a strict embargo in effect, prohibiting any American ships from sailing into foreign waters, Astor had managed to get his vessel, the *Beaver*, to China and back by playing a trick on Jefferson. Foisting one of his clerks off on the government as a Chinese mandarin named Punqua Wingchong who desperately needed to return to China to take care of pressing family matters after the death of his grandfather, Astor had gotten the necessary papers for his ship to sail. The vessel left American waters with money and merchandise and returned full to the hatches with Chinese goods much in demand as a result of the Embargo Act. That shipment alone put Astor well on his way to becoming a millionaire.

And now this unscrupulous, hard-driving, brilliant entrepreneur was getting involved in the fur trade!

"Vanderburg and Drips and their men were waitin' fer us when we rode in. Problem was, Bill Sublette hadn't gotten here with his fourteen wagons from St. Louis—and didn't till day before yesterday.

"Now most of us trappers who float our stick with the Rocky Mountain Fur Company didn't have nothin' to do with Vanderburg and Drips, even though they had plenty of supplies, not to mention likker and tobacky, for trade. But they did talk a bunch of Injuns into tradin' with 'em. You reckon Bill Sublette was hot under the collar about that? Way he sees it, this American Fur Company just sashayed right on in here purty as you please and stole that Injun trade away from 'em. I swear I thought there was gonna be some blood shed over it. But I got to admit, Vanderburg and Drips are cool customers. They didn't get drawn into a fight they couldn't win."

"And Sublette and Fitzpatrick just let 'em stay on?" asked Shadmore in disbelief.

"Well, now, think about it. How would it look in front of our Injun friends? If they thought Bill and them was tryin' to corner the market on their furs, so to speak, they might start lookin' around to see if mebbe there ain't a better deal somewheres else. I hear tell this American Fur Company's got a fort up on the Yellowstone. It's that ol' stockade where the Yellowstone flows into the Missouri. How d' you like them apples?"

"But no Rocky Mountain boys traded with 'em?" asked Fletcher.

"None that I know of. But if they steal the Injun trade away, the Rocky Mountain Fur Company will be hurtin'."

"What else do you know about this new outfit?" asked Zach.

"Rumor has it they're tradin' with the Blackfoot, too."

Shadmore's eyes narrowed. "Them dirty scoundrels!"

MacGregor said, "I canna imagine the Hudson Bay sitting still for that."

"The Hudson Bay Company's pulled back into Canada, they say. Oh, McLaughlin's still over in the Oregon country, but they're pulled out of Blackfoot territory."

"Why come?" wondered Shadmore.

Meek shrugged. "Mebbe they got sick and tired of treatin' with them mangy mischief makers."

"And so the American Fur Company's moved in," mused Zach.

"Like I said, it's a rumor. And I ain't half sure it warn't dreamt up by Dave Jackson to turn the Crows and Flatheads and Shoshones agin Vanderburg and Drips. Also hear that ol' Kenneth McKenzie is runnin' Fort Union—that's what they've named that old fort you boys wintered in back in '23."

"Red Coat himself!" exclaimed MacGregor.

"You know him?" asked Shadmore.

"Aye. Trapped with him up Canada way. A man to ride the river with. Knows more about trapping and Indians than any man I've ever met. If it's true, mark my words, then Mr. John Jacob Astor hired himself a bloody good booshway."

"If you've come to steer us away from Vanderburg," Zach told Meek, "you needn't have worried."

Meek's grin was sheepish. "Bill Sublette's got me runnin' out to meet every brigade 'fore they get in. He's afeared Major Vanderburg will get to 'em fust."

"We gave our word to trade only with Sublette and Jackson and Smith," said Zach. "We've been doing so for years. That should be enough."

"Don't get your hackles up, Zach," said Meek, his tone conciliatory. "Bill Sublette's just been rubbed the wrong way, and he ain't thinkin' clear. Try to make allowances. As for Jed Smith, he done been kilt."

"My God!" exclaimed Shadmore. "How'd it happen and who done it?"

"He was down south of here, on that Santa Fe Trail. Comanches kilt him. I don't know no more than that. But it hit Bill Sublette hard."

"Jedediah Smith was a good man," said Shadmore. "I remember he went through hell to bring word of

Ashley's trouble with the Arikara back in '24," said Fletcher.

Shadmore nodded, morose. "Just a younker then. Used to carry his Bible around with him ever'where he went. No better gentleman, and no braver man."

"Does this Vanderburg have trappers with him?" Zach asked Meek.

"Yeah," growled Shadmore. "I'd like to know iffen we're gonna have to fight over prime beaver valleys next season. Like we ain't got enough to worry about with them bloodthirsty Blackfoot."

"They've got an outfit," nodded Meek, with a sidelong glance at Zach. "And you all know one of 'em, at least. Leastways, that's what Jim Bridger tells me."

"We do?" puzzled Shadmore.

"A feller name of Devlin."

A small cry escaped Morning Sky's lips, for she was close enough to hear Meek, and Devlin's name was like a dagger thrust through her heart.

Shadmore glanced sharply at Zach Hannah. Zach's face was a mask of stone.

III

The summer rendezvous was always held in a valley where there was good water, plenty of graze for literally thousands of animals, and plenty of game near at hand. The upper valley of the Green River filled the bill perfectly, and no one could deny it was a pretty scene as well. Wildflowers were broad splashes of yellow, blue and pink in the tall grass. Cotton-puff clouds scudded across the bright-blue sky, their shadows racing across the valley. On all sides the rugged gray mountains stood in all their majesty, with the green cloak of the forest around their shoulders, and snowfields above the timberline.

Morning, noon, and night, the rendezvous was a lively scene. Most of the trappers had traded their furs upon arrival and they whiled away the rest of their sojourn spending their wages to buy supplies or losing them in games of chance.

Bill Sublette spent the day from sunup to after sundown near his well-guarded supply wagons. The trading was done on a blanket spread out on the grass. A trapper would bring his packs. Sublette would check them and make his offer. There was seldom any quarrel between him and the trapper. He was a meticulously fair man when it came to dealing for fur, and the trappers knew it.

Few Indian trappers let the opportunity pass to complain of being shortchanged. Some of them did so only half-seriously, hoping that they might extort a little more out of Sublette—a hopeless cause.

Occasionally, one would wax genuinely belligerent—usually one who had already had his fill of firewater. But nothing came of these scenes, because two frontiersmen always stood on either side of Bill Sublette, who sat Indian-fashion on the blanket. The bodyguards leaned on their rifles and watched solemnly with eagle eyes, and their presence, coupled with Sublette's unshakable calm, was usually sufficient to deter any dissatisfied customer from forcing the issue.

The packs of an experienced trapper were uniform. Eighty beaver furs made up a pack, or sixty otter, fourteen bearskins, ten buffalo robes. The Indians, more so than the whites, brought fox and muskrat, and a correct pack of fox pelts contained one hundred and twenty skins, while a pack of muskrat numbered six hundred.

The choicest pelts—the plews—were put in the middle of the pack to protect them from the elements. The pelts were always put with the fur side inward, and the whole thing lashed securely with rawhide. A beaver pack weighed in at around fifty pounds.

A pack of beaver this season was bringing two hundred dollars. Otter brought a good price, and bear and buffalo a fair one, as usual. But Sublette could not give much for fox and muskrat. Few of the Indians traded bear or buffalo. Both animals were sacred, or close to it, in the opinion of most of the tribes, and they used the buffalo robes and the bearskins themselves.

In the case of many of the trappers, Sublette did not bother checking the packs closely. Quite a number at the Green River rendezvous were old Rocky Mountain Fur Company veterans. These men Sublette had known for years, and he trusted most of them, and rarely did a Rocky Mountain boy even contemplate cheating the company—not even a character like the notorious Antoine Godin, the half-breed with the temperament of a rattlesnake and the scruples of a coyote.

As for the men Sublette knew less well, he checked each fur, and while some resented this precaution, seldom did anyone make a complaint. Most of the Indians, too, had to wait while Sublette meticulously examined their packs, fur by fur. There were a few he knew he could rely on—Nez Percé and Flathead braves he had dealt with previously.

It was not uncommon for him to find damaged or poor furs in an Indian pack, but he never took offense upon discovery. Trying to put one over on the white man was accepted custom among the Crows and the Shoshones and some of the other tribes. Cheating, like stealing, was a perfectly honorable pursuit. Sublette realized that the Indians respected a white man who proved canny enough to see through a little deceit, so the discovery of a bad pelt was more often than not accompanied by laughter and backslapping. To his credit, Sublette paid his Indian clients on the same scale as he did the white trappers.

Once paid, the trappers headed for the wagons, which had arrived from St. Louis chock-full of merchandise. Since it was impractical for Sublette to haul enough hard money all the way to rendezvous to pay for hundreds of packs brought in, he gave his customers credit with which they could purchase the plunder they needed to get through another season in the high country.

He charged typical "mountain prices" for his

goods. Coffee cost a dollar and a half per pound, as did sugar. Tobacco was running at three dollars a pound, powder at two dollars a pound, and lead a dollar a pound. Fishhooks cost a dollar and a half per dozen, and flints a dollar per dozen. Diluted alcohol was going for four dollars a pint, while honest-to-God rum cost twelve dollars a gallon. Blue cloth brought four dollars a yard, scarlet cloth six dollars, knives two and a half each, and those three-point, blood-red Nor'west blankets so popular among the Indians a whopping nine dollars each.

A man could buy rum or alcohol by the cup, and Sublette did not cheat them by putting a half-inch or so of tallow in the bottom of the cup, as many traders were wont to do. His powder was Dupont, his lead was Galena. Still, he made a huge profit, without having to resort to dishonesty. And nobody begrudged him; bringing the goods all the way across the plains was a tough and risky business, and Sublette and his partners took a chance of losing it all to rampaging hostiles or natural calamity.

The white trappers stocked up on "necessaries"—lead and powder and tobacco and such—and those with squaws to pamper purchased the cloth and the beads and the little tin bells and other trinkets which made the eyes of Indian maidens light up. If they still had any credit left, Sublette's assistants would square the deal with hard money. Sublette had a few thousand dollars in a small iron chest for that purpose. In the past he had been confident he would get most of it back before the end of rendezvous.

The trappers almost inevitably came back for one more jug of liquor or block of tobacco, or fofarraw if they happened to "squaw up" during the "big gather." Many an Indian woman came to rendezvous in the hopes of finding a mountain man to take her on. Generally, they were better treated by a white husband. It was easy to distinguish a mountain man's woman: she was weighed down with about ten pounds of bells and baubles and bracelets, and you could hear them jingling and jangling a mile off.

There, though, was the rub for Sublette regarding the unwelcome presence of Vanderburg and Drips and their outfit. The American Fur Company was undercutting some of Sublette's prices by just enough to garner some business, so Bill and his partners weren't getting back all that coin they were doling out. A trapper might feel obliged to trade his furs to the Rocky Mountain Fur Company, but he didn't necessarily have to spend his hard money with them. For the first time, Sublette was faced with the prospect of having goods left over after rendezvous, and he wasn't happy about it.

IV

The Indian encampments were kept separate from those of the white trappers. This was by mutual preference; still, there was plenty of coming and going between them. And the tribes themselves kept their

lodges apart: the Nez Percé, the Snakes, the Flatheads, the Shoshones, the Crows, even the Sioux.

The camps of the different tribes were scarcely
distinguishable one from the other. Old men sat in
what shade they could find and smoked their pipes,
or strode among the tepees spreading news and lec-
turing the younger and less wise on diverse subjects.
Children played down by the river. Women scraped
hides or cooked or mended or carried firewood and
performed almost all the menial chores, while the
bucks raced their horses or drank themselves into a
stupor or lay in the shade, sometimes with their
heads resting in the laps of their squaws. Young lovers sought seclusion—a difficult task at rendezvous—and usually chose to wrap themselves in a
blanket, their heads covered, while they stood together or strolled along the riverbank.

Zach Hannah picked a spot near the Crow camp
to set up the brigade. He liked the Absaroka, and
they held him in high regard. He had fought well
with them against the Blackfeet in the big fight back
in '23, which was still much talked about. Alone in
the mountains, he had done his share of fighting
Blackfeet, too; in fact, he had become notorious
among the members of that northern tribe, and his
scalp was one of the most sought after by its warriors. Naturally, then, since the Crows hated the
Blackfeet, they considered Zach Hannah one of their
greatest allies. The enemy of their enemy was their
friend.

The Crows were famous thieves. For this reason,

most of the booshways made their camps as far away from them as possible. This arrangement suited Zach right down to the ground. The Crows respected him too much to steal from him or his brigade, and Zach preferred some space between himself and the other white trappers. Indians had never betrayed him, but a white man had. A man named Sean Michael Devlin.

Shelter was made for Sky and little Jacob by securing blankets to poles embedded in the ground. The rest of the brigade slept out in the open. The horses were let loose to graze and the men took turns keeping an eye on them. One by one, each trapper took his share of furs to Sublette and made his trade. Meanwhile, men from other brigades wandered by to pay their respects and speak of their adventures since last summer.

Tom Fitzpatrick had very nearly lost his hair. Seeing Vanderburg and Drips at the rendezvous, he had lit out to intercept Bill Sublette's wagon train, hoping that news of the American Fur Company interlopers would spur Sublette to make all possible haste. After he found Sublette and delivered his message, Fitzpatrick had then turned right around and hastened back toward the Green River, urged by Sublette to remind the Rocky Mountain men of their allegiance.

On the return trip, Fitz had come upon a small party of Blackfeet, suddenly and completely out in the open, with no place to hide. He had turned tail and dusted out; the Blackfeet had given chase.

Abandoning his pack horse, Fitzpatrick had gained the cover of some woods and hidden himself in a rocky ravine until the danger seemed past. Venturing back out into the valley, he had no sooner broken cover than the Blackfeet, who had just recently given up their search for him, spotted him again. This time the chase led higher into the mountains, and Fitzpatrick had been forced to abandon his saddle horse and climb a cliff to reach the shelter of a cave, where he figured to make his last stand.

But the Blackfeet did not find the cave. They scoured the mountainside and the valley below. They lingered for an entire day before abandoning the effort. He remained holed up for most of another day, just to make sure they weren't attempting a ruse to lure him out into the open. Only when he was fairly certain that the Blackfeet were truly gone did he sally forth yet again and manage to make his way safely back to rendezvous.

"I tell you, boys," he said, "those Blackfeet are gettin' to be a mite too pesky for my taste. They're all over the place. Gonna come a time, right soon, when we're gonna have to band together and go on up there north of the Missouri and have it out with them, once and for all. Mark my words. The day's soon comin', and sooner than you might care to know. The best beaver country is up yonder, and 'fore long we'll be obliged to go on up there and get 'em or quit this business."

"Why not let the soldiers do it?" asked Fletcher.

"Soldiers?" Fitzpatrick snorted. "They ain't of a

mind to, first off. Second, I ain't at all sure they could get the job done. Not the whole danged United States Army."

Shadmore nodded. "Remember how Colonel Leavenworth fared with them Arikarees back in '24."

"No," said Fitzpatrick, shaking his head, "we'll have to do it, iffen we ever want them beaver in the north, and iffen we're ever to be free of this Blackfoot plague."

Others came by to visit. Bridger, Beckwourth, Jackson, Godin, Milton Sublette—all men who, like Zach and Shad, had come out with Major Henry on the maiden expedition of the Rocky Mountain Fur Company. Others came who had yondered west in subsequent years, but there was a special camaraderie among the men who had belonged to the initial group.

It was Jim Bridger who drew Zach aside to speak of Devlin.

Next to Shadmore, Bridger was Zach's closest acquaintance in the Rocky Mountain brotherhood. They talked for a while, out of earshot of anyone else. Sky watched them from afar, her features etched with concern. And when Bridger took his leave and Zach returned to her, she asked him what had been said.

The query startled Zach. It wasn't Sky's way to pry. He realized she had guessed the subject of his conversation with Bridger.

"We talked about him," he said. "But then, you must have figured that out."

His tone was a little gruff. At first Sky was hurt by it. But she reminded herself that it would have been unfair to expect Zach to be calm and detached and rational when it came to Devlin, after what Devlin had done.

"What are you going to do?"

"I know what I'd like to do," said Zach, his voice pitched low—which signaled to all who were well acquainted with him that he was truly angry. "He's got a lot of gall, showing up here like this."

"He could not know for sure we would be here."

"I reckon he thought there was a fair chance. Maybe that's exactly why he is here."

"What do you mean?"

"I mean that if he's of a mind to try and make off with you again, I'll kill him."

"Do not say it," whispered Sky, touching his lips with a finger.

Zach's eyes flashed anger. "You trying to protect him? You've got some feelings for him?"

"I do not," she said sternly. "But what you speak of is killing someone in cold blood. You have never spoken in such a way."

"Jim is going to Vanderburg, to tell him he best keep Devlin on a short rein. Or, better yet, send him packing. I gave Jim my word I wouldn't go hunting for Devlin. He seems to think that if I start some trouble, it might trigger all-out war between the Rocky Mountain and American Fur Companies. Seems like we're sitting on a powder keg. But I tell you this. If he comes anywhere near you or little Jacob, he's gone beaver."

Sky nodded sadly. She was glad Jacob was off with Montez, and not present to hear Zach speak such brutal words.

Zach went off to see William Sublette, but not after having a word with Shadmore, and Sky guessed that he had asked the old leatherstocking to keep an eye peeled for Coyote, as Shad called Devlin.

For her part, Sky seated herself in the shade of the shelter Zach had rigged for her and worked on mending a pair of her husband's buckskin leggins. But her mind was not on her work. She kept looking around at the bustle of the rendezvous—looking for Devlin. She was afraid Zach was right. It probably wasn't coincidence that Devlin was here. What did he want? Her? Little Jacob? Surely not his son. Not after the way he had acted when she informed him of her pregnancy. People could change. Panic swept through her. What if he had come to steal her son? She tried to calm herself. Montez would not let anything happen to Jacob. She wanted to run out and find them. But the knowledge that Devlin was out there somewhere frightened her. What if she ran into him instead? And there was no way of knowing where Montez and little Jacob were. So she waited, anxiously, until the Spaniard and her son returned to the encampment, and then she ran out to sweep the boy up in her arms and hold him tight, fighting back the tears.

V

When Sean Michael Devlin was summoned to Major Henry Vanderburg's tent, he found Andrew Drips there too. Vanderburg was seated at a folding table. He was a stern, sour-faced man, his silver hair brushed straight back from a long, sallow face adorned with a luxuriant roan mustache. He had a well-deserved reputation for being hard-driving and unforgiving, and he reminded Devlin of another major—Andrew Henry, who, with Ashley, had led the Rocky Mountain Fur Company. Devlin wondered if that was the way with all military men—arrogant in attitude. He had never felt comfortable around Henry. Always resented the way Henry gave orders, like God had special-made him to lord it over others. Vanderburg was much the same.

Drips was a different story altogether. One could scarcely have imagined a man more unlike Vanderburg. He was short where the major was tall, hefty where Vanderburg was rail-thin. And he was ruddy-complected, while Vanderburg's complexion was like alabaster. He was careless in dress, while the major, though in buckskins, somehow managed to look spit-and-polish. Drips liked a good drink; Vanderburg thought the partaking of liquor a grave sin. He was gregarious; Vanderburg never minced words, and never beat around the bush.

Most important from the viewpoint of a man like Devlin, who required a lot of forgiveness, Drips was easygoing and more than willing to overlook the shortcomings of others—perhaps because he had so many himself, and cheerily admitted as much.

In short, Drips was something of a rogue. Yet he apparently had a shrewd mind for business. A born horse trader, he knew how to make money. Unfortunately, he did not seem to know how to hold on to it. Hence his shabby dress—he was chronically out-of-pocket in spite of his cunning and always willing to lend an ear to any scheme that might turn a fast profit. Devlin suspected that old demon rum of being the real culprit. Liquor could make a fool of the most intelligent of men.

"You wanted to see me?" asked Devlin, a bit insolently. He had responded promptly to the summons because he valued his association with the American Fur Company. He didn't want to lose his job. Yet for some reason he could not bring himself to act subservient in the presence of his superiors, and as a result he barely managed to show respect.

And then there was pride. He liked to think Vanderburg and Drips needed him because they wanted the Blackfeet for allies, and Devlin was a friend of that tribe.

"You told us you worked for the Hudson Bay," said the major, snapping out each word. He spoke like an officer giving a soldier a good dressing-down. "You said you were friend to the Blackfoot."

"I am," said Devlin.

"You never told us about your activities prior to your employment with the Hudson Bay Company."

"You never asked."

Vanderburg's lips thinned. Exasperated, he glanced at Drips.

"These mountain men are an insolent bunch," he remarked to his associate, the words laced with derision.

Drips chuckled nervously. "Got to make allowances, Major. That's what I always say."

Vanderburg grunted and turned his attention back to Devlin. Hands clasped on top of the table, sitting ramrod straight in the folding camp chair, he said, "I am told you came west with the Rocky Mountain Fur Company."

Devlin nodded. "I never tried to hide it. You just never asked. I figured you'd hear about that at this rendezvous. What does it matter?"

"Why are you no longer with them?"

"I killed Mike Fink, for one thing."

"Mike Fink!" exclaimed Drips. "The King of the Keelboat Men?"

"Yep."

"You sound proud of that," said Vanderburg. "I've killed before. It's nothing to be proud of."

Devlin stiffened. The major liked to lecture, but Devlin didn't take to being lectured to.

"It was self-defense," he replied.

"Yet you say it was the reason for your leaving the Rocky Mountain Fur Company."

"It was one reason."

"Zach Hannah would be another, I'd wager."

Devlin's eyes narrowed. After a moment, he breathed, "He's here, then."

"So I have been told."

"Who told you?"

"Jim Bridger. He also told me about an Indian woman named Morning Sky."

The major was watching Devlin like a vulture would watch a body, sprawled on the ground, for any sign of life. Devlin's reaction to the name was so strong that it twisted his burnished features.

"Ah," exclaimed Vanderburg, "so you do know this woman."

"She was my woman," said Devlin coldly.

Vanderburg arched a brow. "Was she now?"

"You saying otherwise?" bristled Devlin.

Drips raised both hands, as though trying to ward off Devlin's hostility.

"Certainly not, Devlin. Are we, Major?"

Vanderburg was grim. His partner had bought Devlin's reputation lock, stock, and barrel. This lanky, redheaded frontiersman was supposed to be a man you didn't want to tangle with. Partly it was a result of his ability to come and go freely among the Blackfeet—a feat precious few white men could duplicate, or would even dare try.

"You claim she was your woman," said the major. "How is it that she is not still?"

"Zach Hannah stole her."

"Did he now? A man like you, Devlin? Well, I would not have thought you'd let that happen without doing something about it."

"I wasn't there when it happened, or it wouldn't have."

"And you did not try to track this Zach Hannah down?"

"I tried. I lost them in the high country."

Vanderburg was impassive. "This is not exactly what Jim Bridger told me. He says you came west with the Rocky Mountain Fur Company back in '23. Major Henry's outfit. He says you were Zach Hannah's friend. That Hannah met and married this Morning Sky. She was with the Absaroka Crows, though born a Blackfoot, with some French-Canadian blood thrown in for good measure. A real beauty, Bridger says. Taken as captive by the Crows when but a child."

"That much is true. Except that she was mine, not Zach Hannah's."

"Bridger went on to say that when Zach and he and most of the others left the post on the Yellowstone to go on the Arikara Campaign—that was '24, if memory serves me—you made off with Morning Sky."

"Bridger is Zach's friend, and a notorious liar."

Vanderburg wondered if Devlin would dare indulge in such bold talk if Bridger himself were present. Among mountain men, the word "liar" often led to bloodshed.

"He told me several Crow warriors set out after you. The Crow, it would appear, think as highly of Zach Hannah as the Blackfeet think of you. You killed one of them, named Rides A Dark Horse."

"That I did."

"Which would account for the Blackfeet calling you their white brother, would it not?"

"It didn't hurt."

Vanderburg smirked. "You knew you would not be safe in Crow country after that. So your only recourse was to cross the Missouri and take your chances with the Blackfeet. There you were fortunate to make the acquaintance of a Scotsman named MacGregor, who was then a Hudson Bay man and who is now, as fate would have it, a member of Zach Hannah's brigade. It was from MacGregor, in fact, that Bridger received much of the intelligence he recently relayed to me."

"I'm not denying I met up with MacGregor. I killed his partner. He was a drunken lout, and he tried to force himself on Morning Sky. So I killed him. Like I killed Mike Fink and Rides A Dark Horse."

"You are a dangerous man," said Vanderburg.

Devlin's blue eyes narrowed. He figured the major was being sarcastic, but he couldn't hear a trace of it in Vanderburg's comment.

"That's been the case," he replied, and meant it as a warning.

VI

"Bridger told me more," said Vanderburg. Devlin's warning had fallen on deaf ears. The major didn't seem to be fazed at all, and that angered Devlin, because his bluff had been called. His reputation and tough posturing hadn't impressed the major at all.

"More lies, I'd wager," said Devlin.

"He told me about a man named Eli Simpson."

Devlin felt the blood freeze in his veins.

Vanderburg continued. "He claims you and a man named Cooper had been out trapping with this man, Simpson, back when all of you were still in the employ of the Rocky Mountain Fur Company. Simpson was hurt by a grizzly, and you and Cooper left him for dead because you feared for your own lives, as there were hostile Indians in the vicinity.

"But Simpson didn't die. By a remarkable feat of endurance and courage, he made his way back to the post on the Yellowstone. At that point, you fled. And you stole Morning Sky while you were at it."

"Black lies!" said Devlin through clenched teeth. "I have never quit on another trapper. Never would."

"I hope not. For a man that would has no place in my company."

"Or in mine," declared Devlin, with righteous indignation.

"This man Simpson was consumed by revenge. He vowed to track you and Cooper down, and make you pay for what you did. Cooper had run south, and Simpson finally found and killed him among the Arapaho. Then he went in search of you. He came across Zach Hannah and his brigade. Murdered one of Hannah's men."

Devlin shrugged. "I wouldn't know. I remember an Eli Simpson. He was with the Rocky Mountain Fur

Company, it's true. But I never trapped with him, never left him to die, and so I can't say I know what the hell you are talking about, Major."

Vanderburg pursed his lips. His dark, hawkish eyes were fastened on Devlin. They were, thought Devlin, disconcertingly keen. He felt as though they could see right through his facade, right down into his soul, where he tried to hide the dark deeds he had done.

Still, he managed to meet that piercing gaze. He did not even flinch. He was lying, and the major was suspicious, at the very least. But Devlin had no choice. He felt as though Vanderburg had lured him into the lie. Asking him why he hadn't hunted Hannah down, for instance, when all along he had known the truth. Devlin had been given more and more rope, and now he was hanging himself with it.

He swore silently, told himself he should have been on his guard the minute Vanderburg had mentioned Morning Sky. For he had known there was a chance—had prayed there would be—of finding her here at rendezvous. But, as usual, he had spoken rashly, without thinking the consequences through.

"So what else did Bridger lie about?" he asked truculently.

"That was all he said. I gathered that he thought it was enough."

Devlin scoffed at that. "Sounds like he did a fair job of smearing my good name. Saying I stole another man's woman. And that I left a fellow trapper to die in the wilderness. I reckon you must believe it, too."

"I never said I did."

"They never liked me—those Rocky Mountain boys—after they found out I was up there with the Blackfeet."

"You think that's why Bridger came to me? To assassinate your character? To make trouble between us?"

"Sure. Why not? You and Mr. Drips here are in competition with the Rocky Mountain Fur Company. They know how valuable I am to you. I can act as your go-between with the Blackfoot Nation. That gives you a big advantage over them. But if you believe Bridger over me, fine. I'll just go my own way. I don't care to work with anybody who doesn't trust me."

Vanderburg's smile was frosty. "I don't have to trust you, Devlin. I recognize your value to this company. You don't need to keep reminding me."

"Thing is," said Drips, his tone a placating one, "we don't want any trouble here."

"We can't afford it," amended Vanderburg. "We're lucky Sublette and his outfit didn't make a fight of it and try to run us off. I thought they might try, and we are outnumbered."

"They're fair-minded men," said Drips, and chuckled. It was no compliment, coming from him. "That makes 'em poor businessmen, which is good news for us."

"But we must behave ourselves," said Vanderburg.

"We must not give them an excuse to take a stronger stance against us."

"What's all this got to do with me?" asked Devlin.

"Let me spell it out for you, Devlin," snapped the major. "Frankly, I don't care whether Bridger is telling the truth or not. Either way, it appears there is plenty of bad blood between you and this Zach Hannah over this Indian woman. Hannah's here. So are you. That's a recipe for trouble. And we won't have any trouble. See my point?"

Devlin nodded, smirking. "You want me to stay away from Zach."

"And the woman. It is not a request. It's an order."

Devlin bristled at that. "I don't have to take your orders, Major. I could quit."

"You could. You could also wind up dead before sunset."

The threat startled Devlin. He stared, then forced a smile and added a laugh for good measure. But the laugh sounded too hollow for his liking.

"You're a ruthless bastard, Major."

"Yes, I am," agreed Vanderburg. "Because I won't let you scotch this up for me, Devlin."

Devlin didn't know how to respond. He could look at Vanderburg and see the man was deadly serious. Obviously the major wasn't impressed by his reputation as a man who made corpses out of everyone who crossed him. That scared Devlin—scared him right down to the ground. Because that reputation, earned largely by accident, was all he had.

The problem was, he had killed Mike Fink in the

blind panic of self-defense, and Rides A Dark Horse too, and even MacGregor's drunken lout of a partner. In every case he would have weaseled out of the fight had he managed to find a way. Sean Michael Devlin lacked courage, and nobody knew that better than he himself.

So how could he get out of this fix with Vanderburg? Just back down and crawl out like a cur dog, tail tucked? The major had threatened him, and Devlin was painfully aware that a man with his reputation was supposed to react belligerently to being threatened. But Devlin didn't react. He couldn't even move. Fear rooted him to the ground. Vanderburg had called his bluff, and there was nothing else to do but fold.

Drips came to his rescue.

"Now, now, friends. No need for this. We're supposed to work together."

Vanderburg stabbed a finger at Devlin. "Just stay away from Zach Hannah and that Indian woman, Devlin. You want a shot at him, and at getting her back? Fine. You'll have it. But when I say so. Not before."

"What do you mean?"

"I mean Andrew and I have hatched a little scheme. When the Rocky Mountain brigades leave here they'll be headed for prime beaver country. Their booshways know these mountains like nobody else, aside from the Indians, and the damned redskins are unreliable."

"So?"

"So we're sending a few men out after every Rocky Mountain brigade. You and Keller and Bledsoe are assigned to Hannah's bunch. You let Hannah lead you to the beaver. Then, once they settle in and lay their traps out, you hie on back to Fort Union and report."

"Then what?"

"Then we lead our Blackfoot friends back to the Rocky Mountain brigades. The Blackfeet will take care of the Rocky Mountain boys, and we'll take the furs."

"That means war."

"A man with your reputation, Devlin, shouldn't mind a good fight."

"That's not sounding like a good fight to me. It sounds downright cold-blooded."

"They're no friends of yours, are they?"

"No, but . . ."

"And you'll be able to get that woman back—the one you say Hannah stole away from you. So, you see? You'll get your chance. But it will be done my way."

Devlin was stunned. He had never heard anything quite so diabolical. And if Vanderburg could discuss full-scale mountain war so calmly, then he was certainly not one to hesitate carrying out his personal threat to kill Devlin if Devlin made trouble.

"Okay," said Devlin. "You're calling the shots, Major."

Vanderburg smiled, warm as winter. "I thought you would see it my way."

VII

It was Zach Hannah's way to trap only as much fur as he needed to trade for necessary items, plus a gift or two for Sky and little Jacob. While most mountain men trapped all they could so that, necessary purchases aside, they would have money or credit left over with which to buy whiskey or indulge in games of chance, these pursuits were of no interest to Zach.

As a result, he trapped less than others, and this in turn gave him more time to do what he preferred: scouting and exploring. He never tired of these activities. Every rock, every tree, every stream was of interest to him. He wanted to know every inch of the high country, the way a man wants to know every inch of the woman he loves.

Apart from that, he did not like the way the beaver were being trapped out. Already he could see the harmful effects of extensive trapping. Many areas once brimming with beaver were completely cleaned out.

"You've brought some fine plews, I'm sure," William Sublette told him. "But not as many as the others in your brigade."

"I never do. You know that. But I need powder and shot and some other plunder."

Sublette nodded. "How's your woman and boy?"

"Well."

"My brother Milton squawed up," remarked

Sublette, with a wry smile. "A Snake woman. Umentucken Tukutsey Undewatsey, they call her."

"Mountain Lamb."

"That's it. 'Course, he almost lost his hair on account of her."

"What happened?"

Sublette scowled. "Damned conniving Rockway Injun name of Gray stabbed him. Claimed Milt insulted his daughter."

"I find that hard to believe."

"So do I. Milt's brigade and Jim Bridger's were trapping together at the time, but they had to move on, on account of those damned Blackfeet had showed up. So when the others moved on, Milt was left behind in the care of Joe Meek. Now there's a man you can float your stick with. Meek stuck by him for six weeks. That's how long it took Milt to heal up. He was in a bad way. Him and Meek became fast friends."

"Joe Meek's got sand."

"Once Milt was well enough to ride, they set out to catch up with Bridger and the rest. They come up sudden-like on a bunch of Snake Injuns. The braves were out watchin' over their horse herd. They lit out after Milt and Meek, who took off like greased lightning. And they let themselves get chased straight into the whole Snake village! Their only chance was to make a run for the medicine lodge. They dashed through the village and ducked into the lodge with them Injuns on their heels. But they were safe inside. Safe as if they was in a church. No harm can be done to any living creature inside a medicine lodge. It's sacred ground. An Injun commits an act of violence there and he loses his soul.

"Them Injuns didn't know rightly what to do. They held a big council right there in the lodge. They smoked the pipe and had a long palaver. Milt tells me they talked it over all day—what to do with the two white men. Milt and Meek sat there amongst them, bold as brass. Where could they go? They took a lot of verbal abuse, of course, but none of the Snakes laid a hand on 'em. Must've been strange, sitting there listening to a passel of redskins talk about skinning you alive and roasting you over an open fire and such. But I bet Milt and Meek acted like they weren't the least bit worried, if I know them. That's the only way to act in the presence of Injuns, you know. Like you ain't got a nerve in your body. They respect that. Show any fear at all and they're on you faster'n a duck on a June bug.

"Most all the council wanted to kill them. One old chief named Gotia, though, voted to let them go in peace. He got shouted down. By sunset the verdict was in. Milt and Meek were sentenced to die. Seems that by some long, drawn-out ceremony the Injuns could get around the problem of the medicine lodge being a safe haven. That done, they was aimin' to come back and lift some hair.

"So Milt and Meek, they decided their only hope was to make a run for it, after dark. The Injuns left the lodge, and on his way out, Gotia made a sign to them—a sign that there was a chance for life. They

didn't see how that could be, but not long after sunset they heard this god-awful commotion. Something
was wrong with the horse herd. Most all the Injuns
in the village went runnin' out to see what the trouble was. A grass fire had done got started, and the
horse herd was stampedin'.

"A few minutes later, Gotia showed up at the
medicine lodge and beckoned for my brother and
Meek to follow him. This they did, and found their
horses in a thicket at the edge of the village. They
were being held by a young Injun woman. You know
her name.

"Now, Milt wanted Gotia and Mountain Lamb
both to come away with him. He didn't give much
for their chances when the rest of the village found
out what the old chief had done to help the hair-
faces escape. But Gotia said he was too old to make
a getaway. He wanted Mountain Lamb to go, though.
But she wouldn't go either. Y'see, Gotia was her
grandfather. Her father was dead and Gotia had
raised her and she wouldn't leave him for nothing.
Brave girl.

"So Milt and Meek set out alone. Eventually
caught up with Bridger and the others. But Milt
couldn't get that Mountain Lamb off his mind. He
lasted a couple weeks. Then one day he told Joe
Meek he just had to go back and find out if Mountain Lamb was alive or not." Sublette shook his head.
"The things a man will do on account of a woman."

"You sound like Shadmore."

"Well, he's my brother, and it was a damfool thing

to do. And Joe Meek was a bigger damfool for going along, but then I reckon it's pretty clear Joe's a true friend. Had to be, to do what he done."

"It must have turned out well," said Zach. "I've seen Joe Meek, and hear tell Milt's been winning horse races left and right ever since he got here."

Sublette chuckled. "Yes! And he's winning those races on Snake horses!"

"Did he steal 'em?"

"They were Mountain Lamb's dowry."

"Never heard of such. You usually have to spend horses to get an Indian bride."

"Milt's always been a lucky coot. You must see that's the gospel, after the story I just told. Anyroad, he and Meek ride back to that Snake village. Milt's of a mind to sneak in under the cover of night just to pay a call on Mountain Lamb. But when they draw near they find a young Snake brave bein' hounded by a passel of Blackfoot. Milt and Joe make short work of the Blackfeet. The Snake boy is mighty grateful. He tells 'em the village is under attack. They make tracks for it. By the time they get there the fight's been fought. The Snakes drove the Blackfeet off.

"When the village finds out how Milt and Meek saved the boy they treat my damfool brother and his damfool friend like long-lost brothers. Tell me honest, Zach. Are Injuns fickle, or what?"

"They just take a little getting used to."

"Sure. If you can stay alive long enough."

"So what happened then?"

"Appears the Snakes had decided that between the white man and them nasty Blackfeet, the white man was the lesser of two evils. So they made Milt and Meek feel right at home. And when Milt started talkin' about maybe taking Mountain Lamb for his bride, them Snakes didn't waste no time. They went for the idea, whole hog. Even gave Milt a few of their best cayuses to seal the bargain! Now the Snakes feel about Milt the way the Absaroka Crows feel about you, Zach. They adopted him into the tribe."

"I'm glad he came out of it with his hair."

Sublette nodded, grinning. But his grin faded fast. "Yes, Milt always seems to come out of things smellin' like a rose. Which is why he'll do better than me in this job."

"What do you mean?"

"He's takin' over for me. I've had my fill, Zach. I'm calling it quits with the Rocky Mountain Fur Company. Selling out my interest."

"Why?"

Sublette shrugged. "I reckon this American Fur Company is the last straw for me. Too much headache. There's a new trade springin' up with Santa Fe. That's what Jedediah Smith got into last year. Only he got kilt by Comanche Injuns down on the Cimarron. Still, there's a lot of money to be made on the Santa Fe Trail, and I have a hankerin' to try my hand at it. Might even head out to California. Like to see that country. But one thing I ain't got a hankerin' for is one more pesky Blackfoot, or any more of Vanderburg and Drips."

"Milt's buying you out?"

"Him and Jim Bridger and ol' Broken Hand Fitzpatrick himself. Might be a couple others. And I was wondering about you. Maybe you'd like . . ."

Zach shook his head emphatically. "No thanks."

"The company would be in mighty good hands if you took the reins along with them others."

"They'll do fine without me, too."

"Who knows the high country better than you, Zach? Or the Injuns, either? All the boys respect you."

"No, thanks all the same."

"Mind if I ask why?"

Zach looked Sublette square in the eye.

" 'Cause there's going to be full-scale war in these mountains, Bill."

"With the Blackfeet? I reckon it's already started."

"That's bad enough. But it's not what I mean."

"I don't follow."

"I mean a war with the American Fur Company. A war between mountain men."

"How do you figure?"

Zach picked up a hairy bank note. "You're paying better every year for these."

"Demand back east is still sky high. Higher than it ever has been before."

"Problem is, there are only so many beaver in this country. Every season we trap out a dozen or so more valleys. Clean 'em out, too, Bill, so that the beaver will never return. And even as they get harder to find, there seem to be more and more trappers out here every year looking for them."

"Milt and Jim and Broken Hand have talked about splitting the country up with Vanderburg. Just to keep things peaceable."

"They can try."

"You sound like you don't think it would work."

"I don't think it would."

"Why not?"

"Because men are greedy. Sooner or later there'll be blood shed over one of these." Zach threw the beaver plew down and stood. "I, for one, don't want to be a part of it. Sorry, Bill. Best of luck to you in Santa Fe."

IX

While the rest of the brigade socialized with other trappers, Zach spent some time with his friends the Absaroka Crows.

Of all the mountain men, Zach Hannah was the one the Crows were most attached to. This kinship was the result of several past events. For one, he had distinguished himself in a big fight seven years previously, siding with the Absaroka against the Blackfeet.

The Rocky Mountain Fur Company had just established the fort at the mouth of the Yellowstone. There Major Henry and his frontiersmen had resolved to spend the winter of '23–'24, while Ashley returned to St. Louis to acquire more horses and more supplies and a keelboat or two—replacements for what had been lost during the journey west that summer, and all of which were necessary in order for the company to proceed to the Shining Mountains.

As they were wont to do, the Absaroka Crows had spent their summer on the high plains further up the Yellowstone. Hearing of the presence of a large group of white men nearby, they investigated. Thanks in large measure to the wisdom of their chief, Iron Bull, their attitude had been friendly.

Iron Bull realized the Crows needed allies in their war with the belligerent Blackfeet, the archenemies of the Sparrowhawk people. He figured the white trappers might be useful in that regard. This the Rocky Mountain men proved to be. A group of frontiersmen, Zach among them, had fought valiantly alongside the Crows to beat off a Blackfoot raiding party. All the trappers were feted by the Crows, but Zach Hannah was perceived as one who had earned special consideration by his valor. Zach had not shared this Crow perception, but he could not deny it served him well in subsequent negotiations for Morning Sky's hand in marriage.

The marriage had met with the approval of both Iron Bull and Major Henry. Both men believed it would enhance the newfound alliance between the Absaroka and the Rocky Mountain Fur Company.

A Crow warrior of great renown, Rides A Dark Horse, had been instrumental in the deal. All Crows hated the Blackfeet—generations of virtually uninterrupted warfare between the two tribes ensured lasting animosity—but none perhaps hated them so fiercely as Rides A Dark Horse. He had lost several family members in the war, and his hatred burned deep. Zach Hannah's prowess in battle had impressed him. He had seen with his own eyes the manner in which the young Tennessean, cool under fire, had dispatched several Blackfeet. He believed Zach's Hawken rifle possessed powerful magic—an instrument of destruction that he desired to see turned again on his enemies. It was his hope that Zach might be induced to become a blood brother of the Crows. At the time, Zach had shunned the idea; Rides A Dark Horse had settled for the marriage to tie Zach to the tribe.

Indeed, in time, it was Rides A Dark Horse who cemented Zach's attachment to the Absaroka. The warrior had made the ultimate sacrifice for Zach's sake. When Devlin had made off with Sky under false pretenses, while Zach was away on the Arikara Campaign of '24, Rides A Dark Horse had tried to stop him. Zach had elicited from the warrior a promise to look out for Morning Sky during his absence, and Rides A Dark Horse put great store by keeping his word. Devlin had killed him, a long and lucky shot. On that day the Absaroka Crows had lost a great warrior, and Zach had lost a better friend than he had realized at the time.

All these factors combined had forged a bond between Zach Hannah and the tribe. Other trappers cursed the Sparrowhawk people as the biggest bunch of thieves on the continent, and Zach did not deny that they were a bit light-fingered. But in every other way he found them of fine character. They were brave, generous, amiable, and as honorable as the noble Nez Percé. He could honestly say they had never done wrong by him.

Iron Bull was still the chief of the Crows, and he treated Zach like a son. They smoked a pipe together, and Zach presented him with some fine plews: mink, ermine, and fox. They feasted and talked candidly of many things. Foremost on the minds of both men was the American Fur Company—in particular, one of its employees, whom both the chief and the frontiersman had good reason to know well.

"My warriors came to tell me the killer of Rides A Dark Horse was here," said Iron Bull. His bronzed, deeply lined face remained impassive, but his dark eyes glittered like black diamonds, reflecting the flickering light of the fire in the smoky tepee.

Zach nodded. "I'm afraid he is."

"They wanted to kill Coyote."

"But you stopped them."

"Broken Hand asked it of me."

"Fitzpatrick?"

"Your people want no trouble with Coyote's people."

Zach knew the chief meant the Rocky Mountain Fur Company when he said "your people."

"They're not exactly my people, Iron Bull. But it is

true that they have tried to keep peace with the American Fur Company. They are even thinking of offering to split the mountains up between the two companies, laying out definite boundaries, to avoid any bloodshed."

Iron Bull shook his head. "Divide the mountains? How can this be done?"

Zach smiled. "It can't, really."

"The mountains belong to no one. The plains belong to no one."

"I agree."

"Most white men do not think the way you do," said Iron Bull regretfully.

"Coyote's people won't take the offer."

"They want war?"

"They'll be afraid of being tricked. They'll figure Broken Hand and Sublette will keep the best beaver country for themselves."

"One day the beaver will be no more."

"I was thinking the same thing myself."

"And then will the white man leave the mountains?"

"Some will. I won't."

"More will come. Many more." Iron Bull gazed into the fire.

Zach made no reply. He figured Iron Bull was right. And he wasn't any happier about the prospect than the Absaroka chief was. A few minutes passed before Iron Bull spoke.

"There will be a fight between your people and

Coyote's people, then. And between you and Coyote."

"I don't know. We were friends once. At one point I reckon he saved my life."

"He was never your friend. If you were a Crow warrior you would have killed him for what he did."

"Ever since I found out he was here at rendezvous, the thought's been crossing my mind," admitted Zach.

"I know many braves who will ride with you to kill Coyote and his people."

Zach shook his head. "I reckon not."

"Kill him," advised Iron Bull. "Do it now, or you will wish you had."

Zach was surprised. "That doesn't sound like you, Iron Bull. You've always talked more peace than war ever since I've known you."

"If you do not kill him now, then come live with the Sparrowhawk people." Affection softened Iron Bull's stern features. "You will be welcome among us, you and your family. Leave these other white men behind you. You are not like them. You love this land as we do. You are an Absaroka Crow in many ways. You have a strong heart. A good heart. Stay with us. Be a blood brother to the Crows. You are a great warrior. You can help us against our enemies, the Blackfeet. And no Coyote will lurk around your tepee in the dead of night."

"Your offer appeals to me in a lot of ways," said Zach. "Except the fighting part. I'd be trading one fight for another, sounds like."

"We will all have to fight the Blackfeet, until they are no more," predicted Iron Bull gravely. "But if you stay with Broken Hand and the others you will also have to fight Coyote and his people."

Zach sighed. "Maybe so. And there's the pity of it, my friend. Because all I want is to be left in peace."

X

Zach was ready to leave the rendezvous as soon as all the trading had been done and he had paid the Absaroka Crows a call. But most of his men were in no hurry to return to the lonesome life of a fur trapper. This was their one chance all year to cut loose, and men like Fletcher and Baptiste wanted to make the most of it. For his part, Montez was indifferent. At first Jubal Wilkes didn't care one way or the other. But then a Flathead woman turned his young head, and he had a sudden strong urge to tarry. As for Shadmore, the old leatherstocking had long ago done his share of whiskey-drinking and woman-chasing, and now the only attractive feature of rendezvous from his point of view was the opportunity to shoot the breeze with other mountain men, catching up on the news and swapping tall tales.

From Zach's perspective it was fortunate they had arrived late. The rendezvous had been going full blast for a whole week prior to their arrival. Already a few brigades were pulling up stakes and heading out. Zach used this fact to justify a prompt departure. They needed to get a jump on the new season. Old Man Winter would likely come early this year. There were signs that this would be the case, and everyone knew them. A couple more days—that was all he would allow them. Then they would blaze a trail.

A couple of days was all Baptiste needed to buy into trouble.

The French-Canadian was an excellent horseman, and he had a good eye for prime horseflesh. He'd made up his mind to come away from rendezvous with an Appaloosa, that special breed so highly regarded for spirit, stamina, and beauty. The Nez Percé had the majority of Appaloosas, though a few had found their way by trade or theft into Flathead hands.

Baptiste could not win one in a race. None of the mustangs in the brigade's cavallard could match a Palouse for speed. The mustang was a good mountain horse, sturdy and surefooted and strong, but not particularly swift. The only alternative left to the French-Canadian, short of thievery, was to win one in a game of chance. This was the strategy he adopted. Trade was out of the question. He had spent almost all his hairy bank notes on liquor and fofarraw for his Shoshone squaw. He had very little to trade with, and an Appaloosa brought a handsome price.

So he lured the owner of the horse he had his eye on into a wager. In exchange for the Nez Percé putting up the Appaloosa, Baptiste put up Flower. This was, of course, without Flower's knowledge. And it was by no means an indication that Baptiste had tired of her company. He did not intend to lose, and would not have upheld his end of the bargain if he had. Losing, though, was impossible, because Baptiste was using loaded dice, while the pair he offered the Nez Percé were not.

The game was over in a moment, and the result never in doubt. A roll of the bones on a Nor'west blanket and Baptiste was the proud new owner of a fine Appaloosa. The loser was downcast, but he honored the deal, as any Nez Percé would. Among his people, honor was everything.

The warrior bemoaned his fate to a white trapper named Laird, who did a little investigating. He happened to be in earshot when Baptiste foolishly boasted of cheating the Nez Percé. The French-Canadian was sharing a jug with a bunch of Rocky Mountain boys around a campfire, and strong spirits tended to loosen his tongue. Laird returned to his Nez Percé friend and enlightened him.

The irate warrior confronted Baptiste the next day. Baptiste emphatically denied having cheated the brave. The Nez Percé would not desist, and made an effort to confiscate the Appaloosa which had been taken by foul means. Baptiste lost his temper and threatened to take the warrior's scalp if he laid a hand on the horse. And so the fight was on, right in the middle of the brigade's camp.

Zach Hannah intervened in time to save the Nez Percé from losing his hair, if not his life. The warrior was courageous but suffered from the inexperience of youth. Baptiste was quick to gain the upper hand; he had the Nez Percé flat on the ground, a knee in the brave's back and his knife ready for bloody work as he grabbed the Indian's topknot and wrenched his head back.

A kick in the side was all Zach needed to apply. The French-Canadian rolled away and came up roaring with rage. All his pent-up resentment towards Zach surged to the surface. Flower was not present to restrain him with a sharply spoken word. He charged Zach with the hot sunlight flashing off the blade of his knife.

Zach eluded the first knife stroke, designed to eviscerate him. The butt-stock of his Hawken rifle struck Baptiste in the groin. This was quickly followed with a sweeping blow to the knees with the rifle, which knocked the French-Canadian's legs out from under him. Baptiste went down, groping his private parts and grunting like a hog.

It was over, quick as a thought. Baptiste had no fight left in him. Zach listened to the angry Nez Percé's story and told the warrior to take the Appaloosa. By this time Shadmore had arrived on the scene. The old leatherstocking impassively watched Baptiste writhing in agony on the ground. Zach told him what had happened.

"Cain't say I'm too surprised," said Shadmore. "Never did entirely trust that pork-eater."

"He's out of this brigade," said Zach.

Shad nodded. "Fair nuff. 'Course, I got to admit, I shore will miss them dough-cakes of Flower's."

"I'm sorry to see her go, myself," replied Zach. "But it's her misfortune to be hitched to such a man."

XI

That very night, Baptiste visited the encampment of the American Fur Company. He was seeking Sean Michael Devlin, and found the man he sought, with several other buckskin-clad frontiersmen, sitting at a crackling fire. Devlin and two of the others were roasting spitted chunks of venison. Blood sizzled in the flames as it dripped from the deer steaks.

"I am looking for a man named Devlin," said the French-Canadian.

"What do you want him for?" asked one of Devlin's companions.

Baptiste surveyed the circle of lean, sun-dark faces.

"Eet is not a fight I bring, but an offer."

"What kind of offer?" asked Devlin, wary.

"Are you heem? Devlin?"

"Maybe."

"I weel talk only to Devlin."

Devlin handed his spitted venison steak to the next man and stood up, draping his hand over the butt of the pistol stuck in his belt. He didn't care to identify himself until he was certain of the French-Canadian's intentions. But he had to. To do otherwise might give his associates around the fire the idea that he was a coward.

"Then talk," he said. "I'm Devlin. And you ride with Zach Hannah."

"How do you know this?"

"I just know," said Devlin, unwilling to admit that he had been skulking around the camp of Zach's brigade just for a glimpse of Morning Sky. Always he had kept a discreet distance, and never had he been seen, because he did not venture near except under cover of darkness.

The risks had been enormous. Not only from Zach Hannah and his outfit, but from Vanderburg, too. But Devlin had felt compelled to take those risks. They were worth running, for a look at Morning Sky.

He had seen her, briefly, on two separate occasions, and he had felt the need to possess her, strong as ever—a need he confused with love. In addition, he had experienced that familiar old resentment directed at Zach Hannah. He would have Sky again, someday. He would win. Zach would lose. These convictions consoled him. He would have her, and this time he would keep her until death parted them.

Once he had seen the boy, and it had been obvious that the lad was Sky's son, and so that meant he was Devlin's flesh and blood too. Devlin wasn't sure how he felt about the youngster. Conflicting emotions confused him. Devlin had never been one for introspection, and he didn't know how to decipher his feelings. He supposed he could tolerate the boy, if upon that tolerance was predicated his keeping

Morning Sky. Clearly he had made a mistake by being honest with her about his opinion on fatherhood. This time, if it meant so much to her—though why it should still perplexed him—he would make certain concessions.

And then he would feel even more resentment towards Zach. How dare Zach act as the boy's surrogate father—and do it well, no doubt. Hannah, damn him, always did well at anything and everything he put his mind to. That boy was a Devlin, and Zach had no right to him. The fact that Devlin had renounced the boy even before his birth didn't enter into the equation. Devlin reckoned it remained his right to claim the boy when he wanted to.

So now here was one of Zach's trappers. What did this bearded hulk of a man want? Was he Zach's agent? Did he bring a challenge? Devlin was a little surprised Zach had not sought him out for a confrontation before now.

"What kind of offer do you have in mind?" he asked, pleased that his voice remained so steady.

"I want to join up with you."

"Why's that?"

"I weel ride with Zach Hannah no longer."

Devlin's eyes lit up. He could hear the hate in the French-Canadian's voice when he spoke of Zach. It was a pure, honest hate. The man held a frontier-size grudge against Hannah. Which was very good news for Devlin.

"Why not?" he asked, relaxing.

"I am done taking orders from heem," replied Baptiste, truculently.

Devlin sensed that the man was in no mood to elaborate.

"So why did you come looking for me?"

"Because you are his enemy? No?"

"You could say that. We don't see eye to eye on much of anything, Zach and me."

"I am his enemy, too," declared Baptiste. "So I will ride with you."

Devlin turned to the men around the fire. "Hank, throw me that jug of corn liquor you've been hogging."

The jug was tossed. Devlin caught it deftly, proffered it to the French-Canadian. Baptiste was quick to take advantage of the offer, and downed a long swig. He came up gasping, wiping whiskey from his lips and beard with the back of a hand.

"You'll have to pass muster with Major Vanderburg," Devlin told him. "He does the hiring. But I'll go along with you. Put in a good word for you. You can join up with me."

"Where will you trap this season?"

Devlin's smile was crooked. "Why, we'll go where Zach Hannah goes. He's gonna lead us to the brown gold. Then we're gonna go in and take it from him. How's that suit you?"

Baptiste looked the other frontiersmen over, judging the fight in them.

"You may need more help, *mon ami*. Make no mistake. It will not be easy to kill Zach Hannah."

"Oh, we'll have plenty of help," said Devlin, and almost blurted out Vanderburg's scheme to employ the Blackfeet for that purpose. But he stopped short of doing so. No point in revealing all the cards in the American Fur Company's hand. He still wasn't completely sure about Baptiste. Oh, the French-Canadian held a grudge against Zach, that was clear as mother's milk. But a lot of mountain men would draw the line at working cheek by jowl with Blackfeet.

Baptiste nodded. "I will join you," he said, and took another drink.

"You wouldn't happen to know when Zach plans to head out, would you?"

"*Oui*. He leaves tomorrow."

"Then so will we," said Devlin, elated.

The waiting was almost over.

Soon he would have Morning Sky in his arms again.

Chapter 3

The Betrayal

I

Zach Hannah led his brigade north from the Green River rendezvous.

They followed the Green to its headwaters, at the southernmost edge of the Wind River Mountains, where the headwaters of the Sweetwater River also lay. Skirting the mountains to the west, Zach intended to take them past the Yellowstone country to the Shoshone Mountains, across the Stinking Water River.

But before they even reached the Wind River Range he had a feeling they were being followed.

He shared his hunch with Shadmore. The old leatherstocking knew him well enough to take him seriously.

It was for the purpose of determining if his hunch was correct that Zach led them through the middle of a valley where tall silver grass sloped gently down to a dancing creek lined with spruce and juniper. The stream curled along the base of a gray-granite escarpment. This was in the morning of the second day out from the rendezvous, and the dew was still heavy in the grass.

The rest of the brigade, apart from Shadmore, wondered what had gotten into their booshway. The rankest greenhorn knew better than to intentionally leave a clear trail in this country. And you never wandered out into such big, wide-open spaces unless you just absolutely had to. On any given day there were probably a dozen Blackfoot war parties out looking for scalps to take. Across the valley from the escarpment was a long ridge covered with golden aspen— perfect cover—and terrain where a trail could be better concealed.

Zach did not bother explaining himself, and traveled on out in the open for several miles before leading them into the creek. They kept their horses wading in the stream for another quarter-mile. It was seldom more than hock-deep. Then Zach turned them up a steep, rocky draw which provided access to the top of the escarpment. They continued north along the flanks of craggy peaks—rough going—and arrived by early afternoon at the northernmost extremity of the valley.

Here Zach finally paused. He had a brief discussion with Shadmore and then, finally, offered an explanation to Morning Sky.

"Shad's going to take you on north a ways. I'm

hanging back for a spell. But I'll catch up with you in a day or two."

"Is something wrong?"

He shrugged, making light of it, not wanting to alarm her unduly.

"Just want to make sure we're not being followed."

"You think we are." She wasn't asking.

"That's what I aim to find out," he said, still being evasive.

"Who would follow us?"

He didn't answer. Just looked her straight in the eye for a long time before finally looking away—and she knew what he was thinking.

"Devlin," she said in a small voice.

"It's probably nothing. I've just got an itch between the shoulder blades. But then, to be honest, I guess it's been there ever since we found out he was at the rendezvous."

He tried to think of something else reassuring to say, because he could see she wasn't convinced—could tell that she was worried in spite of his best efforts to prevent that from happening.

Try as he might, though, he could think of nothing. In truth, he figured if anybody was following them it would be Devlin. And if it was? What would he do about it? He didn't have an answer for that one either. Part of him wanted to confront Coyote and have it out. He didn't want the man shadowing him for the rest of his life. And maybe if he got rid of Devlin he could lay to rest as well the memories of what that man had done to him.

But he wasn't sure he could do the deed.

So he left the others at the notch and returned to the valley. This time he stuck to the aspen ridge and found himself a vantage point, an outcropping of rock, where he could see a large portion of the valley floor laid out below him. He secured his horse and climbed into the rocks and found a comfortable spot to sit, with the Hawken rifle across his knees. No telling how long he would have to wait. It didn't really matter. He had the patience of Job.

Even from this distance he could plainly see the brigade's trail through the tall grass. No way a pursuer could miss it.

The day grew old. The dying sun painted the mountains across the valley blood-red. An eagle soared among the crags. Zach reconciled himself to spending the night. No sooner had he done so then they came into view.

Four riders, leading two pack horses, right on the trail the brigade had left. At this distance, and in the fading light, he could not see them clearly. Yet there was something familiar about three of them.

He would have to get closer.

They reached the creek at the spot where he and his brigade had entered the water. Here they paused, and in the last of the light Zach saw one rider cross the stream and head north along the bank, while another stayed on this side and rode in the same direction. He knew what they were seeking: the place where he and the brigade had left the creek. The other two pitched camp.

Zach soon saw the flicker of a campfire. They were not, it seemed, too worried about Blackfeet. He waited until it was full dark before riding down out of the aspen and across the valley. He knew the moon would rise in a couple of hours. It would be three-quarters full, producing plenty of light, and he wanted to finish the task he had set for himself before that happened.

He entered the trees that lined the creek a couple hundred yards south of the camp. Here he tethered his horse and proceeded on foot, making no sound that was not masked by the song of the nearby creek.

As he got in position to see the camp, the rider who had gone up-creek on this side was just returning. A moment later the other searcher crossed the stream and dismounted to sit on his heels near the fire, where Flower was cooking some of her legendary dough-cakes.

"Find any sign?" asked Baptiste.

Devlin—the man who had searched the opposite bank—shook his head.

"No, I didn't. How about you, Keller?"

The man named Keller was just coming over from securing his pony to the picket line—a rope stretched between two trees. He was tall, lanky, blond-bearded, with pale, icy eyes, a rough look, and a voice to match.

"Yeah. About a quarter-mile up. They were heading north."

"How long ago?"

"Less than half a day."

Zach realized that Keller, at least, was no half-baked tracker. Not only had he found the brigade's trail in the darkness, but he had accurately judged its age as well. Back when he had worked for the Rocky Mountain Fur Company, Devlin had never been much of a sign reader, and Zach was guessing he still wasn't any great shakes. He would have had to do a lot of improving the last few years. As for Baptiste, the French-Canadian was adequate in that department. But Zach knew it must be Keller who was the real master.

Which made him the one Zach was going to have to try to outwit.

Baptiste was shaking his head.

"What is it?" asked Devlin. "Something bothering you?"

"*Oui*. And eet should bother you."

"I don't follow."

"He means the trail," said the laconic Keller.

Baptiste nodded. *"Tres bien, mon ami."*

"Just spill it," said Devlin crossly.

"This Zach Hannah," said Keller, "is s'pose to have boocoo savvy. So why does he leave a trail across this valley that a blind man could follow? And then he goes into yonder crik and pulls a stunt like that? It's like sayin' you want eggs for breakfast and then you go and kill the hen before she can roost. Don't make no sense."

"Ah, but it does," said Baptiste. "Hannah thought he was being followed. So he set it up this way just to see, *comprendez vous*?"

"He couldn't know that," protested Devlin. "We've hung way back. Counting on Keller here not to lose the scent."

"Hannah knows such things," insisted Baptiste. "I rode with the man for years. I am telling you, Devlin. You let your hate blind you to the fact that he is a better mountain man than you. He is better even than me. Better, I think, than all of us put together."

Devlin chunked another piece of wood into the fire, doing it with more gusto than was required and sending a shower of sparks skyward.

"Damn it," he growled. "I'm sick and tired of hearing how great that bastard is."

Baptiste chuckled. "You would give anything to be the man he is, I think."

"You think too much, I think," snapped Devlin. "You don't know what you're talking about, either."

Baptiste gave an expressive Gallic shrug. His smirk was expressive too, and it annoyed Devlin. But the French-Canadian said no more.

Devlin fumed a moment. Keller took out a clay pipe, packed it with tobacco, and fired it with a stick plucked out of the fire.

"Besides," said Devlin, "it doesn't matter how smart he is."

"How you figure?" asked Keller.

"Once he and his men settle in to start trapping, you'll head back to the major, and before you know it, Zach Hannah will be up to his eyebrows in Blackfeet. We'll see how great he is then."

"You should not speak so freely," admonished Baptiste. "These woods, they may be listening."

"He's right," concurred Keller, looking around. "I got a feelin' we're bein' watched. Hannah left that trail on purpose. I reckon he done doubled back to see who come along. He could be out there right now, close enough to shake a stick at."

All three men, and Flower—who until now had been minding her own business, and her savory dough-cakes—began to peer into the darkness.

Zach smiled.

This man Keller had good instincts.

But Devlin didn't. He scoffed and said, "You both are loco. Zach doesn't know about us. I'm telling you, he isn't half as smart as you boys think he is. You'll see. I'm going to outfox him."

I'm going to have to take that as a challenge, Zach thought.

It was time to go. He had heard all he needed to hear.

He slipped away, silent and unseen.

II

Zach caught up with the brigade about noon on the following day. When he told the others that two of their pursuers were Devlin and Baptiste, Shadmore's faded old eyes lit up with savage delight.

"Wagh!" exclaimed the leatherstocking. " 'Pears to me we'll be able to kill two birds with one stone."

"What do you mean, Shad?" asked the young Jubal Wilkes.

"I mean it's time to settle some old scores. Or mebbe it's just one old score and a new one thrown into the bargain. Time to turn around and meet those two scoundrels and have it out with 'em."

"Ambush, you mean?" queried Montez.

"Blazes, no! That's sumpin Coyote and that two-timin' pork-eater might try. Not ussens. Nossir. We'll meet 'em fair and square."

"Well," said Jubal earnestly, "for one thing, there's five of us and only three of them. Not countin' Flower, of course."

"I can't believe Baptiste went to work with that American Fur Company," said a frowning Fletcher.

"He's a dang-blasted turncoat," declared Shadmore, feisty. "I never did trust him a hunnerd percent. As for what you said, Jube, I admit yore cipherin' is right on the mark, and it wouldn' be quite fair, I reckon, when you put it that way. O' course, iffen it was the other way around—iffen they had five and thar was only three of us, I doubt they'd blink an eye, much less try to even the odds. But we kin do it right. Why, we'll draw sticks, see which three git to go."

"I don't reckon so," said Zach.

The others just stared at him.

"We won't fight them," he added.

"Why in blue blazes not?" Shadmore was astonished.

"I fight when I have to—when I'm backed into a

corner and there's no other way out. But there is another way out of this, Shad."

"How?"

"We'll steal their horses."

Shadmore's eyes widened.

"By God, Zach. You're talkin' about thievin'—and you're grinnin' like a fox while you do it!"

"Don't tell me you object."

"Heck no! But I just never honestly thought I'd see the day when you'd suggest horse-stealin'."

"What I wonder is, why are they followin' us in the first place?" asked Fletch.

Zach glanced at Morning Sky.

He knew what she was thinking: that Devlin was after her. She was scared; though she tried to hide her fear, he knew her too well. And the fact that she was afraid made Zach that much angrier at Devlin.

"I reckon they're tryin' to find prime beaver country," said Zach. "They carry no traps. My guess is that Major Vanderburg is letting the Rocky Mountain Fur Company brigades point the way for him. Devlin and Baptiste and that other feller are scouts."

"Well, once they're on foot it won't matter what they're after," said Shadmore. "We'll lose 'em, fer shore."

"Who gets to go with you, Zach?" asked Jubal Wilkes, his boyish features hopeful.

"I do, of course," said Shadmore confidently. "I've done stole more horses in my misspent lifetime than all you pilgrims put together."

"I wouldn't doubt that," grinned MacGregor.

"Montez will go with me," said Zach.

He glanced at the Spaniard, eyebrow raised in silent query. The swarthy Montez nodded once, confirming that he accepted the assignment.

Zach looked next at Shadmore. It was clear by Shad's expression that his feelings were hurt.

"I rely on you to lead while I'm gone," explained Zach. "I entrust my wife and son to your keeping."

Swallowing his disappointment, Shadmore nodded.

"You know where I was headed," said Zach.

"Yeah, you done tol' me."

"If anything happens, just remember Yellowstone country. It's only a few days' ride west of the Shoshone range. Just follow the Stinking Water River. You'll be safe there if Indians are after you. They think that country is haunted, and they won't venture into it, not even for white scalps. At least I've never heard of any doing so, nor seen any sign of them there."

"Don't fret," said Shadmore. "You know I'll keep 'em safe. I'd die 'fore I let anything happen to yore family, hoss, and so would every man-jack here."

"I know," said Zach gratefully.

Shadmore leaned forward in his saddle, his gaze and his voice intense.

"Zach, how come you didn't kill that damned Coyote? Didn't you have a clear shot at him?"

"I guess I did."

"Then why on earth, after ever'thing that man's done to you and yourn, is he still above snakes?"

Zach pondered that for a moment, finally shrugged.

"I'm not sure I could tell you," he confessed.

He said his so-longs to Sky and Jacob; he kissed her and tousled the boy's unruly hair.

Then he and Montez rode south.

That very night they came upon Devlin's camp.

Waiting at a distance, they watched the campfire slowly die and the camp itself grow quiet. Still they waited—until the three-quarters moon had finally crept across the star-spangled sky and descended behind snow-silvered peaks.

They left their horses a good distance away and moved in on foot, careful to remain downwind of the ponies they were after.

Montez handed his rifle to Zach. The Spaniard pulled a knife out of his belt and catfooted to the picket line, while Zach moved off a few yards, with both rifles primed and ready, to keep an eagle eye on the sleeping forms wrapped in their blankets in the camp. There were two blanket-wrapped forms to watch: Devlin was one, Baptiste and Flower together were the other. Zach knew exactly where Keller was.

The man sat with his back to a tree, blanket around his shoulders against the night chill, rifle across his knees. He was the lookout. But he didn't see or hear Zach until it was too late—until the muzzle of Zach's Hawken nuzzled his neck, the barrel resting lightly on his shoulder.

To his credit, Keller didn't move—didn't even

jump. He had good nerves. Zach was impressed. And wary. This was a man it would not do to underestimate. Keller turned his head slowly, raised it, and Zach thought he could see the man's cold, pale eyes glitter in the darkness.

"Don't move," whispered Zach. "Don't make a sound. Slow and easy, lay that rifle aside."

He didn't bother making threats. The Hawken was threat enough. It spoke volumes. He knew he would use it if Keller made a wrong move. To hesitate, with this man, would be fatal.

Keller laid his rifle aside.

Zach kept his attention focused on Keller, and the others who slept in the clearing beyond. He didn't look around to see how Montez was faring with the horses. The Spaniard was good with horses. He knew horse talk, had learned it from Apaches.

Montez had told him that Apaches had a way with horses unlike any other kind of Indian. With his own eyes the Spaniard had seen persuasive evidence of this. An Apache, upon discovering a horse literally ridden into the ground by a white man, could coax the animal back on its feet and into a full-blown gallop for a dozen more miles, and when the horse dropped dead the Apache would cut its throat and drink its blood and go on his way.

So Montez knew about horses—had been tutored by masters—and he could usually mold a pony's will to his own. Which was why the picketed horses were his responsibility.

He had cut the picket rope at both ends with his

belduque and simply led the whole remuda, four saddle horses and two pack animals, deeper into the woods, murmuring unintelligible "horse talk" all the while. As far as Zach was concerned it was gibberish, but it seemed to have the intended effect of soothing the nerves of the animals.

When Zach heard the horses moving off he pressed the muzzle of the Hawken a little harder against Keller's neck. He could feel it, then, if Keller reached for his rifle or made any other move. Zach kept his eyes on the sleepers in the camp, until he could no longer hear the horses that Montez was pilfering.

"Get up," he said.

Keller stood.

He asked no questions, even though Zach figured he was wondering if he was about to get quietly killed. Yes, the man had grit. And he was too proud to ask, for fear that even the asking might be construed as a plea for mercy. And begging was something a man like Keller would never do. He would die first. But he would watch for any slip Zach might make, and use the mistake to his advantage.

"Walk that way," said Zach, nodding.

Keller did as he was told, Zach following with the Hawken planted in the man's back. They put fifty yards between themselves and the camp.

"Far enough," said Zach.

Keller stopped, started to turn.

"Don't turn around."

Keller froze.

"You'd be Zach Hannah," he said.

"Yep."

Keller nodded. "Figured as much."

"I want you to deliver a message."

"To who?"

"Sean Devlin."

Keller drew a deep breath. Now, for the first time, he realized Zach wasn't going to kill him. He couldn't very well deliver any messages if he were gone under.

"Tell him to leave me and mine alone," said Zach, his words as hard as iron. "This is his last warning. I've put up with this as long as I'm going to. Next time he muddies up my water I'm going to do away with him."

"I'll tell him."

"I bear no ill will towards you, but I have a feeling if we meet again one of us will die."

"Yeah. I get that feeling, too."

"So stop tracking me."

"I. . . ."

But before Keller could finish, Zach laid the butt of the Hawken hard against the side of his head. The American Fur Company man crumpled.

Zach moved deeper into the woods and found Montez at the spot where they had left their own horses. Each leading three of the stolen ponies, they rode north and by dawn were many miles away.

III

Devlin was furious.

He was so angry that Baptiste thought the man was going to split a seam. So angry, in fact, that he got in Keller's face and cursed him. If he had been thinking calmly and rationally he would never have done that, because anyone with eyes in his head could see that Keller was no man to tamper with.

"Why didn't you do something?" ranted Devlin. "How could you let them slip up on you like that? My God, I thought you were supposed to be a mountain man."

Keller stood there and weathered this abuse for a while, tight-lipped, his expression stony, but his eyes flickered with an angry fire which burned hotter and hotter as Devlin rattled on.

"Not a shot fired!" exclaimed Devlin. "Not a sound. Not even a shout to warn us."

"Yeah," said Keller, finally. "I'm sartin you'd be shoutin' if Zach Hannah's rifle was stuck in your ear, Devlin."

"I would've done something."

"Sure," said Keller. "Maybe you would have got down on your hands and knees and begged him not to kill you. I think maybe that's what you would've done."

Devlin took a step back and blinked, as though Keller had slapped him in the face.

"I ought to kill you for that," he breathed.

Keller was smirking now. "You ought to," he

agreed. "Wanna try? I'm kinda in the mood for some blood-spillin'. How 'bout you?"

Devlin was silent a moment. He gave Keller a long, hard look and realized that in his blind rage at being outfoxed by Zach Hannah he had jumped into the fire with both feet. Another careless word or two, spoken in bad-tempered haste, would lead to a killing.

"Watch your step, Keller," he said. It was pure bluster, but Devlin had nothing else to fall back on.

Keller snorted. "Don't make me laugh."

Baptiste intervened. "My friends, why do we fight among ourselves? Why does it matter who's to blame for what has happened? What is done is done. Now we must decide what to do next."

"We keep after Hannah, of course," said Devlin.

"On foot?" asked Keller, incredulous.

"Well, I guess so," was Devlin's caustic report. "Seein' as how you let Hannah steal our horses."

"You're crazy," decided Keller. "We get horses first. Then we'll see about following Hannah. I don't cotton to being on foot in this country. Too many bad Injuns. And they'll all be mounted. We stumble on a bunch, and we're dead for sure."

"Major Vanderburg is counting on us to find out where Hannah's brigade is trapping this fall. That's our job, and I intend to get it done."

"Hell. You don't give two hoots about Vanderburg or the American Fur Company, Devlin. You've got some kind of private feud going with Zach Hannah.

That's why you want to keep on his trail come hell or high water, so don't try to tell me different."

"I'm in charge here," said Devlin, "in case you need reminding, and it looks like you do. So since I am, what I say goes."

"If what you said made any sense I'd listen. I'll follow a man who knows what the hell he's doing. But you don't."

"You'll do what I say, if I have to . . ."

"What?" Keller barked a harsh, derisive laugh and made a dismissive gesture. "You're blowin' smoke, Devlin, and we both know it. You can't buffalo me. Let me tell you something—something I'm right certain you already know. Zach Hannah's twice the mountain man you are. And he told me to give you a message."

"Oh. You can be his messenger boy, but you can't watch our damned horses. That's just dandy."

"He said to tell you to leave him and his alone. I think he's about at the end of his rope with you, Devlin. You better leave well enough alone."

"I'm not scared of Zach Hannah," muttered Devlin, through clenched teeth.

"You oughta be."

"I side with Keller," said Baptiste. "We must find some horses first."

"We aren't voting here," snapped Devlin, infuriated. "This isn't a damned democracy. We don't decide on things by committee. The major put me in charge and what I say goes."

"We find horses," insisted Baptiste. "Then, if we

can find their trail, we will learn where Hannah and his brigade are trapping."

"We'll lose his trail," said Devlin. "Besides, where do we get horses around here?"

"We steal 'em," said Keller.

Baptiste smiled. "That seems to be the way one gets horses in this country, no?"

"Steal them from who?" asked Devlin.

"There is a Shoshone village not far from here," said Keller. "We'll help ourselves to some of their ponies. They got plenty. If we do it right, they won't even know we've been there and gone until it's too late."

"No," said Devlin, adamant. "We stick to Zach Hannah's trail."

"You do what you want," said Keller, and turned away.

He gathered up his possibles: rolled blanket, rifle, haversack.

Devlin looked at Baptiste. "What about you? I guess you're desertin', too."

"I do not like Zach Hannah any more than you do," said the French-Canadian. "But I would rather ride than walk. So would my little *fleur-de-lis*." Baptiste nodded at Flower, who stood nearby, impassively observing this heated discussion.

"This is mutiny," said Devlin. "Major Vanderburg will hear about this."

Baptiste stabbed Devlin in the chest with a stubby finger. "I am not afraid of your major. I am not afraid of you, neither. So do not waste your breath with making threats at me."

Devlin realized he was powerless to stop these two from doing what they wanted. All he had was bluff, and bluff didn't work on the likes of Baptiste and Keller. They didn't trust him, and as a result they were not going to follow his lead. He knew now that they had never trusted him, and so he had never really been the booshway of this bunch, except in his own mind. He'd just been fooling himself.

That cut deep. So if he couldn't get them to follow, he would go alone. That was better than being put in these humiliating circumstances.

Going it alone was a daunting prospect, but what were the options? He was sick and tired of standing in Zach Hannah's shadow. He decided right then and there that it would be better to die alone in these godforsaken mountains than to live the way he had been living ever since the day he had lost Morning Sky.

He just had to get her back, or he couldn't go on living. It was as simple as that. He couldn't get her out of his mind. That was especially true of late, ever since he had seen her at the Green River rendezvous. When he'd had her to himself—that had been the only time in his whole life he'd felt complete, like a real man. Having a woman like Sky to call your own did that.

"Fine," he told Baptiste scornfully. "Go your own way. I don't need the likes of you, or Keller. I'm going after Hannah. I don't care if I have to walk. I'll crawl if I have to. But he's not getting the best of me any more."

Baptiste was surprised. "*Sacre bleu!* You mean you will go after Hannah alone? You?"

Disgusted, Devlin gathered his possibles, shoulder-racked his rifle, and headed north on the trail of Hannah's brigade without another word or a single backward glance.

That afternoon, the Absaroka Crow found him.

IV

There were six of them. Their leader was an audacious young warrior called Red Claw. They had been deep in Shoshone country on a horse-stealing excursion. All of them were on the young side, out to make a name for themselves doing what Absaroka Crows were notorious for.

Having successfully raided a Shoshone village and made off with a dozen splendid ponies, they were on their way home. There had been a brief fight and an exciting chase, but nobody had been seriously hurt on either side. Which was fine with Red Claw and his companions. They had been given permission by their chief, Iron Bull, to conduct the raid, on the condition that no Shoshone lives be taken unless absolutely necessary.

The Sparrowhawk people, Iron Bull had told them, were at war with the Blackfeet, and they did not need to start a feud with another tribe. Relations between the Crows and the Shoshones had been fairly good for quite some time. The Crows would steal Shoshone horses every now and then, or even a maiden on occasion, and the Shoshones would return the favor, and while someone got killed every once in a while, everyone accepted this as the price to be paid when indulging in such shenanigans.

Red Claw and his fellow braves were in high spirits as they hazed their twelve newly acquired ponies through a stand of quaking aspen and out into a sun-drenched high mountain meadow. Their village would give them a heroes' welcome. And each of them would be richer by two horses. Red Claw already knew what he would do with his new acquisitions; they were to be part of the price he intended to pay Spotted Owl for his daughter—the young woman who owned Red Claw's heart.

As they emerged from the aspen they spotted a buckskin-clad white man scampering for the cover of trees on the far side of the meadow.

It was Devlin.

He had heard the horses coming through the trees, but too late. Finding himself out in the open, smack-dab in the middle of the meadow, he had made a dash for the nearest place of concealment. But he hadn't made it in time.

One over-the-shoulder glance was all Devlin needed to identify the Indians as Absaroka Crows.

He stopped, turned, lifted his rifle.

The Crows were his mortal enemies. He had slain Rides A Dark Horse, one of the most intrepid and popular of Crow warriors, a hero of the tribe, and he was known to be an ally of the hated Blackfeet.

Red Claw shouted a warning to his companions and followed this with a curt command. He was a born leader—able to make quick, clear, and correct decisions in a split second, and for this reason other braves were willing to follow him.

Four of the warriors turned the twelve stolen ponies. Meanwhile, Red Claw and a brave named Deer Stalker drew their own rifles from fringed and beaded sheaths, preparing to fight.

"It is Coyote!" exclaimed Deer Stalker, suddenly recognizing the white man.

Red Claw shot a sharp look at the other warrior.

He knew who Coyote was. What Absaroka Crow did not? The man who had killed Rides A Dark Horse—a man whose scalp every Crow warrior sought.

Red Claw had never seen Coyote in the flesh, but Deer Stalker had. Deer Stalker was one of the two warriors accompanying Rides A Dark Horse that day six years ago when Rides A Dark Horse had gone after Coyote.

Devlin fired.

The bullet passed harmlessly between the two mounted warriors. Red Claw could actually hear it scorch the air in passing.

He and Deer Stalker fired their long guns almost simultaneously.

When the white powder-smoke cleared, Red Claw saw Devlin plunge into the trees, unscathed.

With a cry of rage, Deer Stalker kicked his pony into a headlong gallop. He was consumed by the thought of killing Coyote and avenging the death of his friend, Rides A Dark Horse. This was the moment he had been hoping for all these years.

Red Claw called to the other four warriors, who had stuck with the stolen Shoshone horses and who by now were back in the fringe of the stand of aspens. At his bidding, they left the horses and struck out after the mountain man. Coyote was a far bigger catch than a dozen ponies. With any luck they could recapture the horses. If not, they could always steal more. But this could be their only shot at the white man most hated by the Sparrowhawk people.

Devlin tried to reload as he ran, weaving through the trees. He didn't have much luck. With half a dozen screaming savages on his heels, and his heart lodged in his throat and strangling him, and his palms so damp with sweat that he could scarcely hold on to his rifle, it was next to impossible to get the job done right.

Swiftly the Crows closed in, before he could get powder and shot tamped down in the barrel and a percussion cap in place. So he whirled and tried to use the rifle like a club, grasping the barrel with both hands and swinging with all his might in an attempt to unhorse the nearest Crow. This happened to be Deer Stalker. But Deer Stalker saw it coming and slipped out of his saddle to cling to the off side of his pony, evading the blow as he galloped past the cornered mountain man.

In the next instant Devlin found himself on the ground, the earth spinning and tilting madly beneath him, and white-hot pain lancing through his body.

Red Claw checked his pony sharply and raised his tomahawk high overhead. He had discarded his own rifle, knowing it would be next to useless in the trees, and resorted to the war hatchet. Striking Devlin a glancing blow on the skull, he had counted first coup, a great honor. Turning his horse, he uttered an exultant whoop. Then he saw Deer Stalker leap from his pony and, drawing his knife, pounce on Coyote, intent on lifting Coyote's hair.

"No!" bellowed Red Claw.

Deer Stalker froze. He had grabbed Devlin's sandy-colored locks in one hand and had the knife at the man's hairline. The edge of the blade had pierced the skin already. A rivulet of blood snaked down Devlin's forehead and into his eye. Devlin was still stunned by the blow from Red Claw's tomahawk—he was not resisting.

Red Claw jumped off his pony. He was furious. He had expected the tomahawk blow to be fatal— and so had thought himself, for one brief, wonderful moment, the slayer of Coyote, already anticipating, in those few seconds of premature elation, the glory which the feat would bring him.

In his fury he had prevented Deer Stalker from finishing Coyote off, which Deer Stalker had a perfect right to do. Deer Stalker had stayed his hand, though, out of respect for Red Claw as the leader of the group. But he quickly reassessed the situation and began to realize he had been robbed, that Red Claw had no right to claim Coyote's death.

Deer Stalker had taken one look at Red Claw's wrathful expression and stepped away from Coyote. Now, though, he stepped forward again, to stand face to face with Red Claw. Devlin slumped in a half-prone position on the ground between them.

"I will take his scalp," declared Deer Stalker.

Red Claw made no reply. He didn't have a leg to stand on to support his claim anyway, and he knew it. The only recourse left to him was to strike first.

He bent down, grabbed Devlin by the arm, and dragged him a little ways. Then, straddling Coyote, he raised the tomahawk.

With a shout, Deer Stalker lunged forward and blocked Red Claw's arm before he could bring the war hatchet down. Red Claw tried to shoulder him out of the way, but Deer Stalker wouldn't budge. A struggle ensued. Deer Stalker hooked Red Claw's leg with his own and they fell. Red Claw managed to get the upper hand, and again raised the tomahawk.

Aghast, the other four warriors looked on. Red Claw and Deer Stalker were quarreling over the mountain man like two dogs fighting over a bone. They were trying to kill each other for the right to kill the white man.

But Red Claw came to his senses in time. He lowered the tomahawk, rose, and stepped away from Deer Stalker, mortified by the realization of what he had been about to do.

"I am wrong," he admitted flatly. "Forgive me, my friend."

On his feet again, Deer Stalker stared at Red Claw with newfound respect. Red Claw was a proud man, and Deer Stalker knew it wasn't easy for him to admit his mistake.

"The honor belongs to you," he said. "You should be the one to take Coyote's life. His scalp should be on your shield, Red Claw."

By this time Devlin was fully conscious. He knew enough of the Sparrowhawk dialect to comprehend the gist of the discussion. These two red bastards were arguing over who would kill him! He gathered himself up and tried to make a run for it. But one of the other warriors saw it coming and stepped in to hammer him to the ground again with the stock of his rifle.

Devlin shook the cobwebs out of his head, blinked his vision clear, and looked up to see all of the Crow braves standing around him.

"We will take him to Iron Bull," decided Red Claw. "Then all of us will be honored equally. Let Iron Bull decide his fate."

Deer Stalker and the others voiced their assent.

Devlin was securely bound with strips of rawhide ordinarily used to hobble horses. He tried to think of some way out of this dilemma. There had to be a way out. If he didn't come up with something, he was a dead man.

"You better let me go," he told Red Claw, verbally stumbling over the Sparrowhawk lingo, but managing to make himself understood. "My men are nearby. A whole brigade. A dozen men. Let me go and they won't bother you. You have my word."

"You lie," said Red Claw flatly. "You are alone."

"Yes," admitted Devlin, suddenly contrite. "It's true. I did lie. I am alone. But my brigade is not far from here. I was scouting. Got separated from my horse. Rattler spooked her and she threw me and then ran off."

He paused, checked the circle of grim, fierce, bronzed faces.

"It would be foolish to kill me," he said. "You will profit more by letting me live. Take me back to my brigade and I'll see to it you get plenty in return. Rifles, powder and shot, traps, blankets, whatever you want you will get. You have my solemn word on it."

Red Claw told one of the warriors to stand watch over Coyote. He sent three more to round up the Shoshone ponies. Then he and Deer Stalker moved off out of earshot to talk things over.

Devlin watched them anxiously. His gaze was riveted to the two Indians, who he knew were deciding his fate.

All the while he wondered if they would fall for it.

Eventually Red Claw and Deer Stalker returned.

"We will take you to your men."

"Good!" exclaimed Devlin. "I was right on their trail. Reckon they're only a day ahead."

Red Claw gave a curt nod. He and Deer Stalker walked away to gather up their own ponies.

Devlin was gloating. The ignorant savages had

played right into his hands. By God, he wished Shadmore was here to see him living up to his nickname. The old leatherstocking had been the first to call him Coyote, that night on the Mississippi when the Rocky Mountain Fur Company had just departed St. Louis, back in '23. Devlin had left camp that night and returned with a chicken stolen from a nearby farm. This thievery had prompted Shadmore to give him the name.

Yes, he had outsmarted these Absarokas, sure enough.

They thought they were stringing him along, pretending to accept his offer, when all along they really intended to let him lead them to his brigade, at which time they figured to harvest some white scalps. They knew he was working for the American Fur Company, and they probably knew the American Fur Company was in cahoots with their enemies, the Blackfeet, so they believed his men to be fair game.

What they couldn't know, of course, was that the brigade he would lead them to was Zach Hannah's.

It was perfect. The Crows would take him to Hannah, which was where he wanted to go anyway.

But then, what would Zach do?

According to Keller, Hannah was primed to kill him if they met again.

Devlin wasn't so sure. There was a fair to middlin' chance that Hannah would save him from these Absaroka savages. He wouldn't let any white men die at the hands of Indians. He was too decent a man for that. He had too much compassion. He was too honorable for his own good.

Devlin tried to suppress a self-satisfied smirk.

Yes, these Crows would be furious when they discovered he had outfoxed them, and they would want to murder him on the spot, but Devlin was betting Zach would stop them, and they would listen to him.

And after Hannah had rescued him, Devlin was going to repay him by taking Morning Sky away from him again. This time it would be for good.

V

As Zach had promised, they found a valley chock-full of beaver in the Shoshone Range. The glacier-fed creek which rambled through the valley emptied into a tributary of the Stinking Water River. It was the consensus of the brigade as a whole that no trapper had ever set foot in the valley. They anticipated having a fine haul to take to next summer's rendezvous.

There was plenty of beaver sign all along the creek. A dam, a slide, a lodge, shavings near a tree, or a tree cut down altogether. Zach let the men trap in pairs, and each team selected its own stretch along the creek. Most of the time they set their traps at the foot of a slide. The trapper would select a trap, spread the jaws, set the trigger, and place it under water. The trap's chain was attached to a notched stake, usually willow, which was secured in the bottom of the creek. Then he fastened a smaller stick, called a floater, to the chain with a long piece of stout chain. If the beaver manage to swim away with the trap, the floater would mark its location.

Every trapper carried a horn vial filled with castor. A bait stick was dipped into this "medicine" and then stuck in the bank so that it leaned out over the creek where the trap had been concealed. Whether playing on the slide or attracted by the scent of the castor, a beaver sooner or later encountered the trap. The pain would cause it to dive deeper into the creek. This made the ring at the end of the chain slip along the stake and catch in one of the notches, which prevented the animal from reaching the surface, and it soon drowned.

As usual, Zach did not do much trapping. Fletcher and Jubal Wilkes formed one team, Montez and MacGregor the other. Shadmore was Zach's partner, but Zach spent most of his time scouting, and the old hivernan was quite content to trap on his own. He didn't need a partner to watch his backside. Zach didn't figure there was an Indian alive who could sneak up on the old man.

Before long, Zach knew the valley like the back of his hand.

There were two ways out to the south, and one to the north, the latter leading deeper into the mountain range, while the southern passages debouched into the floodplain of the Stinking Water. There was also another exit—a high saddle between two peaks to the west, if a man was willing to leave his horse and possibles behind and make a difficult and oftentimes perilous climb. Zach tried it once, and reached the top, but it was slow going, and he nearly fell more than once.

When the snows came this route would be impassable, as would the northern passage. For this reason Zach decided they would have to winter elsewhere. He thought the Yellowstone country would be a good place. But this valley surely would not be. With only the southern passes open, the valley was a potential death trap. The brigade would have a couple of months to trap before they had to leave. Then they would cache what furs they had gleaned, winter in the Yellowstone, safe from Blackfoot depredations, and return at "green-up."

The third day after the brigade's arrival in the valley, Zach was scouting the southern passages when he crossed paths with Red Claw's bunch.

He knew at a distance that they were Crows, his friends. This he could ascertain from their garb, and the paint on the ponies they rode.

For this reason he had no qualms about approaching them openly. While still some distance away, he rode his horse in a broad circle. In this way he signaled that his intentions were peaceful.

The Indians stopped. Zach noticed that there was a white man among them. At this distance he could not identify the man, but there was definitely something familiar about him. The Crows also had ten spare horses with Shoshone paint markings.

The circumspect, almost wary, behavior of the

Crows perplexed Zach. Holding his pony to a walk, he ventured closer, wondering what was amiss. Then he sharply checked his horse as one of the Indians raised a rifle as though to fire on him. Zach held up a hand and shouted a greeting in the Crow dialect.

Deer Stalker reached across to push aside the rifle which the warrior next to him had brought to his shoulder and aimed at Zach.

"It is Hannah," declared Deer Stalker. "Friend of the Absaroka Crows. Killer of our enemies, the Blackfeet. Do not shoot."

Zach rode up. Now he could see that the white man, mounted on one of the Shoshone horses, was Devlin and that his hands were tied behind his back. He also recognized Red Claw and Deer Stalker and one of the other braves. He deduced that the Crows had recently stolen the ponies, but he couldn't figure how Devlin had come to be their prisoner.

The man just kept turning up, like a bad penny.

He soon learned the truth. Red Claw exchanged greetings with him, and then related to him the events which had led to their capture of Coyote and how Coyote had promised to lead them to his brigade.

"Coyotes are tricksters," said Zach, "and there aren't many trickier than this one. It's my brigade you've trailed, and you brought him right where he wanted to go. Coyote works for the American Fur Company."

"This we know," said Red Claw. "They are our enemies. They trade with the Blackfeet."

"They also want to find the best beaver country, and they figure on letting us Rocky Mountain boys lead them to it. Coyote's been on my trail. I thought I'd shaken him off." He glanced across at Devlin and then switched to English. "You outsmarted me this time, didn't you?"

Devlin's smile was cold. "Yeah, I believe I did just that."

"Only thing is, these fellers have a strong hankering to kill you. You are not well liked among the Sparrowhawk people."

"I don't think you'll let that happen, Zach."

"No? You found out where my brigade is laying out its traps. That's what your Major Vanderburg wanted to know. Well, I reckon he never will if Red Claw here sends you to meet your Maker."

"You can't just turn your back on me. It would cut too much against the grain."

"When I heard you were at the rendezvous I thought about killing you."

"But you didn't."

"I want you out of my hair, Devlin. Out of my life. Red Claw can do that for me."

Devlin shook his head. "You won't let him." He sounded utterly convinced.

Zach felt like swearing, long and loud. But he didn't. Didn't utter a sound for a full minute. Just sat his horse and stared grimly at Sean Michael Devlin, thoroughly disgusted.

He knew Coyote was right.

VI

Red Claw was incensed. His wrath was the quiet, dangerous kind, simmering just beneath the surface—the kind that, when it erupted, did so with the violence of a volcano.

Coyote had fooled him, and Red Claw's first, and almost overpowering, inclination, was to take his tomahawk and bury it in Devlin's skull. Zach could sense this, and smoothly persuaded him to sit and talk it over. They built a small fire and passed a pipe around. Two of the warriors watched the horses. Two more stood flanking Devlin, who sat cross-legged in the grass within earshot of Zach, Red Claw, and Deer Stalker, who shared the pipe and engaged in the parlay.

It was Red Claw's opinion that Devlin should be put to death immediately. Deer Stalker thought the original idea was still the best: to take their prisoner to Iron Bull and let the chief decide what to do with him. In that way, all six of them would receive an equal share of the glory.

But Red Claw did not want to take any chances. Coyote was too tricky. What if he escaped? Then he and Deer Stalker and the others would face scorn and ridicule from the rest of the tribe. No, it wasn't worth the risk.

Zach listened for a while before speaking up, and when he did, what he had to say profoundly shocked Red Claw and Deer Stalker.

"Coyote must live."

"But he is your enemy as much as ours," protested Red Claw.

"He stole your woman. And he killed Rides A Dark Horse," added Deer Stalker.

Zach nodded. "No denying it. Coyote has caused me a lot of grief. And Rides A Dark Horse was a true friend."

"Then why do you speak for Coyote now?"

"Because he once saved my life," replied Zach. "It was the winter before he killed Rides A Dark Horse. He and I were far from the fort on the Yellowstone River. My horse slipped on ice and in the fall I broke a leg. Devlin was with me. We lost our horses. We got caught in a blizzard and for a spell lost our way. It looked pretty bad for us. And I was slowing us down with that busted leg. Coyote would have stood a better chance of surviving had he left me behind and struck out for the fort on his own, but he wouldn't leave me on my own stick. I told him to go, but he refused. If he hadn't stuck by me I reckon I would have been gone beaver."

Red Claw and Deer Stalker exchanged solemn glances.

"So you see," continued Zach, now stating the obvious, "I am honor-bound to return the favor."

Frowning, Red Claw mulled this over in his mind. He could well understand the concept of honor, and he had tremendous respect for Zach Hannah. Zach had used the only argument that would have any impact on the Crow warriors.

Finally, Red Claw nodded. There was only one thing to do.

"Coyote will live," he muttered.

Deer Stalker jumped up and walked towards Devlin with long, angry strides. Zach watched him with anxious eyes. He wasn't sure what Deer Stalker intended. The warrior was agitated, that much was clear. But Zach didn't move. If Deer Stalker intended to kill Devlin, defying Red Claw in the process, Zach wasn't going to interfere. He had done all he was willing to do for Devlin. He wasn't going to fight one Absaroka Crow to save him.

Devlin cringed as Deer Stalker approached. But the warrior merely spit on him, and cursed him virulently, casting aspersions on Devlin's manhood as well as the legitimacy of his parentage. Then he walked away.

"Deer Stalker was a good friend of Rides A Dark Horse," Red Claw told Zach, in a roundabout apology.

"I know."

"We go," said Red Claw curtly. He stood and, cupping his hands around his mouth, uttered a piercing cry similar to that of an eagle. The two mounted warriors assigned to the horses brought the cavallard near.

Zach stamped out the fire and watched the Crow braves mount up. Red Claw made the sign for "friend": holding his right hand up, palm outwards, with index and second fingers extended upwards, he raised the hand until the tips of the fingers were as high as his head.

Zach answered with the same sign.

And then the Crows were gone, driving their stolen ponies ahead of them.

Zach sighed and walked over to Devlin, who still sat in the grass with his hands bound.

"I knew you'd come through for me, partner," sneered Devlin. "I know you wouldn't let those stinking savages lift my hair."

"Those 'stinking savages' are some of the best people I've ever run across," snapped Zach.

"Sure. Just cut me loose."

Zach drew his knife.

But he just stood there a moment, staring at Devlin, his expression inscrutable.

Trying to mask his nervousness, Devlin laughed, because the look in Zach's gray eyes worried him, but the laugh sounded a little forced and ragged.

"Nice blade," he said. "I recollect I bought that for you back in St. Louis."

"I remember."

"So what do you aim to do now? Cut my throat with it?" Devlin shook his head. "No, you won't do that, Zach. So don't bother trying to scare me. You just haven't got it in you to kill me."

Zach lunged. Devlin uttered a strangled cry as Zach pushed him down on his back, planted a knee in his chest to pin him to the ground, and then put the point of the knife to his throat.

"This is your last chance," growled Zach. "I don't

ever want to see you again. Stay away from Morning Sky. And little Jacob too. He's my son now. You got no rights as far as he's concerned. Not anymore. You hear?"

Devlin nodded, unable to speak.

"I swear to God," breathed Zach, trembling with violent emotion, "the next time I see you I'm going to kill you, Devlin."

He got off Devlin's chest, rolled him over on his belly and with one quick slash severed the rawhide binding Devlin's wrists together. Belting the knife, he hauled Devlin to his feet and gave him a hard shove. Devlin staggered, caught himself, and half-turned to glower at Zach.

"Walk away," rasped Zach. "Walk away or die."

Devlin's eyes were hooded, unreadable.

"You win," he said, and walked away.

VII

Zach hunkered down next to the fire and waited a couple of hours—time he measured precisely by the movement of his shadow across the ground. He tried to calm down. It scared him, how close he had come to killing Devlin. In cold blood.

He wasn't used to hating that hard, and he didn't like the feeling. Not one bit.

Eventually he mounted his horse and followed Devlin's trail. He held his pony to a walk, not wanting to catch up with Coyote, not wanting to lay eyes on the man, because he knew that if he did he would unlimber the Hawken and put a bullet through his heart. He'd have a hard time living with the deed on his conscience, but he'd do it anyway— he'd have to.

But he never saw Devlin, and was relieved to find Coyote's trail leading directly out of the valley. Relieved, but disturbed, as well, because somehow he knew it wasn't the last he would see of Devlin and that really he had only prolonged the inevitable final—and fatal—confrontation.

At last he turned back and headed for camp.

All the way back he debated whether to tell Shadmore and the others what had occurred. None of them would understand, he decided. Least of all Shad. He realized there were striking similarities between this situation and the events of the previous winter, when he had spared the life of the Blackfoot warrior called Long Runner. Then, the others in the brigade had leaned towards executing the Indian, and they'd had a valid point. Everyone had expected Long Runner to inform his fellow Blackfeet of the brigade's presence. Against their better judgment, and some might say against all common sense, Zach had spared Long Runner's life. Knowing all along that in doing so—by letting the warrior go free—he had put the life of each member of the brigade at risk, not least Sky's and little Jacob's.

Now he was letting Devlin go free, and Devlin would return to Vanderburg and inform the major of a valley where the beaver were plentiful and where

Hannah's brigade had settled in for the season. Then what would happen? Would Vanderburg's men come in and try to take the valley by force? Would they wait until the end of the summer and then try to slip and steal the brigade's fur packs?

Any way you looked it, it looked like trouble.

But in the end, Zach did not tell anyone what had happened.

He tried to act as though nothing had occurred. But he couldn't fool Shadmore. He should have known better than to try. Shad knew him entirely too well.

It wasn't until they were lounging around the campfire that night that Shadmore made any comment. Everyone else had turned in. Montez and MacGregor and Fletch and young Jubal had put in a long day, from "can see" to "can't see," wading in ice-cold water laying or checking traps, and they were bone-tired. Shadmore had done his fair share of trapping on the day too, but he didn't sleep much anymore—the older you got, he said, the less sleep you required to keep going. As for Zach, he wasn't the least bit tired.

"So what did you find out there?" asked Shad, out of the blue.

The query caught Zach off guard. He hesitated, staring at the old leatherstocking, and then, realizing that he just could not look Shad square in the eye and lie, he averted his gaze and pretended to take particular interest in the fire dancing between them.

"Green grass and blue sky," he said lamely.

Shadmore chewed reflectively on the tip of his pipe.

Zach glanced at him again. Shad's silence was reproachful, and Zach knew the gray-bearded mountain man wasn't buying it for a minute.

But Shad didn't press the issue, which surprised Zach, because his friend and mentor was nothing if not persistent and forthright. In fact, Shadmore's silence worried Zach. Made him edgy. A few minutes later, unable to sit still any longer, he rose, stretched the kinks out of his back, and shouldered his rifle.

"Turnin' in?" asked Shadmore.

"No. Reckon I'll take the first watch."

"It's my turn."

"I know. But I'll take over for you, if you don't mind. I'm not tired."

Shadmore shrugged. "Suits me. I'll spell you in a few hours." He looked at the stars, the equivalent of setting his watch.

Zach walked off, beyond the reach of the campfire's light. The campsite he had selected was on a high, dry meadow enclosed on two sides by the bending creek and on the third by a stand of conifers. Beyond the trees was a bluff, with a game trail which led to the rim. This Zach took. Once on the rim of the bluff he could look down over the tops of the evergreens and see the entire camp, and the shallows of the creek beyond, the water like molten silver in the light of the full moon. He had an excellent view in all directions from the top of the bluff.

A while later he saw Morning Sky stirring in the

camp. She disappeared into the trees. A moment later, having climbed the bluff by way of the game trail, she was with him.

"Can't sleep?" he asked.

"I was waiting for you."

"Sorry. I took over for Shad."

She sat down beside him. He put an arm around her, and she rested her head against his chest, and they stayed like that with no words passing between them for quite some time. Later, she lifted her head and looked at him with those violet-blue eyes of hers—looked deep into his eyes, as though she could read the thoughts in his mind. Then she brushed her hand lightly across his forehead, where the lines of worry furrowed deep.

"Something is wrong," she said. She was stating a fact, not asking a question.

"Just got a lot of things on my mind." He gave her a squeeze. "Don't worry. Everything will be fine. You'll see."

"Will it?" She sighed. "I am afraid."

"There's nothing to be afraid of."

"I think something will happen. Something bad."

Zach tried on a reassuring smile. It wasn't a comfortable fit.

"You haven't had another visit from that spirit-wolf of yours, have you?"

It was meant for a joke, but he had misjudged badly, and knew it right away by the expression on her face, and he felt like kicking himself for being such an insensitive lout.

"No," she replied at length. "But I think someday soon I will see him again." She said it in a resigned way.

"This is no way to live," said Zach, suddenly angry. He wasn't sure exactly what he was angry at. Maybe the situation. Or the Blackfeet, for being so dedicated to the proposition that every white man who ventured west of the Big Muddy had to die. Or Devlin, for being obsessed with having everything he had.

"I wish we could just be alone," he added. "Up here in the mountains, you and me and little Jacob. Somewhere where nobody could find us."

"I wish for the same. Can we not find such a place? Before it is too late."

Zach nodded. "Maybe so. After this season."

"Why wait? We should go now."

"The others are counting on me, Sky. I'm their booshway. I brought them here. I've got to see them through the season. Then I'll quit. Shoot, a lot of others are quitting. Bill Sublette, for instance. Major Henry's out of the business. What do you say? I'll get the brigade through the winter and then we'll be finished."

Sky was silent for a while.

Then she rose quietly, and bent down to brush his lips with hers.

"I fear it will be too late," she whispered.

She left him then, and he watched her go, and he was genuinely afraid, because he couldn't shake the feeling that their days together were numbered.

VIII

Weeks passed uneventfully.

The trapping went well. Shadmore predicted this would be their best haul yet. Spirits ran high—with the exception of Morning Sky and Zach Hannah. Both of them suffered from a premonition of disaster. They hid their anxieties from the others. And they loved each other with a tender, almost desperate, intensity, the way lovers do who know they will soon be parted from one another.

The days grew shorter, the nights colder. Summer was over. There was a saying in the high country that July, August, and winter were the only three months. Zach kept an eye on the weather, and watched the animals, for animals knew before humans when the seasons would change.

"Another fortnight," Zach told Shadmore, "and we'll have heavy snow. It'll be time to cache our packs and make a trail for the Yellowstone country."

Shadmore nodded, concurring with this prediction.

"We've done ourselves proud this season, hoss," declared the old leatherstocking. "We've got us a lot of plews and not a speck of trouble. Reckon our luck'll hold?"

"I hope so."

In fact, Zach could hardly wait to quit the valley. Almost every day he rode to the southern passages and checked for sign.

He saw the Blackfeet only a week before the time

he had set in his own mind for pulling up stakes and making tracks for the Yellowstone country.

Fortunately he was in the cover of some trees when he saw them. They were out in the open, having just come through one of the southern passes.

There were twenty of them, and they were painted for war and armed to the teeth. Zach made note of the fact that all of them had rifles.

But what he noticed first and foremost—the thing that made his blood run cold—was that Devlin rode with them. Coyote, and another white man in buckskin garb.

Zach didn't recognize the second man. He scarcely paid him any attention at all. He stared at Devlin. Then he raised the Hawken and drew a bead on Coyote.

But he didn't shoot.

It was all he could do to refrain from killing Devlin right then and there.

Just in the nick of time—even as his finger whitened on the trigger of the plains rifle—he considered the consequences.

At this range, about five hundred yards, he could plug Devlin. But then what? His chances of eluding the Blackfeet were slim. They would probably catch him, and if they did they would surely kill him. And if he perished, who would warn the rest of the brigade? No, this time he couldn't do what he should have done before with Devlin. Now that he was finally reconciled to taking Coyote's life, circumstances prevented him from doing so.

He lowered the rifle, mounted his horse, and rode back to the creek.

The section Fletcher and Jubal Wilkes were trapping was the closest. Zach found them within an hour of sighting the Blackfoot war party. Fletch was wading in the stream, checking traps, while young Jubal stood guard from the bank, eyes peeled. Even though they had been working the valley for over a month without any trouble, every member of the brigade knew better than to let down his guard.

When Zach rode up, both Fletch and Jubal took one look at him and knew the brigade's luck had run out.

"Blackfoot war party," announced Zach. "Devlin and another American Fur Company man with 'em. Just came through the south pass an hour ago."

"I'll be damned," breathed Fletcher. "So that's their game. That bastard Vanderburg is gonna turn his Blackfoot dogs on us."

"Looks that way," said Zach.

"How many are there?"

"Too many," was Zach's grim reply. "And they're headed straight up the valley. No way they can miss our camp if they keep on."

"What do we do?" asked Jubal.

"You head up-creek. Find Montez and the Scotsman, and then Shadmore, on your way to camp. Move as quick as you can. Forget the furs. Forget everything except your lives and your rifles. Take Sky and little Jacob and get out of here, fast. Use the northern pass if you can, but if not, leave your horses and go over the mountain."

Jubal knew what "over the mountain" meant. Zach had told them all of the way across the western line of mountains, the climb up over the saddle between two snow-clad peaks.

"What about me?" asked Fletch.

Zach looked him straight in the eye.

"We've got to buy Jube and the others some time."

Fletch nodded, and said nothing more. He realized right then and there that the odds of his getting through this day alive were right slim. But he accepted that. Fighting hostiles, and maybe dying in the process, was a fact of life for any mountain man, a reality he had to live with.

"What do I tell Sky?" asked Jube, as he mounted his horse.

"Tell her I'll see her soon," said Zach.

He didn't really think he would, though. This was the day he had been trying to prepare himself for all along. The day he had been dreading. But all the preparing hadn't worked.

"Can't we wait for you?"

"No," snapped Zach.

"But . . ."

"Get going. Don't look back. Fletch and I will catch up if we can. You understand?"

Jubal nodded. He understood very well. And he looked at Zach and Fletcher like he was looking at dead men.

"It all depends on you, Jubal," said Zach. "You've

got to get through. Don't let anything stop you. The lives of the others hang on it."

"I'll get through," was the young man's resolute promise.

"Yeah, I reckon you will," smiled Zach. "One more thing. Remind Shadmore about the Yellowstone country. The brigade will be safe there. That may be the only safe place in the high country anymore."

Jubal Wilkes nodded.

He raised his hand, reined his horse sharply, and galloped up-creek.

Zach turned to Fletch. "You ready?"

"Hell, yes," growled Fletcher. "Let's go welcome them Blackfeet to our valley."

IX

Zach and Fletcher rode hard until they found the Blackfoot war party.

As Zach had predicted, the Indians were headed straight for the brigade's camp. Unless they were slowed down or drawn off in another direction, Zach figured they would reach the vicinity of the camp before Jubal could round up the rest of the men and get there himself.

In which case, Sky and little Jacob would be at the mercy of the Blackfeet. And Blackfoot mercy was a critter that just didn't exist. Maybe Devlin wouldn't let anything happen to Sky and his son—or maybe he would be powerless to stop his Indian allies from doing anything they had it in mind to do.

The two men cut the war party's trail and closed in from behind. Once they'd spotted the Indians and their two companions from the American Fur Company, they checked their tired horses. Fletch turned to Zach.

"How do we start the shindig?" he asked.

Zach dismounted. He drew his Hawken plains rifle from its fringed and beaded sheath. Reins in his left hand, he turned the horse broadside, rested the rifle in the curve of the saddle, and drew a bead on the rearmost Blackfoot in the war party.

It was a long-range shot—Fletch calculated it had to be close on to a quarter-mile. But Zach made it. The Hawken spoke. As the powder-smoke cleared, he saw the warrior slump forward and then slide sideways off his pony.

"Good shootin'," said Fletch.

The other Blackfeet were milling around on prancing ponies, trying to figure out where the shot had come from. Then a cry rose up as they spotted Zach and Fletch. An instant later they were galloping across the open ground, straight at the two mountain men.

Zach calmly reloaded. His hands, like his nerves, were quite steady. Fletch raised his rifle and fired. Another Blackfoot hit the ground dead.

Once the Hawken was reloaded, Zach climbed on his horse and looked for Devlin. But Devlin and the other American Fur Company man were trailing along behind the ragged line of charging Blackfeet. Zach was disappointed at not having a clear shot at Coyote. He hated Devlin now with a hate that burned like a hot and steady flame in his heart. And he cursed himself for having missed the chance to kill Devlin.

"We got 'em turned around!" shouted Fletch.

"Let's give them a run for their money," said Zach.

The two mountain men kicked their horses into a gallop and headed south, the pack of screaming hostiles right behind them.

Both men carried flintlock pistols. Zach did not resort to his, concentrating instead of riding, low in the saddle, a firm hand on the reins, an eye on the terrain in front of him. He realized his chances of hitting anything from the back of a hard-running horse were slim indeed.

Fletcher, though, did draw his pistol, and fired at their pursuers, holding the reins in his teeth. The range was too long, and he didn't hit anything. But worse than the waste of powder and shot was the timing—he was looking over his shoulder as he came upon a deep gully. Zach had seen it, and kicked his horse into a jump that cleared the obstacle with room to spare. But Fletcher didn't know it was there until too late.

His horse, left to its own devices, decided to negotiate the gully rather than jump it. As it descended the embankment, soft earth gave way beneath its weight, and it stumbled and fell, throwing its rider.

Fletch struck the opposite bank, lost his grip on

both rifle and pistol, and rolled to the bottom, momentarily stunned. He gained his feet and tried to catch his horse, but he was still groggy, and stumbled, and the horse eluded him and crow-hopped down the gully. Cursing vehemently, Fletcher grabbed his rifle and reloaded. He got off a shot that dropped another Blackfoot.

Zach looked back, realized Fletcher's predicament, and without a second thought turned his horse and headed back to stand with his friend.

He arrived only seconds before the Blackfeet. Fletcher had just finished reloading his rifle again. He brought it up and fired point-blank into the body of a warrior leaping off his pony. The Blackfoot died in midair, but his corpse struck Fletcher and knocked him to the ground.

Fletch rolled the dead Indian off of him and got to his feet—just in time to catch a bullet between the shoulder blades. He dropped to his knees. The warrior who had fired the shot cast aside his empty rifle, jumped off his pony with an exultant cry, and ran to the rim of the embankment, brandishing a tomahawk, intent on finishing Fletcher off. Zach plugged him right between the eyes. The impact of the bullet picked the Blackfoot up off his feet and slammed him to the ground.

Zach made a running dismount, leaped into the gully. Some of the Blackfeet were also dismounted, sensing that the chase was over and the finish was near—now the fight would be hand to hand. Zach tried to reach Fletcher, but a Blackfoot appeared suddenly in his path, raising his rifle. Zach had the flintlock pistol in his left hand; he carried the empty Hawken in his right. He and the Blackfoot fired simultaneously. The warrior's shot clipped Zach's buckskin tunic but didn't scratch his skin. Zach's shot was true—the Blackfoot crumpled. Zach hurtled the body and kept running for Fletcher.

Yet another warrior had closed in on Fletcher with tomahawk raised for the killing blow. Zach yelled hoarsely. It was all he could do. Both pistol and rifle were empty, and he wasn't close enough to use knife or fist to stop the Blackfoot. The tomahawk swept down, striking Fletcher at the base of the neck, and nearly decapitating him.

Fletcher's corpse pitched forward. The warrior raised the bloody tomahawk and uttered a bloodcurdling yell. Zach saw the Indian had a terrible scar across one cheek.

Then the warrior bent over Fletch, a knife in hand now, and lifted the dead trapper's scalp.

Zach kept running. All he thought about was reaching the scar-faced warrior and paying him back for taking the life of his friend.

Before he could get to the Blackfoot, another one stepped in his way, crouching, war club in hand. Zach slammed the barrel of the empty Hawken into the Indian's gut. The Blackfoot doubled over, and Zach hit him in the face with the butt of the plains rifle. The warrior fell backwards, blood spewing from his ruined mouth and smashed nose.

Zach let out a guttural cry of his own as he closed with the scar-faced warrior.

The latter whirled. Drawing his knife, Zach charged straight at him. The warrior had picked up Fletcher's rifle. He used it like a club. The stock hammered Zach in the shoulder and sent him sprawling. He rolled and bounced to his feet. But the scarred Blackfoot was quick. He drove the butt of the rifle into Zach's chest. Zach went down again, the wind knocked out of him. Before he could get up a second time, the warrior struck once more, hitting Zach in the head with such force that the stock of the rifle splintered.

Zach's world turned black.

X

"We've got to go," Shadmore told Sky. "Right now, gal."

She stared at him, and then at the three mounted trappers behind him—Montez, MacGregor, and Jubal Wilkes. Her expression was stricken.

"I will not go without my husband," she replied, lifting her chin a defiant inch.

"Zach wants you to go," said Shadmore. "He told us to take you to safety. I reckon that's what I'm gonna do."

"I will wait for him," she insisted, her heart racing, her stomach twisted into knots, her eyes hot with tears that she fought to keep back. Disaster had struck. She would never see Zach again. Somehow she knew this, just as she had known that this day would come.

And so, at that moment, she was monumentally unconcerned by the prospect of the Blackfeet coming, even though she knew they would kill her.

"Wimmin!" growled the perturbed Shadmore. "They ain't worth a fraction of the trouble they cause. I've allus said so."

"Save yourselves," urged Morning Sky. "Take little Jacob with you."

"No!" cried the boy, who was clinging to his mother's leg tighter than a Number Five steel trap. "I won't leave you, mama."

"Little Jake needs you, Sky," said Shadmore. "What would Zach want you to do? Think, gal! He'd want you to raise the boy, not abandon him."

Morning Sky gasped. She could no longer hold back the tears. Sobbing, she covered her face with trembling hands. Shadmore placed a consoling arm around her shoulder.

"You are right," she whispered. "I am ashamed. I was thinking only of myself, not the welfare of my son."

"Don't fret. You warn't thinkin' clear. And don't count Zach out of this hyar world yet, Sky. You'd've felt right foolish staying put and lettin' them Blackfoot kill you and then ol' Zach shows up the next day, fit as a fiddle, now wouldn't you?"

She nodded, unable to speak.

"Now come along," said Shadmore gently. "Git

yoreself and the younker up on that cayuse so's we
kin dust out of hyar."

Sky obliged him, mounting the pony held by
MacGregor. Shadmore lifted little Jacob up to her,
and she placed him in front of her. The Scotsman
surrendered the reins.

Shadmore mounted his own horse. His heart was
heavy, for he, too, feared that he had seen the last of
Zach Hannah. But he didn't let on. His weathered
features were stoic as he led the others north out of
camp.

An hour later, Devlin and the Blackfeet rode into
the camp from the south.

Devlin leaped from his horse and checked every
lean-to, throwing aside the deerskin covers and peer-
ing in, cursing every time he found one empty.

Some of the Blackfeet started to dismount, intent
on looting, but a curt word from Scar kept them on
their ponies. He impassively watched Devlin run
from one lean-to to another.

Behind him, belly-down across the painted war
pony of one of the warriors who had died earlier that
day, was an unconscious Zach Hannah.

The other American Fur Company man, whose
name was Bledsoe, noticed that blood from Zach's
head wound had splattered all over the side of the
horse. Bledsoe figured if Zach wasn't dead, he soon
would be. The thought didn't bother him much. In
fact, very little bothered him. Bledsoe was a laconic,
come-what-may kind of man. He had fought under

Old Hickory Jackson at the Battle of New Orleans and then gone on to engage in a little smuggling in the Mississippi delta country. As a result, he had seen more than his fair share of bloodshed.

Devlin returned to stand between the still-mounted Scar and Bledsoe.

"She's not here," he rasped. "She's gone."

Bledsoe looked curiously at Devlin. Devlin had a strange, wild-eyed look to him, and Bledsoe wondered how a man could get so worked up over a woman. But he didn't voice this opinion. Devlin looked more than a little crazy.

"Maybe so," he said, "but over yonder's a fine bunch of plews. That's what the major sent us all this way for, ain't it?"

"That's what you came for," growled Devlin. "I came for Morning Sky."

"We came for white men's scalps," said Scar. "We have only one. Six of our brothers are dead, for only one white scalp."

"They can't be far," said Devlin. "There are four more you can take. See, here's their sign. Four more scalps, if you want 'em. But the woman—you don't lay a hand on her."

"Or those plews yonder," said Bledsoe. "That was part of the deal."

Scar glowered. "Six dead," he repeated.

Bledsoe shrugged. "You tangled with the great Zach Hannah, chief. What did you expect? But you got the sumbitch. Thar he is, in the flesh. Though why you ain't lifted his hair yet is beyond me."

"I take him alive to my people," replied Scar. "All Blackfeet will share in the glory of his death."

Devlin grunted. That was exactly what Red Claw and his Absaroka Crows had wanted to do with him, before Zach had intervened and saved him.

He looked at Zach, draped over the Indian pony, bleeding bad, and he felt a pang of genuine remorse.

"Well," drawled Bledsoe, addressing Scar. "If you ask me, seems like six dead's a small price to pay for the glory of being the one to count first coup on Zach Hannah. Especially iffen it's six others and not you that's gone under. You'll be a big augur, Scar, when you haul him back to your village."

Scar nodded. "It is so." He turned to Devlin. "We go back now."

"No!" shouted Devlin. "We're going after the rest of Hannah's brigade."

Scar shook his head. "You want the woman, you go get her," he said adamantly. "We have done all we will do."

"Look, you dirty . . ."

Bledsoe interrupted him. "Devlin, for Chrissakes, keep a civil tongue in yore head, or they'll take two more scalps back with 'em—yours and mine."

Devlin clamped his mouth shut. He was fuming, but he could see the sense in what Bledsoe was telling him. Riding with these Blackfoot devils made his skin crawl anyway. Let them go, and good riddance. At least now Zach was out of the way for good. This was the end for the great Zach Hannah. He would find Morning Sky, and when he did she would be his forever. It would be better this way. He couldn't trust these red rascals not to kill her anyway.

"Fine," he said, with a dismissive gesture. "Go ahead and ride out. You've done your part."

Scar reined his horse around and without another word led the war party out of the camp.

"Reckon that's the last we'll see of Zach Hannah," chuckled Bledsoe. "Hell of a mountain man."

"Shut up," snapped Devlin crossly.

Bledsoe smiled coldly. "You won, Devlin. Reckon you ought to be happy."

Devlin reckoned he ought to be.

And wondered why he wasn't.

Chapter 4

The Captivity

I

When Zach came to, his first reaction was surprise—that he was still above snakes was surely a true wonder.

Surprised, yes. Happy about his prospects, not in the least. Because the first thing he became aware of—the same thing that had brought him around—was the fact that a Blackfoot was pounding on him with a heavy stick.

Of course, his instinct was to get on his feet in a hurry and defend himself. But he couldn't move. His ankles and knees were tied with strips of rawhide, and his hands were bound behind his back. He didn't have a stitch of clothes on, either. He was trussed up like a Thanksgiving turkey with all the feathers plucked.

He tried to roll away, but the Blackfoot laughed—an unpleasant sound—and just kept pummeling him. Only when the warrior was exhausted did the beating stop. Zach was in the process of checking for broken bones—trying, gingerly, to move his arms and legs—when several more braves arrived. One proceeded to kick him, aiming for the ribs and crotch, and spit on him for good measure. Another one picked up a few convenient rocks and hurled them at Zach. The third used a willow branch on Zach's shoulders and back as Zach rolled over on his chest and tried to draw up his knees up, endeavoring to protect his rib cage and private parts.

No question but that the Blackfeet had a real poor opinion of him. It was, however, no poorer than the one he had of them. He cursed them, in English and in their own tongue. No cry of pain, no plea for mercy, not so much as a groan escaped his lips. He refused to give them the satisfaction.

The kicks and the rocks and the switching that laid his flesh open all hurt. But the worst hurt of all was the throbbing pain in his head. Zach figured he would have to get better to die. Felt as though his skull was about to explode. One of his eyes was swollen completely shut. Blood kept getting into the other.

Lost in a world of agony, Zach was slow to realize that the warriors had stopped kicking and stoning and whipping him. He warily unlimbered his aching body, just a bit, and risked opening that squeezed-shut good eye.

A fourth warrior had appeared, and he was giving

the three tormentors a good dressing-down. Incensed, he even gave one of them a hard shove.

"I want him alive when we reach our village," he said.

At first, Zach couldn't figure out why the fourth warrior was intervening on his behalf. The smoothest confidence man in the world couldn't have convinced him that a Blackfoot knew the first thing about compassion. Or had one drop of human decency in his blood.

"He is Longshot—the enemy of our people. He has killed many of our brothers," protested one of Zach's tormentors.

"That is so. But all our people will share in the glory of his death. All the Blackfeet—and the Bloods and the Piegans, too—will come to witness it."

The one who had called Zach "Longshot" started to argue further, but the fourth warrior cursed them fiercely, and the other Blackfeet took this violent upbraiding with silent, if sullen, resentment.

The warrior doing all the yelling was the one who had taken Fletcher's scalp. He wore deerskin leggins, breechclout, and moccasins—in his garb he was no different from the others. His necklace was the jawbone of a wolf, the teeth intact, tied to a rawhide thong. He wore three eagle feathers, attached to a hammered silver disk in his hair. A warrior rewarded with an eagle feather had demonstrated extraordinary valor in battle. In a tribe whose men were known for their courage and feared for their warlike nature, an eagle feather was a telling mark of distinction. To have three of them was noteworthy indeed.

The Blackfoot's most remarkable physical feature was that savage scar reaching from the bridge of his nose, diagonally across his cheek, to the jaw.

Eventually Scar led two of the chastised warriors away. The one left behind sat on his heels ten feet from Zach and glowered.

Zach studiously ignored his guard and tried to get his bearings. They were in a patch of trees. Day was drawing to a close. Somewhere nearby, a creek murmured. The sound made Zach aware of his raging thirst. Over yonder were a bunch of ponies, painted—like their Blackfoot masters—for war. Zach counted fourteen horses. He could smell meat cooking. At least he wasn't starving. His stomach was twisted into knots of fear. They intended to make his execution a big event. Escape appeared impossible. But as long as he drew breath there was a chance. His reputation was keeping him alive. Any other trapper would have been killed on the spot. He had never much cared for his reputation as one of the greatest enemies of the Blackfeet; now, for once, he was glad of it.

He considered the name they had given him. Longshot. No doubt it was the result of his prowess with the Hawken.

It was not for his own life that he feared. All he could think about was Morning Sky. Would he ever see her again? He was afraid not. Was this the end of them? The ending he had been dreading, and he

had been trying to prepare himself for, since their reunion three years ago? Were three years of happiness
all he was destined to have?

And then they came: the words he wished he had
said, the opportunities for tender moments with Sky
which he had let slip by. He had not touched her
enough, or kissed her enough, or told her that he
loved her enough times. These thoughts made him
so wretchedly miserable that he could scarcely endure it.

Night fell, dark as his mood. A pair of warriors
came over from the campfire. Zach braced himself,
expecting more abuse. Instead, they dragged him by
his heels to the nearest tree, sat him up with his
back to it, and lashed him to the trunk with a horsehair rope around his throat, the rope so tight that the
slightest movement on his part caused him severe
discomfort. Satisfied, they returned to the fire.
Zach's guard left him, too. Or so it seemed. Zach
couldn't shake the feeling that he was being watched
from somewhere in the darkness.

The war party was huddled over near the fire.
Zach counted thirteen warriors. They were having a
high ol' time. Voices were raised in shouts and laughter. They were regaling themselves with tales of their
bravery in the recent fight. They weren't the least bit
concerned about discovery. And why should they be?
wondered Zach. If they were still anywhere near the
Stinking Water River there wasn't another brigade of
white trappers within fifty miles in any direction, as
far as Zach knew.

The night got colder. Zach began to shiver uncontrollably. He clenched his teeth to keep them from chattering. He knew it wouldn't get so cold that he would have to worry about frostbite, but it was plenty cold enough to guarantee extreme discomfort.

The Blackfeet were crowing over Fletcher's scalp. Poor Fletch, thought Zach. He never had a chance. And it doesn't look as though I do, either.

Brandishing Fletcher's topknot, Scar came over and shook it in Zach's face.

"I kill your friend," he taunted, his features contorted with hate. "I take his scalp. I cut out his heart."

In spite of the dryness of his throat, Zach managed to gather enough saliva to spit in the warrior's face.

Enraged, the Blackfoot screamed like a panther. He slapped Zach in the face with the scalp. Zach lost his temper. Roaring incoherent rage, he strained against the rawhide which bound him to the tree, oblivious to the fact that his exertions cut off his wind. He didn't care. He didn't mind choking to death; all he wanted to do was get his hands on the Indian.

Two more Blackfeet ran over from the fire. One carried a burning brand. The other hefted a tomahawk.

Zach figured he was gone beaver for sure.

But instead of burying the tomahawk in Zach's skull, the warrior struck with the pipe side of the weapon.

The blow sent Zach spiraling back down into the bottomless black pit.

II

It was morning when Zach came to.

The Blackfeet were untying him from the tree. They cut the bindings on his ankles and knees. But they left his hands tied. Another rope was lashed around his neck. A warrior arrived on his pony and took the other end of the rope, which was about twenty feet long. He gave the braided horsehair a sharp tug, almost pulling Zach off his feet. The Indians had a laugh at that. The mounted brave then kicked his horse into motion. Zach tried to walk, but the circulation had not yet returned to his legs, so he fell. The Blackfoot didn't check his pony, and Zach was dragged across the rough ground by the neck.

It occurred to Zach that he might as well just lie there and choke to death. His immediate future promised only further torment and humiliation, culminating in a slow and agonizing death. But then he thought about Morning Sky and little Jacob. He had to look beyond the immediate future. He had to convince himself that, in spite of all the odds against him, he could somehow survive and escape and find his way back to his wife and son. He had to live for them and endure whatever the Blackfeet could dish out.

He would just have to cheat death.

He'd done it before. Maybe he could do it again. So he got back on his feet.

The rest of the war party mounted up. The scar-faced warrior led the way. Zach's captor fell in behind him. The others followed in ragged single file.

Before long they emerged from the trees, into a clearing on the shoulder of a mountain, made long ago by a rock fall or snowslide. The sun had not yet ascended above the gray peaks of the valley. But Zach was able to confirm that they were headed in a northerly direction. He recognized the mountains. They were deep in the Shoshone Range. About twenty miles from the ambush site. He figured the war party would leave this valley by a high pass a half-day away. It would be a rough climb for a man afoot and shoeless. But he had a hunch that the climb would amount to nothing compared to the other torments he would suffer.

Two days, he figured, and they would be in Black-foot country.

Late that afternoon, storm clouds began to fill the sky. Zach thanked the Lord Almighty for that. The day had grown downright hot. The sun had blistered his body. A strong wind began to whip around, howling through the lofty crags above them, seeming to come from all directions at once. It would be a real frog-strangler. Zach looked forward to it. He hadn't had a sip of water since yesterday morning. His throat was parched, his tongue swollen, and his lips chapped and split and bleeding.

He hadn't had any food, either, since supper day before yesterday. So by the afternoon he was about at the end of his strength. They had stayed on the slopes, well above the valley floor, and then begun the ascent to the high pass at the north end of the valley. It was hard walking. But Zach prevailed. He just concentrated on putting one swollen, bleeding foot in front of the other all through the long and painful day. He did not let himself think about the thousands of agonizing steps ahead of him. Instead, he kept telling himself that at least one step successfully taken was one closer to reunion with his family—and one less step he would have to take to reach freedom.

An hour before dark they reached the crest of the pass. When Scar made the rim he let out a whoop. A moment later Zach reached the crest and looked down the other side and saw the flicker of a fire in the purpling plain below.

It proved to be the camp of another Blackfoot war party.

Zach had figured it would be—Scar's reaction demonstrated that a rendezvous had been planned. There were ten warriors in the second band. That stacked the odds even higher against Zach. He had already decided that his only chance lay in making good his getaway prior to their arrival in a Blackfoot village. But now he had ten more warriors to worry about.

Night fell before they reached the camp. The overcast sky meant a particularly dark night. The rain finally came, after sundown. It soothed Zach's burned and bruised body.

They bound his ankles and knees again. He held his head back and opened his mouth wide, savoring every sweet drop of rain he could get. It wasn't anywhere near enough to slake his raging thirst, but it was the only drink he was likely to get.

Zach might have passed out from exhaustion right then and there. But the two war parties were making a lot of noise. Warriors recounted their exploits, and Zach heard enough to gather that the second war party had attacked a brigade in a valley near the western end of the Beartooths. There had been a fierce fight. Two warriors had lost their lives. The leader of the war party bragged to Scar that three mountain men had perished. Yet he had only one scalp to display. He explained this discrepancy by stating that the surviving trappers had carried off the other two dead white men before more topknots could be harvested.

Zach was surprised by this rendezvous. War parties did not usually work in tandem like this. It was too organized to make sense to anyone who knew anything about Indian nature and customs. A proven warrior would get it in his head to take the warpath; he would seek out volunteers to join him; if he could recruit enough enthusiasts, and gain the approval of chief or council for the venture, he would strike out on the path to glory. Usually, he had no specific target in mind. The war party would scour the countryside looking for prey, and strike at the first opportunity. Often enough, the warriors would find no victims, and they would soon grow disgruntled, and at some point the leader would have to give up and return home, lest his band disintegrate on its own.

So what was happening here? Were the Blackfeet going to wage a different kind of war than they had in the past?

Most of the second war party walked over to look at Zach. All of them either kicked, cursed, or spat on him. One of Scar's band sat on his heels nearby, watching—Zach's guard. He laughed at the abuse the other Blackfeet heaped on his prisoner. Zach scarcely felt the kicks, and the curses and spitting failed to move him to anger. He was past the point of wasting what little strength he had left just to indulge in futile struggle. Besides, any reaction from him would only provoke them.

Eventually Zach drifted off, lying on the ground in the rain, naked and bruised and bleeding. Disappointed that they could not get him to beg for mercy, or at least to curse them, the warriors stopped tormenting him.

Then someone was shaking him awake.

Zach cringed, expecting a rock or a stick or a good hard kick.

"Easy, hoss."

Zach started, tried to sit up.

The man spoke English!

The fires were still burning, in spite of the rain,

and the flickering light from them was just enough for Zach to see by.

Sure enough, a white man was hunkered down beside him. A rangy, big-boned character in age-blackened buckskins and flop-brimmed hat. Most of his face was concealed by a shaggy black beard and mustache. Pale, piercing eyes glimmered like the tempered steel of a good knife blade. A pistol and belduque were stuck in his belt.

Zach was astonished. Here was one of his own kind, and the Blackfeet weren't paying him any mind.

"Who are you?" asked Zach. His own voice startled him—it was a croaking travesty of its former self.

"Name's Bushrod Jones. What's yore handle?"

"Zach Hannah."

"Huh. Heard of you. Explains why you're still alive. Ol' Scar, the ugly bastard, he wants to show you off to the whole damned Blackfoot nation. Looks to me like you've been clear through hell and gone back for seconds."

"You work for Vanderburg?"

Bushrod glanced at the Blackfoot sitting on his heels a few strides away. The hair on his face parted, and Zach saw teeth flash in a wolfish grin.

"I'm in over my neck, hoss, same as you," replied Bushrod Jones. "I signed on with the American Fur Company, yes. Come to find out Vanderburg's cut a deal with the Blackfeet. This is how it works, in case you're interested. Vanderburg sends us out to follow the brigades of yore Rocky Mountain Fur Company to wherever they settle down to do some trappin'. Then we send word back to the Blackfeet. They got a big encampment up on the Judith. Then they sashay in with a war party and drive you boys out. After that, we move in and take over. The Blackfeet got their scalps and we get the fur."

"Bastard," breathed Zach.

Bushrod scowled. "Don't go judgin' me, Zach Hannah, till you've walked in my moccasins. I ain't no knight in shining damn armor, and I ain't never claimed to be. So get that straight right now or you'll rile me."

"I got it straight," Zach snapped right back. "And you better hope I don't get shed of these ropes and get my hands on a knife. 'Cause if I do, I'll come lookin' for you."

III

Bushrod chuckled.

"You got some hair on yore chest, don't you, hoss? I'll give you that."

"I can understand the Blackfeet doing what they do. But not a mountain man who turns on his own kind. And I don't care what company he's signed up with."

Bushrod's expression darkened.

"Yeah. Well, we all got rules we try to live by. I can live with a fair fight, but this—what they're doing to you—ain't fair, and it rubs against my grain. A moun-

tain man don't ask for nothin' but a chance to die
with a rifle or knife in hand. Now, I rode with these
Blackfoot bastards to hit Jackson's brigade, knowin'
there'd probably be some blood spilt. Long as I didn't
have to take a hand in it. Yore friends gave as good
as they got, and just between you and me, I'm glad
it went that way instead of t'other. But either way,
s'long as it was a fair fight, I knew I could sleep."

"You draw a fine line," said Zach.

"Everybody draws his own line," insisted Bushrod.
"So I can go a little farther before steppin' over mine
than you can go 'fore you step over yourn. Over here
a man lives a hard life and generally dies an ugly
death. That's the way of things out here in the high
country."

Zach did not immediately respond. He puzzled
over Bushrod's words. The man seemed to be ram-
bling, and Zach could make precious little sense of
the point he was trying to make—if indeed he had
one. All the same, Zach figured he would do well to
cease judging this man, and thereby antagonizing
him, just because he was in cahoots with the Blackfeet. For whatever reason, Bushrod's conscience was
bothered by the treatment Zach was receiving, and
Zach decided it would be worth allying himself with
the devil himself if it might lead to escape.

"Just sit tight, hoss," said Bushrod. "Mebbe I kin
get you a blanket and a bite to eat."

"How about a knife?"

But Bushrod seemed not to hear this request. He
stood and bent his steps toward the fires.

Zach watched him converse with the warrior named Scar. After a short but animated discussion with the Blackfoot, Bushrod repaired to his horse, and then returned to Zach bearing a wool blanket. Brandishing a long knife, he cut a foot-long slash dead-center of the blanket, then draped the blanket over Zach. Zach's head fit through that middle cut.

"There," said Bushrod. "Now you got what them Mex folks down south call a *serape*." He leaned closer, with a surreptitious over-the-shoulder glance at Zach's guard. He held out a strip of venison jerky. His body blocked this from the guard's view.

"Ol' Scar gave in about the blanket, but I reckon he'd pitch a conniption if he knew I was feedin' you, too. Here. Take it. Don't let nobody see you eat it, though."

Zach sat with his knees pulled up, ducked his head, and worried a piece off with his teeth. It was like biting into old whang-leather, and just about as tasty. But beggars couldn't be choosers.

"So can you help me out of these ropes?" asked Zach as he chewed.

With a grimace, Bushrod shook his head. "Cain't do her, hoss."

Zach could tell the man was plenty bothered. But apparently Bushrod had done all he could do. He'd climbed out on a limb with the venison jerky, and he wasn't going to go out any further. So Zach settled down and counted his blessings.

"Well, thanks for the blanket and jerky, anyway," he said.

"Eat it all, Zach Hannah. A better meal ain't likely to come yore way tonight."

Zach tore another bite off the strip, worrying it like a dog might worry a bone.

"Sorry, hoss," muttered Bushrod. "Hate like holy hell to leave you like this. But I got no choice. Were I to try and set you loose we'd both die. This ain't easy for me, but I made my bed so I reckon I've got to lay in it. I know you don't feel too kindly towards me right now, and I don't really give a damn."

Zach nodded. "Reckon you'll sleep tonight, then."

Bushrod's eyes glittered behind a veil of rain dripping from the sagging brim of his hat.

"You'd best try to get some shut-eye yoreself, Hannah," he suggested. "You'll need all your strength for tomorrow."

With that, he turned and walked quickly away.

Dawn found them on the trail north.

The two war parties were traveling together from now on. All day long Zach trudged at the end of the horsehair rope tied around his neck. He saw no sign of Bushrod Jones, and though the frontiersman had made it clear he had done all he would do for Zach's benefit, Zach missed him regardless.

Much to his surprise, his captors permitted him to keep the blanket-*serape* Bushrod had provided him. He was also surprised to find himself making it through that second day in pretty good fashion, feeling marginally stronger than he had the day before.

By his best calculations, Zach figured they would

reach the upper Missouri by nightfall. Tomorrow would find them in Blackfoot country. In spite of the twenty-three warriors in the band, he decided he would have to make a bid for freedom, somehow, before tomorrow's sunrise. The odds, steep as they were, would only worsen if he delayed.

He was right on the mark—they reached the river at dusk and camped on the south side of it. The Missouri was running high and wide. There had been summer storms up in the mountains, and the river was on the rampage.

Scar and several other warriors engaged in a heated discussion concerning where and when to cross. Zach's resolve to escape tonight was strengthened by the prospect of the river crossing. He wasn't sure he could survive it. Even in the best condition and unbound it would be a perilous endeavor, and he wasn't sure but that the Blackfeet might toss him in tied hand and foot and just haul him across at the end of a long rope. And if that happened, and he survived the ordeal, and reached the other side alive, he would simply have to cross the river again, assuming he made good his escape and was heading south. No, better to try a getaway now.

When night fell, the darkness was absolute, as the sky had remained overcast. Most nights Zach could see as well as a cat. But tonight he couldn't make out anything that was much beyond arm's length.

That day he had watched the ground, looking for a rock. Not just any rock—one he could grip easily, and which could be concealed in the palm of his

hand, and finally, one with a sharp point or edge to
it. When he saw one that appeared to fit the bill, he
stumbled and fell and rolled over on top of it, hoping
to snare it in his grasp. The first attempt was a failure. The Blackfoot in charge of the rope around his
neck kicked his pony forward and gave the rope a
malicious pull as Zach hit the ground. He had no
idea what Zach was up to; he was just trying to inflict more pain on his prisoner. Zach was dragged forward before he could clutch the rock, and all but
strangled to death before he could regain his feet.

But he wasn't deterred. Three times he fell, hoping to snare a rock without being discovered. The
third time was the charm. The Blackfeet thought
nothing of his apparent clumsiness. They laughed at
him, believing him to be on his last legs and rejoicing
in his suffering.

The rest of the day, Zach kept the stone in his fist.

That night they tied him, sitting up, to a willow
tree. Scar did not bother posting a guard to watch
over him. A fire was built. Fresh-killed meat was
cooked. The mood of the band was reserved. It had
been a long trail, and the weather didn't help. They
were close to home now—spent, relaxed, and—Zach
hoped—a little off their guard.

He waited several hours. The fire died down. The
camp grew still as the Blackfeet rolled up in their
blankets and slept. Each warrior kept his pony near
at hand, as was their habit on the warpath. Scar sent
one mounted guard south, to watch their backtrail in
case of pursuit. This sentry was posted too far away

to see Zach, or to hear any noise he might make as he sawed at the rawhide around his wrists with the sharp-edged rock.

IV

Having been wet, the rawhide binding Zach's wrists together had shrunk to bite deep into his flesh. It had long ago cut off the circulation to his hands. Having no feeling left in his fingers made gripping the rock a tricky business. He wished the same were true of his wrists. He had to cut into his own flesh just to get to the rawhide. There was no help for it. In minutes his hands were slick with warm blood. But Zach scarcely noticed the pain. He didn't know if pain could even faze him anymore. He had endured a surfeit of pain. It had become a part of his life. He wasn't sure if he remembered what life was like without it. He was beginning to take it for granted, and it just didn't impress him all that much anymore.

Ten minutes later his hands were free. Then he started on the horsehair rope tied around his neck and secured to the trunk of the willow. While he worked, Zach strained to see in the heavy darkness. Without the fire's light, he could scarcely see twenty feet. Last of all, he cut the rawhide binding his ankles. He sat there a few minutes to let the feeling return to his hands and feets.

When he did start catfooting in the direction of

the nearest pony, he almost stumbled over a slumbering warrior. For an instant he considered bending down and cutting the Indian's throat with the sharp, jagged edge of the rock. It would be one less Blackfoot to deal with later. But he couldn't bring himself to do it. He remembered last winter, when the brigade had captured the Blackfoot warrior named Long Runner. Baptiste had wanted to kill the Indian outright and be done with it—and the French-Canadian would have done the deed with no more thought than he would have given to snuffing out the life of a timber rattler. No denying that the suggestion had had some merit, considering the circumstances. But Zach hadn't been able to get around the fact that it was cold-blooded murder, circumstances notwithstanding—and no matter that sparing Long Runner's life had jeopardized the brigade.

Similar considerations applied now. From a purely objective standpoint, Zach could see the value in killing this man while he slept. If he did manage to escape and there was pursuit—and there almost certainly would be—it would mean one less pursuer to elude. If he were captured, what would they do to him by way of retribution for the killing that they weren't already planning to do? Perhaps he could slip through camp, from one sleeping warrior to the next, cutting every throat. He could take his first victim's knife and go to work. But the mental image he conjured up of his embarking on such a bloody deed made him shudder, and he knew he just didn't have it in him to pull it off.

Zach turned his attention to the warrior's pony. As he reached out, the horse snickered and jerked away. Zach's heart nearly jumped right out of his throat. He moved closer, inch by laborious inch; no sudden moves. He shushed, real low and soft, but the pony would have nothing to do with him and his horse-talk. It sidestepped and jerked its head again, and the braided horsehair reins linking the Indian bridle to its owner's wrist were pulled taut. Zach braced himself, expecting the Blackfoot to awaken and pre-paring himself to rip the man's throat open with the sharp-edged stone.

But the warrior did not stir.

Zach decided to try a different approach. He knelt, saw the sheathed knife at the warrior's side, and slipped the blade, slowly, slowly free. He used the knife to slice the horsehair reins. He had to do a little sawing—the blade was not as sharp as he would have liked it to be, less keen than he would have kept his own. He held the reins firmly to keep from jostling the Indian's wrist as he worked.

Once the reins were cut through he led the horse away. The pony followed without raising a ruckus. In a moment he was deeper into the trees, out of the camp proper. Hope welled up inside of him. He hadn't dared to hope before but had simply made the attempt without bothering to consider the chances for success. It would have been self-defeating to do so—the odds were astronomical against his making good an escape.

And then he heard the mounted guard, coming

through the trees, coming back to camp, heading in his direction.

He could try to hide. But hiding the horse he had just stolen would be a problem. Precious seconds were wasted as he stood stock-still in the nocturnal gloom, straining his ears, trying to determine the guard's exact course. Why was the Blackfoot lookout returning to camp? There was no sense of urgency in his progress through the trees. But what did it matter? He was heading pretty much straight on at Zach, and Zach didn't know whether to move to his left or to his right or simply to stay where he was, because a man on horseback moving through trees was liable to make a dozen little changes in direction.

One thing was certain: if the warrior saw him, Zach would have to use the knife. Hopefully before the Blackfoot could cry out an alarm.

Zach made up his mind on a course of action. It was not his nature to stand and wait for something to befall him. Tethering the Indian pony to the nearest tree, he went forward on foot. Better, he decided to be the predator than the prey.

A minute later he saw the mounted Blackfoot, at first no more distinctly than as a moving black shadow in a world of black stillness. Zach angled through the woods to intercept the rider. He got so close that he could have reached out and touched the guard's pony—yet it was so dark that the Indian did not see him.

The warrior's horse, however, could sense him, perhaps smell him. The pony gave a nervous nicker, a toss of the head. The Blackfoot spoke to his mount. Zach made his move. There was no turning back now. Knife in hand, he vaulted onto the croup of the horse, behind the Indian. The latter uttered a single sharp sound of alarm before Zach's hand clamped over his mouth. A heartbeat later, cold steel slipped to the hilt between the warrior's ribs, piercing his heart.

The Blackfoot's body jerked convulsively and pitched violently sideways. As the knife had entered, he had grabbed Zach's forearm in an iron grip. Zach was pulled off the horse with him. He hit the ground hard enough to drive the wind out of him. Wrenching free of the warrior's death grip, he got to his feet, laboring to drag air into his lungs, and took two long strides towards the horse. But the pony was spooked. With a shrill whinny it bolted—straight for camp!

Zach cursed under his breath and headed at a flat-out run for his own mount. He tripped over an exposed root, fell hard, got up quickly, kept running. His sense of direction was flawless. He knew right where to find the pony, even thought at first he could not see it.

As he ran, weaving through the trees, he heard a shout from the direction of the camp. He reached the pony, pulled the slip knot of the tether. But before he could mount up, a warrior came charging at him, emerging from the darkness, uttering a war cry that sounded like a panther scream. The sound, and the Blackfoot's sudden appearance, startled Zach and sent a chill down his spine.

The warrior had his tomahawk raised. Zach turned to meet him, stepping in at the last second to plant a shoulder in the Blackfoot's chest, ducking under the down-swept tomahawk. The collision sent both men reeling. Zach steadied himself and braced to meet another onslaught. The Blackfoot was coming at him again. This time, Zach reached out to grab the warrior's arm as he brought the tomahawk down. As they collided, Zach drove the knife into the Indian's belly and ripped him open. The Blackfoot collapsed, writhed, then lay still.

The pony, untethered, had wandered, but not far. Zach breathed a sigh of relief and moved slowly towards it, thinking it might bolt if he made a run at it. As he came within reach of the animal, it sidestepped, whinnied. Zach could hear more Indians thrashing through the woods, searching for him. He didn't have time to play games with a skittish horses. It was all or nothing. He made a lunge for the horsehair reins. The pony bolted, pulling him completely off his feet. Zach fell under its hooves, rolled desperately, almost lost the knife, and came up in a graceless, stumbling run, holding onto the knife for dear life. The pony veered sharply, its straightaway run blocked by a tight clump of trees. Zach kept running full-bore and hurled himself onto the animal's back. The pony reared up on its hind legs. Zach grabbed a handful of mane, locked his legs as tight as he could around the pony's barrel, and somehow managed to hang on.

The pony came down running.

For one brief moment Zach thought he would actually make it.

Then he heard the *crack*! of a rifle report and saw the powder-flash out of the corner of his eye, not twenty paces to his left.

The pony died in midstride. Zach thought he could feel the bullet strike, and was sure he felt the horse give a massive shudder. As it collapsed, Zach went flying. The ground rushed up to meet him. He lay there, stunned, fighting for air. Tried to get up. Couldn't. He heard a shout, managed to lift his head. It took a lot of effort, but he wanted to see death when it came for him. He knew he was done for. He had made his bid for freedom, for life, and come up short. He wasn't afraid. Again he thought of Morning Sky, and little Jacob. He wondered what day it was. He saw, as through a haze, the face of a Blackfoot warrior. The Indian's features were twisted with hate. He was brandishing a war club. Zach watched the club descend with terrifying swiftness. An explosion of white pain was the last thing he knew.

V

When they were close to the Blackfoot village, Scar sent a warrior on ahead to inform his people that he was bringing in as his prisoner one of the most hated of all the mountain men.

Zach figured there was a better-than-even chance

he would die before the day was done. Scar had accomplished what he had set out to do: deliver Zach Hannah—Longshot—to his tribe, alive. The feat would bring him great honor. It would be an exploit worthy of retelling around the council fires for generations to come. Now that it was done, Scar would be indifferent to Zach's fate. And Zach doubted there would be a single soul in the village likely to take a benevolent interest in his welfare. It was really just a question of how long they would take to kill him.

The warriors in Scar's band had come close to killing him earlier that day. They had tried to drown him in the hair-raising crossing of the high-running Missouri. But Scar had intervened. Zach couldn't blame the others for their homicidal frame of mind. He had killed two of their number in his escape attempt, and without Scar's determination to obtain the signal honor of bringing him in alive for all the tribe to vilify and torture and, ultimately, execute in the most diabolical way the Indian mind could devise, he would have been gone beaver, for sure.

But now he was at the end of the trail, in more ways than one, and as he looked down at the village, nestled between grass-covered slopes, and calculated that there were at least a hundred tepees, which mean three to four hundred Blackfeet, at least, he felt the sinking finality of utter despair. He'd had his chance, and he'd failed. This was where it would end. All he could hope for was to die with dignity. That would be hard to do, because dignity was what they would try to strip from him. But he would do

Sky proud. If she heard of his death, and got a true rendition of the event, she would at least be able to hold her head high knowing he had died well.

They proceeded down the slope, into the valley filled with wood-smoke haze, and a dozen warriors rode out to meet them, and then a dozen more, and there was a great deal of whooping and hollering. The warriors from the village spit on Zach and cursed him and kicked him, but Zach was oblivious.

He walked behind Scar's horse. Ever since the incident at the river, Scar had taken personal charge of him. His hands were bound in front of him. The rope was still around his neck—Scar had the other end of it.

As they neared the village he saw the people swarming to meet them. A double line of men and women, old and young, developed in their path. Zach figured it was a good three hundred yards long—a couple of hundred Blackfeet at least. Every last one of them had something in hand—a club, a stuck, a strip of rawhide, a rock.

He didn't need to be told what was about to unfold.

It was the gauntlet.

The gauntlet was a tried-and-true Indian tradition, and more tribes than not used it, in some form or fashion. It was a test of courage. Some tribes used it to initiate warriors into special societies, whose members generally had to be the bravest of the brave, the strongest of the strong. Sometimes the gauntlet was employed to determine the guilt or innocence of a man, or women, accused of some crime. And sometimes, as now, a tribe's captured enemies were forced to prove themselves by running the gauntlet.

Zach figured there had never been a gauntlet like this one. Looked like the whole village was wanting a shot at him.

Scar dismounted near the beginning of the line. The Blackfeet set up such a hue and cry of adulation for him and his band that Zach's ears were ringing. Scar received this approbation with grave dignity. His was the air of a man scarcely even grateful for this outpouring of feeling, since it was his due.

Approaching Zach, the warrior drew his knife. He stood very close to his prisoner. His dark eyes were aflame with fierce elation, and fierce hatred. The way he held the knife made Zach wonder if, for some reason, Scar had changed his mind about handing him over to the village—if he had instead decided to kill his captive right here and now. But Zach stood tall and unflinching, with defiance in his steady gaze.

The corner of Scar's mouth curled, a sardonic smile. Zach's attitude seemed to amuse him. He brought the knife to Zach's throat. Still, he got no response from his prisoner. Zach's eyes said *go ahead and kill me*.

Scar cut the rope around Zach's neck, one quick flick of the blade.

And then the warrior pointed down the gauntlet—

that long, narrow path between two rows of yelling, taunting, eager Blackfeet.

"You run, Longshot. If you fall you will die."

"And if I reach the end?" asked Zach. "You'll let me go free." He said it with sarcasm; he knew they would never let him go.

"If you fall you die," said Scar. "If you reach the end you still die. But maybe you die tomorrow instead of today."

There was really no hope of his reaching the end of such a gauntlet, and he knew that. He was going to die. He knew it. Accepted it. That didn't mean he wouldn't fight to the last breath. With acceptance came a sudden calm. His fear melted away.

Looking back, he had only one regret.

In the three years he had been reunited with Morning Sky he had tried to prepare himself for this—for being parted from her again, but this time forever, because it would be death that parted them. To a degree, he had withdrawn into himself and that approach had colored his relationship with her. He had held back from her, a little, when he should have given his all.

"I'm sorry, Sky," he murmured.

"Run," said Scar.

Zach gave the warrior a cold look.

"Go to hell," he said.

Clenching his bound hands into fists, he struck Scar across the face. Scar crumpled. Some of the mounted warriors behind Zach yelled in outrage and kicked their ponies forward, their weapons raised.

Zach didn't wait for them to strike. He took off sprinting down the gauntlet.

He was quicker than the Blackfeet expected him to be. With bounding strides and elusive feints he made fifty feet before a single Indian managed to land a blow. Even then it was a glancing blow to the back, a club grazing his shoulders. He stumbled forward, found his balance, surged ahead.

Weaving and dodging, he made another fifty feet with only minor damage done. He was quick and agile and elusive—considering the ordeal of the past few days, it surprised him that he could move so well. It surprised and infuriated the Blackfeet. One hefty squaw was so bent on stopping him that she stepped out of line and planted herself squarely across the path, brandishing a club. There was no room to get around her, so Zach lowered his head and plowed right into her, bowling her over. The club came down across his back with such force that he dropped to one knee.

He was up again in a heartbeat, hurtling the fallen woman, who was clutching her midsection and making strange noises. Zach felt no regret about hurting a member of the opposite sex. That was no longer a consideration. She was a Blackfoot—she was the enemy—and she was trying her best to kill him. None of the other Blackfeet came to her aid. She had dishonored herself and the tribe by stepping out of line; for this reason she would get no sympathy or assistance now, and in days to come would face ridicule and contempt.

Zach made it a little further before suffering his first serious injury. A switch caught him across the face. The blow itself was not all that painful, especially to a man virtually inured to ordinary pain, but it laid a deep gash across his forehead and the bridge of his nose, and the wound bled profusely, as head wounds do. The blood blinded him. He veered too close to one of the lines as he tried to wipe the blood out of his eyes with his still-bound hands. A club caught him squarely in the chest. The blow stopped him, rocked him backwards. Another blow to the legs felled him. He was down, and by the rules of the game, the Blackfeet were free now to leave their lines and converge on their victim like a pack of wolves moving in for the kill.

He tried to get up, but the blows kept raining down on him. Rolling up into a tight ball, he covered his head with his arms and took the punishment without a whimper. A club came down hard on his left arm below the elbow. He felt the bone snap. A wave of blackness enveloped him and he welcomed it, believing it was death. He did not fear it, but rather embraced it, because he had died well.

VI

Zach came to feeling the gentle, unmistakable touch of a woman. He thought he was dreaming. "Sky," he whispered. For a moment he thought he was with her, safe and sound in her arms. Then he opened his eyes.

He was lying in a tepee, stretched out on a buffalo robe, with another covering him. His arm had been set, and tightly bound. A woman knelt beside him, applying a cooling salve to the bruises, cuts, and abrasions on his chest and shoulders. He could tell that the salve had already been applied to other parts of his body, and he blushed furiously.

"Who are you?" he asked, in the Blackfoot tongue.

He knew then what had happened, though he could scarcely believe that it had—he was still alive. He was glad to be above snakes, and in another way not glad at all, since he was still a prisoner of the Blackfeet and the death they were determined to inflict upon him yet loomed in his future.

"I am Moon Singer," she replied, her gaze shyly downcast. She was pretty—almost as pretty as Sky, he thought.

"Why are you helping me?"

An explosion of angry voices outside the tepee intervened before she could answer. Moon Singer glanced with sharp apprehension toward the deer-skin-covered entrance. The glance told Zach a number of things. For some reason the tepee was a haven for him, a safe place in the enemy camp. Yet it was a precarious haven. Someone had interceded on his behalf, and that someone—and Moon Singer, too—were risking a great deal, because the wrath of the rest of the village would be turned now against them.

But why?

Who was this mysterious benefactor, and why would a Blackfoot risk so much for his sake?

The deerskin flap was brushed aside, and a warrior entered the tepee.

"You!" breathed Zach.

It was Long Runner.

The warrior whose life Zach had spared the winter before now had a tomahawk in his hand, and Zach surmised that he had been brandishing the weapon to drive his point home in the argument which had just occurred outside the tepee.

So Long Runner had saved him.

But the warrior's expression was one of such bitter resentment that Zach suddenly wondered if he was reading this right. And when Long Runner took a menacing step towards him, with tomahawk raised, Zach raised an arm to fend off the blow he thought was coming. It was an ineffectual gesture, a reflex action, and perfectly useless, but Zach was simply too bone-tired to make a real fight of it.

Moon Singer threw herself across Zach's body. Draped across his chest, her face turned up to Long Runner, she raised her own arm, as though she, too, expected the tomahawk to come sweeping down.

"Brother, no!" she cried.

With a guttural sound that was half-growl, half-groan of pure anguish, Long Runner hurled the tomahawk across the tepee, a gesture of utter frustration. Trembling violently, he dropped to his knees, fists clenched so tightly that the knuckles were white, lips drawn back from gritted teeth. He stared at Moon Singer, and his eyes reflected the agony gripping his soul, and then he lowered his head, in the attitude of one who is praying.

At that moment the deerskin flap was thrown aside again.

Bushrod Jones entered the tepee.

Long Runner jumped to his feet. His hand flew to the knife sheathed at his side. This aggressive move triggered an equally belligerent response from the frontiersman, who leveled his rifle at the Blackfoot.

"Howdy, Hannah," said Bushrod, his pale eyes glimmering like sunlight on polished steel. "My Blackfoot ain't as good as I've heard yourn is, so why don't you tell this feller to ease off, else I'll have to blow a hole in him so big you'll see next year through it."

Zach was mighty confused by the whole business, but he tried to gather his wits and consider how to address Long Runner. What could he say? Merely relay Bushrod's threat? Tell him that the mountain man meant no harm? That he was a friend? How could he be certain that any of that was true? Fact was, he didn't have an inkling as to what was going on here.

But Long Runner eased off on his own initiative before Zach could say a word. He took his hand off the knife. Bushrod lowered the rifle. From outside came the babble of angry voices.

Bushrod's grin was lopsided. He sat on his heels

just inside the tepee entrance and gestured over his shoulder.

" 'Pears to be half the Blackfoot Nation out yonder, worked up to a slim frazzle," he remarked. "I'm surprised they ain't come bustin' in here and dragged you out by your heels, Hannah."

"Why haven't they?"

"This one here's to thank for that." Bushrod nodded at Long Runner.

"I figured that much. What happened? Last I knew, I was running the gauntlet. They knocked me down. Somebody hit me with a club. Broke my arm. I couldn't get up. Thought I was gone beaver."

"Well, I warn't here day before yesterday, so I honestly couldn't . . ."

"Day before yesterday!"

Bushrod nodded. "You've been walkin' around in the land of dreams for two days, hoss." He looked, sly and sidelong, at Moon Singer. The glance was appreciative. "This here punkin's been takin' care of you like you belonged to her."

Zach looked at Moon Singer. She was sitting on her heels beside him. She could tell the two white men were talking about her, and she blushed and refused to look either one of them square in the eye.

Bushrod chuckled. "She's this feller's sister, by the way. From what I hear, Long Runner stepped in and stopped all them folks out there from poundin' you into bloody pulp. But don't ask me why."

"I reckon it's because I didn't kill him last winter when I had the chance."

Bushrod hiked bushy eyebrows. "You didn't? Why the hell not?"

Zach told him all about it—how the band of Blackfeet, rousted from their own wintering ground by treacherous Gros Ventres, had come waltzing through the valley where his brigade had set up winter camp. Long Runner's wife had been mortally wounded in the fight with the Big Bellies. The band had been forced to leave her behind to die in the valley. Long Runner had remained with her.

Trailing the Blackfeet, Zach and his men had come upon Long Runner and his dying wife. Baptiste, the French-Canadian, had wanted to kill Long Runner outright. Instead, Zach had taken the warrior prisoner and, later, released him, even though by doing so he had taken a terrible risk. Long Runner could have betrayed the brigade's presence to the other Blackfeet.

"Looks like he didn't," remarked Bushrod, with a curious glance at Long Runner.

"Reckon not," said Zach.

"So he figures he owed you a life."

"Guess so. Though he paid me back by keeping his mouth shut about me and the rest of the brigade."

Bushrod grunted. "Huh! Then I wonder how come he was out there a minute ago tellin' everybody he wanted you alive so's you two could fight a duel to the death when you was well enough to give a good account of yoreself?"

VII

"I don't understand," said Zach. He looked at Long Runner, who was watching him, unblinking. "You saved my life just so you could kill me yourself?" he asked in Blackfoot. "Why didn't you just kill me a minute ago? Sure looked like you had a mind to."

"I owed you my life," was Long Runner's grave reply. "I have paid what I owed."

"What did he say?" asked Bushrod. "Somethin' about owin' somethin'?"

"He says we're even," said Zach. "I saved his life, he saved mine."

"Don't make much sense," mused Bushrod.

"Maybe it does, though. You see, I don't reckon he could tell his people about what happened last winter. How could he? How could he admit to them that he knew my brigade was in that valley but didn't say anything about that at the time?"

"Well, I can see that much," allowed Bushrod. "But why the duel?"

"Because I've put him in a bad fix. His honor required him to step in and save my bacon . . ."

"Honor?" Bushrod scoffed at that. "Hell, Hannah, he's a damned Blackfoot."

"He's a man, and he knows what honor is. Maybe more than you."

"Get off my back."

"I know," said Zach. "You're just doing what you have to do, and I shouldn't judge you till I've stood in your moccasins."

Bushrod scowled. "You ain't easy to make friends with, Hannah."

"Didn't know you wanted to be my friend, Jones."

"I don't."

"Fine. Long Runner hates my guts, too. In that respect, he's a good Blackfoot."

"I don't savvy why you didn't kill him when you had the chance."

"At first it was because we couldn't risk firing a shot. The rest of his outfit was somewhere close by. We knew that much. They'd have heard the shot, and we'd have had a fight on our hands. Considering how many of them there were, it would have been a fight we probably couldn't have won."

"So you took him without a shot fired," said Bushrod. "Why didn't you cut his throat and be done with it?"

"I won't kill a man in cold blood," declared Zach, his voice as hard as stone.

Bushrod cast a speculative glance at the sullen Long Runner.

"Reckon he wouldn't have thought twice."

"You might be wrong."

"He's the one wantin' a fight to the death, remember, hoss?"

"So he does. And he has a right to ask for it. But it'll be up to the tribal council to say yes or no."

"True enough. He'll have to have a damned good reason for having you all to himself and spoilin' everybody else's fun, else the council won't buy it."

At that moment, Scar called to Long Runner from

outside, requesting permission to enter—for to enter another's tepee uninvited was forbidden. Bushrod Jones had barged in without a by-your-leave, but then what could one expect from an uncouth white man?

Zach figured Scar had aspirations of being more than just a warrior of repute. For that reason, he had to observe the proprieties. He had to keep the respect of the tribe, because his ascension to a seat on the council, if that was what he was after, would be decided by a vote of all the adult members of the tribe, subject to the approval of those who were already council members. In many ways, tribal government was every bit as democratic as the system by which citizens of the United States governed themselves. When a place on the council became available, two or three likely candidates would step forward. The supporters of each candidate would line up behind their choice, and a head count would resolve the election.

Long Runner called out to Scar and bade him enter.

Zach's captor gave Bushrod an unreadable look, glared malevolently at Zach, and then sat cross-legged just inside the tepee entrance.

"I have a hunch we'll find out what Long Runner's reason is right here and now," Bushrod told Zach.

Though he pointed an accusing finger at Zach, Scar kept his eyes fastened on Long Runner.

"This one is my prisoner. I captured him." The

warrior struck his chest with a fist. "I decide his fate. Not you, Long Runner."

His tone was belligerent. In contrast, Long Runner's voice was thoroughly calm and without rancor.

"Longshot is a brave man. He deserves at least to die with dignity. Are the Blackfeet cowards that the whole village is needed to kill one white man? And must his hands be bound, and empty, without a weapon with which he might defend himself? Is the village afraid of this one white man? In this, is there any reason for the Blackfoot Nation to be proud? Is there any honor in it? I say there is no honor. And I am not afraid of him."

Scar was scowling. "He has killed many of our brothers, Long Runner. Many are the nights we have heard a woman wail because Longshot has killed her man."

"I never looked for a fight," said Zach. "I tried to avoid one whenever possible."

"Silence," snapped Scar.

But Zach kept on. He figured he might as well have his say and try to get things straight just for the record—he couldn't be sure he'd have another opportunity. Besides, he wanted to provoke Scar. He'd taken a strong dislike to the man.

"Your warriors kept coming into the high country after my scalp," he said. "I went out of my way to stay clear of them. But sometimes I couldn't. Sometimes they found me. And then I had to kill them, in self-defense." Zach's smile was bitter. "Thing is, the more I had to kill, the more came looking for the glory they would reap from being the one to bring back my scalp."

Scar stared at him with cold disdain. In his case, Zach's defense was falling on deaf ears. Long Runner didn't seem any more receptive than Scar. He did not even glance at Zach—he was watching Scar like a hawk. Moon Singer's eyes, though, told Zach that she believed him.

"He must die," said Scar flatly.

"He will," said Long Runner, with quiet resolve. "Or I will."

"The council will not allow it," predicted Scar. "You have no reason, and so no right, to ask for a fight to the death with Longshot."

"He killed Red Hawk, my brother."

"You have no proof of that."

Long Runner turned to Zach. "Did you not kill a Blackfoot warrior in the Absaroka Mountains, two springs ago?"

"I could not have done so," said Zach with certainty. "Two springs ago I was down on the Rolling Fork. I was nowhere near the Absarokas."

"He lies," Long Runner told Scar. "I know it was he who killed my brother. Red Hawk was young and foolish, untried in battle. He sought the glory of being the Blackfoot who killed Longshot. He left with that purpose in mind, with three companions. Two of them I can present to the council. They will tell how Red Hawk died. A long rifle shot—a shot I believe only this man could have made."

"It's not true," said Zach.

"He ain't the only good shot in this neck of the woods," said Bushrod. "I been known to pluck a prairie hen at a couple hundred paces."

Zach knew Long Runner was lying. Maybe he had lost a brother in the manner he had just described, but it had not been Zach's finger on the trigger. Of that Zach was certain. Only once had he killed a man at long range.

No, Long Runner was just manufacturing a plausible reason for the fight to the death. The real reason was finally clear enough to Zach, now that he'd had a little time to do some pondering on the subject. Alive, he was a constant reminder to Long Runner of the time when the warrior, out of a sense of honor, had compromised his own people—had betrayed them—by failing to tell them of the presence of Zach's brigade. That same sense of honor had compelled Long Runner to step in and rescue Zach from the gauntlet. Long Runner was sick and tired of being impaled on the horns of a moral dilemma. By killing Zach with his own hands, he thought, he could possibly redeem himself, or at least atone for the sins he had committed.

Scar spoke. "Long Runner, I will speak against you in the council meeting. That is all I have to say."

He rose and left the tepee.

A moment of tense silence later, Long Runner departed too.

"Well," drawled Bushrod. "These fellers are fallin' all over themselves just for a chance to put you under, Zach Hannah."

VIII

The tribal council met the very next day. Bushrod
came to Long Runner's tepee at intervals to keep
Zach apprised of what was going on. But Zach was
ambivalent.

"It doesn't matter one way or the other," he told
Bushrod, who seemed to find the situation exhilarat-
ing. "If Long Runner gets his wish, and we fight, and
I kill him, I'll still wind up burnt alive—or whatever
Scar has in mind for me."

Bushrod frowned. "Now, that's a mighty poor attitude, if you ask me. Iffen I were you, I'd be prayin'
for a shot at Long Runner."

"How come?"

"Two reasons. One is, he won't fight till you're
healed up, and by the looks of you, it'll take you a
while just to stand up, even though that lil
punkin'—" he winked at the omnipresent Moon
Singer "—has been takin' mighty fine care of you."

"So I'll have a few days' grace."

"A few weeks, lessen yore bones somehow heal up
faster than mine do. Longer, iffen you make up yore
mind to heal real slow like."

"And the other reason?"

Bushrod got real solemn. "You'll get a chance to
die with a knife in yore hand. I'm assumin' Long
Runner will pick knifes, iffen the council gives the
duel the go-ahead. But be it knives, or tomahawks,
or rifles at fifty paces—who cares? That's all a true
mountain man asks for when his time comes—to go

out fightin'. That should be what you want, Hannah."

"The idea of fighting Long Runner just doesn't suit me."

"Why not? No, don't tell me. Let me guess. Cause he saved yore bacon a few days ago? He sure as shootin' didn't want to, that's plain to see. He did it 'cause he owed you, and he hates yore guts for puttin' him in that position in the first place. That's what you told me, leastways."

"He's a decent man."

"He's a damned Blackfoot."

"Blackfoot or not, it doesn't matter. He stuck with his wife when she was dyin', and had to be left behind. And he puts a lot of stock in honor."

Bushrod shook his head. "Lord, you done made another fool. Fight him, Hannah, iffen you get the chance, and kill him, and then, even if they do put you under, you'll go down knowin' you took at least one of these varmints with you to hell."

Zach glanced at Moon Singer. "Lucky for you, Bushrod, that she doesn't understand English. I mean, you're supposed to be a friend of the Blackfoot. What would they think if they heard you talk that way about them?"

The frontiersman's expression darkened. "I ain't no such thing and never have been. And I wouldn't be hangin' around this here den of thieves and cutthroats except for you."

"Don't stay on my account."

"You don't like me much, do you? Well, to hell with you, then."

And Bushrod Jones left in a huff.

But he was back a few hours later, his eyes twinkling with excitement.

"Long Runner got his way!" he exclaimed. "It went over a lot easier than I expected. You're all set for a knife duel with this lil punkin's brother. Soon as you're healed up, that is."

Zach looked grimly across at Moon Singer.

"You *are* gonna fight, aren't you?" asked Bushrod, suddenly worried.

"What do you mean?"

"I mean that funny look on yore face is worrisome to me," snapped Bushrod.

"Reckon you'd be disappointed if I didn't hold my own against Long Runner."

"Reckon I would, indeed. Ain't much I like better than a good fight."

"Why should I fight?" asked Zach. "Why should I try to kill her brother? That would make me a pretty poor guest, wouldn't it? Trying to stick a knife in my host."

"I can think of one damned good reason. 'Cause he'll be tryin' to do the same to you."

Zach shook his head. "What difference would it make? If I put Long Runner under they'll kill me slow. At least he'll do the job quick."

Bushrod was flabbergasted. "Good God. What did I tell you before, hoss? He's a Blackfoot, and . . ."

"He's Moon Singer's brother. I won't do it, Bushrod."

"Yes you will. You'll protect yoreself when the time comes."

"Reckon not."

"You'll just stand there and let him run you through?" cried the other, thoroughly exasperated.

"My mind's made up."

Bushrod stared at him for the longest.

"You're plumb crazy," decided the frontiersman.

"It's the best way for all concerned."

"Well, I know one thing," said Bushrod, with a gusting sigh. "I ain't never in my livelong days run across the likes of you, Zach Hannah."

He left, shaking his head in wonder.

Some time later, Long Runner arrived. With a grim glance at Zach, the warrior informed Moon Singer of the council's decision. Upset, she pleaded with her brother not to go through with it. The more she pleaded, the angrier he became.

"Why do you protect him?" snapped Long Runner. "He has killed many Blackfeet. He is our enemy. He must die."

"I do not want either one of you to die."

"He will be the one who dies. And it will bring much honor. Why do you care what happens to him? How can you?"

Moon Singer looked long and hard at Zach with tear-glistening eyes.

"Because he is a good man. I know this in my heart. He is the best man I have ever known."

"You are a fool!" shouted the agitated Long Runner.

"I cannot help the way I feel."

The warrior stormed out.

Moon Singer moved to the other side of the tepee from where Zach lay. She diligently applied herself to mending a pair of her brother's leggins. She was embarrassed to look his way. For a spell, Zach was too astonished to speak. When he finally did address her, he spoke slowly, picking his words with the utmost care, because the last thing he wanted to do was hurt her.

"Moon Singer," he said softly, "I'm right flattered you feel about me the way you do. But you really ought not to. There sure isn't any future in it."

"I cannot tell my heart not to feel the way it does," she shot back heatedly.

Zach smiled. "No, I guess you can't do that. Lord knows, a heart does what it wants to, and seldom will listen to the head. But, for one thing, Moon Singer, I'm hitched. I'm married to a woman I love more than life itself. You're a lot like her. If I'd never met her, I reckon I'd have strong feelings for you. You're a kind and beautiful and gentle woman, and one day a feller will come along that's right for you. But I'm not that feller. In fact, I reckon I'm a dead man."

"No," she said emphatically, denying it.

"I promise you one thing," he said. "Your brother will live. No harm will come to him by my hand."

Her eyes were wide and bright in the smoky gloom of the tepee, and he knew she understood what he intended to do.

No more words passed between them. Zach eventually drifted off to sleep. Now that he knew how it would end, he felt a vast relief. He had made up his mind, and he knew it was absolutely the right thing to do. It was a comfort, too, knowing that his death would count for something. He slept well, untroubled, and woke but once—when Moon Singer kissed him softly, her lips brushing his, and a hot tear fell from her cheek onto his.

IX

Zach's arm healed quickly.

The day after the council meeting which had decided his fate, he prevailed upon Moon Singer to let him walk outside the tepee. She feared for his safety, but he was confident, and insistent. He refused to spend the few days remaining to him cooped up inside. The weather was fine, and he gazed long and appreciatively at the blue sky, and at the green cloak of the forest on the hills surrounding the village, and at the prairie grass as the strong, clean wind rippled through it.

Moon Singer walked with him. Some of the Blackfoot women, and even a few of the men, hurled cruel insults at her, but she paid them no heed. Zach's heart went out to her. He admired her pluck. And her devotion to him was touching. She was indeed a lot like Morning Sky, and her presence was a real comfort to him. He was glad for the way things had worked out. Somehow it made what he had to do, and what would inevitably happen to him, easier to handle.

Several braves screamed curses at him and made threatening gestures. When they stood in his path he went around them with a cool glance and the smile tailor-made to infuriate. One brave charged at him, uttering a bloodcurdling war cry, his tomahawk raised. Zach stepped in front of Moon Singer, sheltering her, and stood fast, unflinching, confronting this onslaught with such nerveless aplomb that murmurs of admiration escaped the lips of some of the Blackfeet who witnessed the scene.

The warrior pulled up short, his bluff called. Zach had been fairly certain that he had been bluffing. The Blackfoot had hoped to intimidate him or, at best, provoke some belligerent response from Zach which would justify his taking the mountain man's life in the guise of self-defense. Zach was counting on the fact that no warrior would lay a hand on him now that the council had made its decision. To go against that decision would bring dishonor upon the village, and would result in banishment, at the very least, for the offender.

So Zach walked freely about the village, certain that no harm would befall him, apart from an occasional stone thrown by child or squaw and a thousand insults and taunts, as long as he made no attempt to escape. In a way he was taunting the Blackfeet himself, and he knew this and liked the feeling.

The Blackfeet were not sure what to make of him. His courage daunted them. They expected him to cower in Long Runner's lodge. Or make a dash for freedom. Or beg for mercy. But he did none of these things. They could not intimidate him, or break his spirit. They could not make him break out in a cold sweat, or even bat an eye. Truly, he was a great enemy, and as the days wore on, more and more of them grudgingly gave him their respect.

And as the days passed, Zach became, if anything, more comfortable with the situation. He accepted the fact that there was no chance for escape. They watched him like hawks. Day and night, young braves encircled Long Runner's tepee. This ring of sentries was not by council decree. There was no need for such an order to be given. The young warriors were there of their own volition, hoping he would try to flee. Then they would have the right to strike him down, and to the one who delivered the death blow would go the scalp of Longshot, and the glory that came with it. During his daily walks they shadowed him—behind, and to either side— watchful, waiting, weapons in hand. But he disappointed them. He was not going to play into their hands. instead, he tormented them in his own cunning way, and was resolved to do so for as long as he could. Then he would let Long Runner kill him.

For his part, Long Runner was in a perpetual state of high dudgeon. Patience deserted him. But there was nothing he could do to hasten the date of the duel. He could not fight a man whose broken arm was not completely healed. That would be dishonorable. So he had to wait, though he was in no mood for waiting. He wanted to get it over with, one way or the other. Whether he lived or died really made no difference to him. Either way, he would be relieved of the doubts and demons which plagued him.

Moon Singer told her brother what Zach intended, but Long Runner refused to believe it. He could not comprehend a man entering a fight with the intent of letting his adversary win. It could not be so. But Moon Singer was convinced, and more doubts beset Long Runner as a consequence, until finally, some days later, when he could stand it no longer, he confronted Zach.

"I reckon you'll win," allowed Zach.

"You must fight," insisted Long Runner.

Zach was implacable. "I won't fight you."

"Then you take from me the honor of killing you," growled the warrior.

"Guess that's right," replied Zach coolly. "So maybe I'm the one who'll win, and you'll be the loser."

"You will fight!" raged Long Runner, as though merely by saying it he could make it so.

"I've made up my mind," said Zach with a calm that infuriated the warrior, "and that's my final word on the subject."

* * *

Weeks passed. Members of the council visited Long Runner's lodge periodically during this time, checking on Zach's progress. Eventually they reached the conclusion that in five days he would be fit enough to fight.

"That's fine with me," said Zach. In truth, he was a little weary of the nervy game he had been playing. He was a condemned man, awaiting execution, and while there was no outward manifestation of it, his nerves were beginning to fray.

The day before the duel was to take place, Sean Michael Devlin rode into the village.

X

He rode in on a rangy claybank, leading a pack horse laden with gifts, which included ten Mackinaw guns, some powder and shot, and two dozen of those three-cornered, blood-red Nor'west blankets always highly sought after by Indians.

"I thought you was down in the Shoshone Range," Bushrod said, walking out to greet his American Fur Company colleague.

"I'm not much for trapping," said Devlin. Still mounted, he looked out over the heads of the Blackfeet flocking from all points of the compass—they knew him, and knew he always brought gifts. "Where is he?"

"Who?"

"Don't play games with me, Bushrod." Devlin's

tone was sharp. "You know who I mean. I heard about it two weeks ago, when I got back to Fort Union. They've got Hannah here. Or . . . They haven't put him under yet, have they?"

Bushrod cocked his head to one side, squinting slyly up at Devlin.

"Would it bother you if they had?"

Suddenly on the defensive, Devlin asked, "Why would it?"

"I've heard tell you two were pardners, once."

"We were friends, or at least I thought we were. But he betrayed that friendship."

"Well, it depends on who you talk to about that."

"I don't follow."

"I have heard it told two different ways."

"I'm telling you the way it happened. That ought to be good enough for you. If it ain't, then we have a problem, don't we?"

Bushrod bristled, and flashed that wolfish grin. "You don't really want to tangle with me, Devlin."

"Or you with me."

"Oh, I've heard, Devlin. I've heard all about you. The man who killed Big Mike Fink. And Rides A Dark Horse. Yes, indeed, you have quite a reputation."

"I earned it."

"I ain't but half scairt," said Bushrod sardonically.

Devlin swung a leg over the high pommel of his Indian saddle and dropped to the ground.

"You must be tired of working for the company, Jones."

"You sayin' you can fire me?"

"One word from me, and Major Vanderburg will put you out."

"Will he now?" Bushrod rubbed his bearded chin. "Mebbe you could do that. You throw a lot of weight, don't you? On account of how these damned Blackfeet hold you in such high regard."

"They do. And no one knows that better than the major. Makes me worth a dozen of the likes of you."

"Say the word, then, Devlin. Get me drummed out of this godforsaken company. I ain't no quitter. Never quit nothin' in my whole life. But I won't lose no sleep iffen you and your blessed major, damn his eyes, toss me out of the company. I ain't exactly in love with the way you boys do business. It's my bad luck I didn't hitch up with a booshway like Zach Hannah. He's twice the man you are, Devlin. Why, he's got more grit and gumption than the whole goddamn American Fur Company put together."

Devlin was livid. "So he's still alive."

"Hell, yes. I'm beginning to think nothin' can kill him. He shore has turned the tables on these Blackfoot bastards you call your friends. They don't rightly know what to think about him anymore."

A woman was fingering the blankets strapped down over the packsaddle of Devlin's second horse. He barked a curt reprimand at her, and she withdrew into the crowd pressing in around the two frontiersmen.

"What do you mean?" asked Devlin.

"I mean he's got them buffaloed. He's plumb hard

to kill. I think some of 'em are wonderin' if he ain't immortal. Some kind of god."

Devlin swore under his breath. "He's just a man."

"Not just any man."

Devlin stared at Bushrod, incredulous. "Sounds like he's got you buffaloed too."

"I know brave men when I see 'em," laughed Bushrod, and the expression on his face as he gave Devlin the once-over made it clear he did not think Devlin fit into that category.

"I ought to take you down a notch," said Devlin.

"You're welcome to try," drawled Bushrod, delighted. "My mama was a she-wolf with a poor disposition, and my pa was half alligator, and folks were sayin' I was twice as mean as both of 'em put together, and that was before I even got shed of the cradle. But, hell, Devlin, that don't scare you none. Not a feller like you, with the reputation you got."

Devlin clenched his fists. Bushrod was taunting him. His reputation, and his standing in the American Fur Company, did not seem to count for much as far as Bushrod Jones was concerned.

"I would do better than try," he declared. "Except that Major Vanderburg wouldn't stand for it. There's to be no quarreling amongst the men on his payroll. He's made that plain."

"But I don't work for the company no more, remember? Feel free, Devlin. Have at it." Bushrod threw his arms wide. "Take your best shot."

Devlin was rescued by the arrival of the village chief, the council members, and several of the leading warriors, Scar among the last. He gave two Nor'west blankets and a Mackinaw gun to the chief, and one blanket and one gun to each of the others. When he came to Scar, he told the warrior he wanted to see Zach Hannah.

"He is in the lodge of Long Runner," replied Scar.

"But I heard you brought him in."

Scar frowned. "He and Long Runner fight to the death when the sun rises again."

"But you can arrange for me to see him," said Devlin. "I've got extra powder and shot says you can."

Scar's eyes gleamed with greed. "I will see what I can do," he said.

XI

"Glad you could make it," said Zach.

The sun was going down and the day was fast cooling off, and there was a small, warm fire going in Long Runner's skin lodge. Zach sat across the fire from Devlin.

He was surprised to see Devlin but hid it well, and that offhand remark rang true.

"I wouldn't miss this for anything," was Devlin's equally dry retort.

He glanced at Moon Singer. The Blackfoot maiden's eyes were wide as she looked from one mountain man to the other and back again. There was a tension between these two that was almost tangible; it electrified the air inside the lodge, and she could feel it. She sat very still, scarcely breathing, not knowing what to expect.

"Now look at this," said Devlin. "You sure do have a way with the women, don't you, Zach? Even here, in a Blackfoot village, with one foot in the grave, you manage to find the prettiest girl in the village to shack up with."

"It isn't like that," snapped Zach.

Devlin's empty smile broadened. He had hoped to get Zach's dander up, and the snide comment about Moon Singer had worked. That made him feel good. The knife was in up to the hilt, so he decided to twist it.

"Wonder what Sky will think when I tell her about this?" he asked.

"Have you . . .?" Zach stopped short of asking Devlin if he had seen Sky. That would be playing Devlin's game. Devlin had certainly phrased his remark as though he expected to see her. But Zach had a hunch Coyote was just being clever again.

Zach had wondered, every minute of every day, what had become of Morning Sky. Had Shadmore taken her into the Yellowstone country, as they had planned to do if anything befell the brigade?

Of only one thing could he be sure: Neither Scar's band, nor any other from this particular village, had found Sky and Jacob and the rest of his brigade. If they had, he would have learned of it by now. But he could not be certain that Devlin hadn't hunted for her and tracked her down; while Zach had faith in Shadmore, and confidence that the old leatherstocking would die before letting Coyote get his hands on Sky and the boy, there was really no way for him to know what had occurred in his absence.

Devlin with Sky. The idea lurked in Zach's mind, and prowled through his dreams sometimes, so that occasionally he woke with a start, shivering, in a cold sweat.

"Have I what?" asked Devlin. "Come to save your bacon?"

Zach breathed easier. Devlin was off the mark.

"I wouldn't expect that from you," he said.

"You wouldn't?" Devlin's smile melted. A furrow creased his brow. "Sure you would. You saved me from those damned Absaroka Crows, didn't you? So why don't you think I'll rescue you from these Blackfoot friends of mine?"

"That just wouldn't be like you, Devlin."

"You bastard," hissed Devlin. "Why don't you just come out and say it? Because that would be the honorable thing to do, and I don't know the first thing about honor. Isn't that what you were thinking?"

"Your conscience bothering you?"

"I hate your guts, Zach."

"I noticed."

"Know why?"

"Tell me."

"Because you think you're so much better than everybody else."

Zach shook his head. "That's not true, and even if it was, it wouldn't be why you hate me."

Devlin abruptly changed the subject. Zach figured the words were cutting too close to the bone for Devlin's liking.

"That was mighty rich beaver country you led up to this season. My boys'll add ten, fifteen packs to the ones we took from your brigade, come next spring."

"What are you doing here? A booshway should stick with his men."

"I wish you wouldn't keep preaching to me," said Devlin crossly. "It just so happens I don't go in much for trapping. Not my cup of tea. I rode back to Fort Union to report to Vanderburg, and to find out about you. Heard Scar had brought you here. So I gathered up some trade goods and came on. Hoped to get here in time to say good-bye."

"You just made it. Tomorrow's the big day."

"You're mighty cool about it."

"Why worry about something you can't change?"

For a moment Devlin was quiet. When next he spoke, his tone had lost all the cocky belligerence. His demeanor was pensive.

"I remember the day we met, back in St. Louis. That gamblin' man, Tyree, had set a bunch of rivermen after me. Had me cornered in an alley, as I recall, when you came along and lent me a hand."

"Because you had stolen Tyree's money. I didn't know that until later. Maybe if I had I would've just walked on and let you take your comeuppance."

"No, you wouldn't have. Because it was four to

one against, and that ain't fair, and fair means everything to you, doesn't it, Zach?"

"Too bad it doesn't mean much to you."

"And then when I bought you that knife, you said
you didn't want it 'cause it was purchased with stolen money. But you took it anyhow. And we took an
oath to be blood brothers, just like a couple of fool
kids."

"I remember," said Zach.

Devlin shrugged. "Seems like a hundred years ago.
I recall when we tried to sign up with Major Henry,
and he said he could only take one of us, and you
were willing to stay behind so's I could go."

"Had you stayed, you would've have ended up 'ga-
tor bait. Tyree would have seen to that."

"I guess things were all right between us until
Morning Sky came along."

Zach said nothing.

"Reckon you wanted to kill me, after I took her
away from you and all," said Devlin.

"The thought crossed my mind."

"I love her, Zach. Love her just as much as you do.
Maybe I do have a funny way of showing it. And that
boy . . . he's my son. I want him back."

"You didn't want anything to do with him before
he was born. What's changed?"

"I have," said Devlin. "I've changed. I was wrong.
I admit it. But I . . . Tell me where they are, Zach."

"No."

"You've got to. You're going to die tomorrow. Let

me take care of them. I will, you know. I promise I will."

"No."

"You selfish bastard," snarled Devlin, standing, fists clenched.

"You'll never have her."

"I'll find her."

"No you won't."

"I will. I'll find her and the boy if it takes me the rest of my life. She'll belong to me again."

"She doesn't love you, Devlin."

"Once you're dead she will."

"That's not how it works."

"I don't care. I want her. And tomorrow, as you die, think of this: While you burn in hell, I'll be laying in Sky's arms."

Through clenched teeth, Zach said, "I should have killed you last summer at the Green River rendezvous."

Devlin threw back his head and laughed.

"You had your chance, Zach. Tomorrow, you run out of chances."

With that, he left the skin lodge, still laughing, and his laughter clawed at Zach's soul.

XII

They came for him at sunrise, four warriors decked out in full regalia. He wore moccasins, leggins, and breechclout, made for him by Moon Singer. He said his good-byes to her, and she kept her composure, as he had expected her to do, at least until he was gone from Long Runner's lodge.

The four warriors escorted him through the village, two in front of him and two behind, to the clearing in the middle of the camp, where the medicine lodge stood. Dozens of villagers followed. Strangely, none hurled taunts or insults at the mountain man. The Blackfeet were oddly subdued. They watched his every move, some with hostility, others warily, and still others with wide-eyed wonder and respect.

Long Runner stood alone near the scalp-pole, located in front of the medicine lodge. He faced the village chief and council, who were seated in a half-circle. Behind them stood the crowd, hundreds of Blackfeet—men, women, and children. No one wanted to miss this historic event. Only a handful were not present: a few too old or infirm to leave their lodges, and the young braves who were watching the horse herd.

There had been omens. A woman had given birth to twins in the early-morning hours, one dead and one alive. And a pack of wolves had been spotted in the gray gloom just before the sunrise. The wolves had circled the village and spooked the horse herd. One big silver male had ventured forth to bring down a colt. While the herd guard had tried to keep the rest of the cavallard from stampeding, the wolf had dragged its kill into tall grass. An eagle had then appeared out of nowhere. The two predatory animals had hotly contested the colt's carcass. The eagle and the wolf fought to a draw. The return of one of the horse guards had sent the wolf into the brush and the eagle soaring skyward. Some said the eagle represented Long Runner, while the wolf represented Zach Hannah. To those who put great stock in such things, the incident was seen as prophecy, and they predicted that Long Runner and the mountain man would kill each other.

Scar served as master of ceremonies. He brandished a strip of braided rawhide about three feet long. The ends were tied to the left wrists of the combatants. Two knives were stuck in the ground five paces from where Zach and Long Runner stood facing one another. Scar stepped away and glanced at the chief. The chief nodded gravely. The crowd waited with breathless anticipation for Scar to give the word.

"Fight."

The crowd roared. Long Runner lunged for the knives. Zach went right along with him and, timing it perfectly, knocked him sideways as the warrior reached for one of the knives. They fell in the dust. Zach scrambled to his knees and stretched for the knives. Long Runner pulled hard on the rawhide binding them together, and Zach missed his grab, fingertips brushing the bone handle of a knife.

He rolled over and kicked Long Runner in the face, then powered to his feet and literally dragged the stunned warrior along behind him. But the Blackfoot was quick to recover. He kicked Zach's legs out from under him. Zach ate dirt, clawed at the ground as Long Runner tried to haul him back, away from the knives.

Then the warrior pounced on Zach's back and tried to wrap the rawhide around Zach's throat. Zach bucked like a greenbroke horse and dislodged him. Once more, Zach stretched for the knives. This time he got one. On his face, he turned as Long Runner plowed into him. The impact picked Zach up off the ground. Legs churning, Long Runner carried him ten feet and then slammed him down. Zach got his knees up between his body and Long Runner's and catapulted the warrior over his head. Scrambling, Zach straddled the warrior's chest before Long Runner could recover. A cry rose up from the crowd as he raised the knife. Everyone expected him to deliver the killing blow.

Instead, with one swift stroke of the blade, Zach cut the rawhide and freed himself from his Blackfoot adversary.

A dozen warriors surged forward, brandishing knives and tomahawks. By cutting the rawhide, Zach had broken the rules, and now it was open season on him.

He broke for the entrance of the medicine lodge, remembering the story Bill Sublette had told him at the Green River rendezvous—about his brother Milton and Joe Meek finding refuge in the medicine lodge of the Snake Indians.

He could only hope the Blackfeet played by the same rules.

Because he suddenly wanted to live. It was Devlin's unexpected visit that had wrought this change. Devlin . . . and his talk about Sky. There was no chance of escape from the village—so maybe his only escape lay within the village. In the medicine lodge.

As he dove through the flap over the entrance into the lodge, the warrior closest behind him raised a tomahawk to throw it. At such close range he could not miss. But the Blackfoot chief was on his feet now, and roared a stern command. The warrior refrained from hurling the tomahawk, and Zach disappeared inside the medicine lodge.

Sprawling on the ground inside the lodge, Zach laughed.

He was on sacred ground.

They could not touch him here. He was safe, as long as he remained within the lodge.

Only problem now was how to get out of the village, safely away from these Blackfeet, and back to Morning Sky—before Devlin found her.

XIII

The medicine man, Blue Elk, was both physician and prophet. He came from a long and distinguished line of doctor-priests, for the source of his powers was a sacred sack, which he wore around his neck and which had been passed down from generation to generation in his family. The sacred sack, it was said, had been given by the Great Spirit, and no one knew what it contained, for it had never been opened, least of all by Blue Elk, for to open the sacred sack would visit great calamity upon the entire tribe.

Blue Elk had seen many winters. He was wizened and gray and more than a little eccentric. And he had great influence in the village. His father had taught him well all the secrets of the trade—how to concoct curative potions, and how to perform varied and sundry ceremonies, with a little magic and sleight of hand mixed in, designed to impress the people. He was well versed in the use of herbs and roots; he knew which plants could be used as sedatives, and which as cathartics or stimulants.

Yet most of what Blue Elk practiced was not medicine at all. It was flummery, pure and simple— because Blue Elk in fact knew precious little about disease. Like most Indians, he diagnosed an illness as the work of evil spirits. Quite often, Blue Elk's prescribed remedy was to frighten away the spirit possessing the body of his patient with a noisy and usually very strenuous demonstration. He would yell, wail, growl; he would dance, cavort, or posture in imitation of a wolf or grizzly; he would brandish a stick and simulate striking the ailing person where he or she hurt. Quite often he worked himself into such a frenzy that he would collapse from exhaustion.

One of his best tricks was to pretend to suck the evil spirit out of the patient's body. He used this kind of hocus-pocus when his chants and potions failed to work; he knew it was essential to maintain his image.

He would spit out a pebble or bone fragment, which was, of course, the form which the spirit took after being drawn from the body of its victim.

Blue Elk did believe he was possessed of special powers. The people of the village believed it, too. That faith, above all, was the reason for quite a lot of the medicine man's success in healing others. If a sick person believes he will be well again, and that the treatment will work, then half the battle is won, and the patient embarks on the road to recovery before the very first poultice is applied.

The duties of a medicine man went beyond healing the sick. He was called upon to give his blessing to many and various events. The leader of a war party would always come seeking his blessing before striking out on the warpath. Blue Elk would bestow his blessing if he favored the warrior, or if the warrior was willing to resort to bribery. Sometimes Blue Elk would hazard a prediction regarding the success or failure of the venture, but not often, and only when he calculated the odds were strongly in favor of his being right. He was also called upon before a marriage, or a buffalo hunt. One negative word from him and a wedding might be called off, or a hunt postponed until such time as Blue Elk judged the omens were more auspicous. In short, his influence in the village was great—in some ways equal to that of the chief.

Naturally, then, his people turned to him when Zach Hannah took refuge in the medicine lodge.

The village wanted him to do something to remove the mountain man from that sacred ground.

Blue Elk appeared confident that he could accomplish what was asked of him. But he didn't feel nearly as confident as he looked. By now he was firmly convinced that Zach was possessed by powerful demons. How else could one explain the mountain man's survival? His audacity? The man was not altogether human.

Still, Blue Elk agreed to see what he could do. His reputation depended on it.

He spent an entire day and night preparing. He chanted. He mixed potions. He put himself in a trance. He painted unusual symbols all over his body in black and vermilion-red. He did not eat or drink anything—he purged his body of all impurities with a potion which made him vomit, and took the extra precaution of a little bloodletting.

While Blue Elk was making himself ready to take on the demon white man, Zach Hannah had other visitors.

A number of warriors, Scar among them, entered the medicine lodge. They cursed and insulted him. They painted graphic word pictures of what they would do to him when the time came for him to die. They made threatening gestures, wielding their weapons as close to him as they dared without touching him. For that they could not do. So Zach sat there, cross-legged near the fire-circle in the center of the lodge, and let them rant and rave; he did not speak or flinch.

For the time being he was safe. But what next?

Milton Sublette and Joe Meek had had help escaping from the medicine lodge of the Snake Indians. Mountain Lamb and her kindhearted grandfather had risked their lives to get them out. But who would help him? Moon Singer? She might try. He prayed she would not. It was too risky. The medicine lodge was ringed about with scores of angry, vigilant warriors. How long would he last without food and water? It looked like he needed a bona fide miracle to get out of this fix.

Later that day, Bushrod Jones appeared at the entrance of the medicine lodge. He sat on his heels in the slanting sunlight and peered into the gloom within. At first he could not see Zach.

"Hannah, you in there?"

"I'm here."

Bushrod chuckled. "Hoss, you beat all I ever seen. What you aim to do now?"

"Got any suggestions?"

"Nope. I'd come in and join you, but us hair-faces ain't allowed in there. So if I come in, I git kilt quick when I come out. Just like you will be."

"Where's Devlin?"

"He rode out last night. Didn't stick around to see your fight with Long Runner. I thought he would."

"I didn't see you there, either."

"You told me it warn't gonna be much of a ruckus, so I slept in. I didn't know you were gonna try something sneaky like this."

"Devlin say anything to you?"

"We're not exactly on speakin' terms. Why?"

Zach was silent.

"You still there, Hannah?"

"Where would I go?"

"You're one hard-to-kill pilgrim, I'll give you that much."

"I've got to get out of here, Bushrod."

"You askin' for my help?"

"Would it do any good to ask?"

"No." Bushrod was suddenly solemn. "I cain't do it. Like to, but I value my scalp more'n yours. Not to mention my skin, which they'd peel off me in little bloody strips iffen I tried to help you. You're gone beaver, but you gave 'em a helluva run for their money. Once I git finished tellin' ever'body what I seen here, you'll be downright famous."

"That's comforting."

"I know you don't like me worth spit, Hannah, and it won't make no difference to you, I reckon, but I'm shed of the American Fur Company."

"How come?"

"Devlin and me had a fallin'-out. I don't care. It suits me. So I'm ridin' out myself, tomorrow. Just wanted to say so long."

Zach made no reply. He didn't know why he felt like Bushrod was deserting him, when the man wasn't going to do anything to help him anyway, but that was how he felt all the same.

"Anything I kin do 'fore I leave?" asked Bushrod.

"Yeah. Tell Moon Singer to stay clear of me."

"Oh, Long Runner won't let her anywhere near you. But I'll tell her. Good luck, hoss."

Bushrod rose and started to turn away.

"Jones."

Bushrod hunkered down and peered inside the medicine lodge again.

"Thanks," said Zach.

The frontiersman flashed a grin. "See you on the other side, Zach Hannah."

XIV

The medicine man came at dawn.

Catfooting into the medicine lodge, Blue Elk made no more sound than a wraith. He hoped to catch Zach Hannah—and the demons which possessed him—asleep and off guard.

Much to his consternation, he found the mountain man sitting cross-legged at the stone-rimmed fire-circle, facing the lodge entrance.

Zach took one look at the slightly bent, white-haired old Indian with wizened features, his frail frame draped with a long woolen robe decorated with fox and otter fur and horsehair and owl feathers, and knew him for what he was.

"Reckon you're the shaman," said Zach. "Maybe you could conjure up a small fire from these ashes. It got a mite cold last night."

"Leave this place," commanded Blue Elk, his rasping voice authoritarian.

"Can't do it," said Zach amiably.

"Then I must drive you out."

He sat across the fire-circle from Zach. From beneath his robe he took a pipe. A twist of human hair and the tail feather of a spotted owl dangled from the long stem. Blue Elk held the pipe at arm's length over his head and muttered an incantation which was gibberish to Zach. Lowering the pipe, he took a pinch of tobacco from the bowl and placed it on one of the stones of the fire-circle. He then passed a gnarled hand over the bowl several times. A wisp of smoke curled out of the bowl. He looked at Zach with a gleam in his dark, sunken eyes, just to see if his captive audience of one was suitably impressed.

Zach smiled wryly.

"Neat trick," he said. "What's next?"

Blue Elk drew smoke from the pipe. He blew three puffs skyward, three more downward, and then three to the left and three to the right—before sending a cloud of smoke into Zach's face.

Zach's head reeled from the sweet, pungent smoke. He squeezed his eyes shut, held his breath until the smoke had cleared, and then inhaled deeply, trying to clear the cobwebs. He wondered what the medicine man had mixed with the tobacco. Whatever it was, Blue Elk was impervious to its deleterious effects.

The medicine man dumped the ashes on the stone where the pinch of tobacco had been deposited. Chanting low and monotonously, he dipped his fingers in the ashes, stirred them, then rose to execute a shuffling dance which took him completely around the fire-circle and behind Zach. Zach sat perfectly still and did not turn to look around. Not even Blue Elk could touch him here. At least, he was counting on that being the case.

Brandishing a rattle drawn from beneath his robe, Blue Elk circled twice more, still chanting. Zach began to feel drowsy. Before long he was fighting to keep his eyes open. His eyelids felt like lead weights. He realized Blue Elk was trying to mesmerize him. Put him to sleep. And he figured if he went to sleep that would be it. He would not wake up, ever. But the monotone chanting, the shuffle of the shaman's moccasined feet in the dust, the rhythm of the rattle—all worked in concert to push him closer and closer to the brink of oblivion.

In desperation he used the knife he had acquired in the duel with Long Runner, cutting open the palm of his hand. Lancing pain jolted him awake. He squeezed the hand shut. Warm blood leaked through his fingers.

Enraged, Blue Elk screamed at him. Zach made no reply. He watched the medicine man, grim, wary. He had underestimated the shaman. Blue Elk had real talent. Zach was determined to be ready for his next piece of treachery.

But Blue Elk was out of tricks. He had tried to drug Zach and failed. He had tried to hypnotize the mountain man, without success. Now all he could do was resort to histrionics.

He barked, yelped, screamed, and growled. He got

down on his hands and knees and clawed the ground. He scooped up handfuls of dirt and hurled them at Zach. He danced like a mad dervish around the lodge, calling on the spirits in the heavens to help him vanquish this white demon.

For a quarter of an hour he persisted in these antics, at the end of which time he dropped, exhausted, to his knees across the fire-circle from Zach, slump-shouldered, head down, drool leaking from the corner of his mouth.

Zach hadn't moved a muscle.

Slowly, Blue Elk raised his head. There was a glimmer of fear in his eyes as he stared at Zach, as though Zach were some hideous, unearthly, monster.

"All I want," said Zach, very quietly, "is to ride out of here."

Blue Elk stared at him for a long time. Zach thought he could almost hear the old shaman's brain clicking. He figured the medicine man was trying to think of some way to explain his failure.

At length, Blue Elk rose and shuffled out of the medicine lodge.

All that day and the next night no one ventured near the lodge. Zach paced restlessly. Sometimes he would hunker down just inside the entrance, push aside the flap, and peer cautiously outside. That night the Blackfeet built fires all around the medicine lodge. Scores of warriors gathered round them, waiting, watching, grimly silent.

It was Zach's second night in the lodge. His stomach felt like it was tied up in knots. His throat was so parched he could scarcely swallow without pain. He felt weak and dizzy when he moved around too much. A person could go a month without food, but only three or four days without water.

He didn't have much time left.

He'd bought himself a few more days by seeking refuge in the medicine lodge. For over a month he had been a captive of the Blackfeet. He had survived an ordeal few men could have endured. A lot of it was luck. Long Runner's intervention the day he had run the gauntlet was a case in point. The broken arm he had suffered had given him a few more weeks of life. But his luck had run out. There would be no more good fortune. He was at the end of his string.

Before long he would have to make a break for it, even though there seemed to be no chance of getting past this cordon of Blackfoot warriors, every last mother's son of them itching for a shot at him. And he would have to do it soon, while he still had a little strength left.

Tomorrow. Early. He would have to go for it.

In the early-morning hours a horrible keening sound woke him from a light sleep, sending chills up and down his spine. He identified it as a woman wailing. Someone had died. The wailing went on for quite some time. He tried to go back to sleep but couldn't.

He could not know that the deceased was one of the chief's wives. Early the previous day she had become suddenly and violently ill. Wracked by high fever and chills, she had developed ugly black boils in her armpits and groin area and, finally, had begun hemorrhaging black blood. A few hours later, she passed away.

Blue Elk had been called. He had known in a glance that this was something for which he had no cure or incantation. never had he seen anything so virulent strike so swiftly. It scared him.

Worse, the chief's wife was not the only victim. Five more villagers had identical symptoms, and one of them died not an hour later.

The next morning, before sunrise, Bushrod Jones returned to the medicine lodge. Zach was sitting just inside the entrance. One glance at Bushrod's features warned Zach that something momentous had occurred. Bushrod looked downright grim.

"What is it?" asked Zach. "What's happened?"

"The plague."

"What?"

"Plague, Hannah. Seen it before. It's here in this village."

"My God. Are you sure?"

"When I seen it before, up Canada way a few years back, some trader had hauled a pack of infected blankets into this Injun village. A fortnight later all but a dozen or so was dead. And it's an awful, ugly way to die, hoss."

"Blankets? Devlin told me he packed in some trade goods . . ."

Bushrod nodded. "Yep. He shore did. And, best I can tell, there's a dead or dyin' redskin in every tepee one of them Nor'west blankets of his went into. 'Course, that's just where it starts. It'll spread to every livin' soul in this place. Includin' me and you."

"Where does it come from?"

"Hell, I ain't no doctor," said Bushrod crossly. "All I know is it kills quick and sartin, and I aim to put as many miles between me and this place as I can."

"Then what are you waiting for?"

Bushrod grimaced. "I'm gonna have to take you out with me."

Zack was startled. "Why the change of heart?"

"I've been puttin' off leavin' here for a spell, in case you hadn't noticed. I finally figured out it was because I knew I couldn't leave you in this fix you're in."

"Well, it's a little late," snapped Zach. "Maybe that rainy night on the trail, when you gave me that blanket, we could have slipped away. But how do you aim to get me through them?"

He pointed at the warriors ringing the lodge. Bushrod cast a quick glance over his shoulder. When he looked back around he was grinning ear to ear.

"You know me, Hannah. Never do want to miss a good fight."

XV

"I wouldn't call that a fight," said Zack. "More like a massacre."

Bushrod shook his head. "I swear, hoss. You got a

mighty poor attitude for a mountain man. Iffen I'd survived all that you've lived through these past few weeks, why, I'd feel downright invincible."

"Invincible?" Zach smiled. "Give me that horse pistol stuck in your belt and let's go find out."

"Now, that's more like it!"

But before Bushrod could transfer his flintlock pistol to Zach, Blue Elk, Scar, and the village chief broke through the cordon of watchful warriors and advanced on the medicine lodge.

Scar stepped in front of the others to threaten Bushrod with his tomahawk.

"Stand aside!"

Bushrod took a step back and yanked the pistol out of his broad leather belt.

"Now's as good a time as any to show you how much I dislike you, Scar," he drawled.

"No fight!" exclaimed the chief, whose handle was Whirlwind. He said it in English first, for Bushrod's benefit, then repeated himself in Blackfoot, so that Scar would understand.

Both the warrior and the frontiersman restrained themselves, but it wasn't easy for either one of the them—that much was evident from their truculent expressions.

The chief entered the medicine lodge. Zach moved back away from the entrance, out of the way. Blue Elk followed, and Scar came in last.

The three Blackfeet walked to the fire-circle in the center of the lodge and sat around it. Only Scar paid Zach any attention whatsoever—bestowing a murderous glance on the mountain man.

Zach wasn't certain what to do in this situation, so he settled for moving a little closer to the trio before sitting on his heels to watch and listen.

The three Indians shared a pipe. After this ritual had been tended to, Whirlwind spoke.

"A great and terrible curse has been brought upon our people. Already four have died." Grief twitched the corners of the chief's eyes and mouth, but he kept his stoic composure and went on. "Many more are sick. They too will die, because the medicine of Blue Elk is powerless against this curse."

"We have brought this upon ourselves," said the old shaman defensively. "Evil spirits I can vanquish. But this curse has been visited upon us by the Great Spirit Himself. He has done this because we have done wrong. This one . . ." Blue elk pointed a gnarled finger at Zach ". . . is favored by the Great Spirit, and we have tried to take his life. The Great Spirit is angry with us for trying to do this thing. That is why my medicine was powerless against him. And that is why our people are dying."

"What must be done?" asked Whirlwind.

"He must be set free, unharmed."

"No!" exclaimed Scar.

Whirlwind's eyes flashed anger. "You dare speak against Blue Elk?"

"I do," said Scar, full of venom. "He is an old fool. He knows not what he says. If the Great Spirit is angry with us it is because we failed to kill this white man, the enemy of our people, and allowed him to enter into this sacred place. His presence is an insult to the Great Spirit."

Blue Elk gravely shook his head. "It is not so. If that was true, my medicine would have worked against Longshot. But his power is too great, and such power can only come from one source."

"You cannot let him live!" shouted Scar, leaping to his feet.

"I decide what will be done!" barked Whirlwind. "Take care what you say, Scar."

"You are both cowardly old women," declared Scar. "All of the warriors will obey me."

"They will obey *me*!" said Whirlwind, striking his chest. "If you doubt that, Scar, we will go out from this place, and you will tell them to strike me down, and I will command them to kill you, and we will see who lives, and who dies."

Scar was silent a moment, weighing carefully Whirlwind's offer.

"What will it be?" snapped the infuriated chief.

Scar sat down.

"It will be done as Blue Elk says," decided Whirlwind. "The white man Longshot will be set free. No harm will come to him while he remains on Blackfoot land. Then the Great Spirit will lift this curse from us. Is that not so, Blue Elk?"

Blue Elk was always careful to hedge his bets. "It is our only chance. The Great Spirit is very angry with us. Who can say what, if anything, will cool his anger?"

"How is it that the great Blue Elk failed to see this before?" sneered Scar. "Is he not a great prophet? Does he not know all?"

"I see only what I am meant to see. I know this: The Great Spirit is particularly unhappy with you, Scar. You are the one who captured Longshot. You brought him here. Are you not then responsible for what has happened to our people?"

Scar scoffed at this. "I brought great honor to this village. It is you who bring great shame."

"I have spoken," said Whirlwind sternly.

Scar rose and stormed out of the medicine lodge without sparing Zach a glance.

Whirlwind and Blue Elk stood and confronted Zach.

"A horse will be brought to you," said the chief. "You will go from this place, and you will take this curse with you."

I wish I could, thought Zach, his mind turning to the women and children of the village who were destined to die horrible deaths.

But he said nothing, and the chief and the medicine man left the lodge.

Whirlwind spoke to the warriors outside. He told them to go to their lodges and see to their families. He said that the Great Spirit had decided that Longshot should live, and that the plague was among them as a consequence of their attempt to take the life of one favored by the Great Spirit. If any harm came to Longshot, he warned, then all the village would perish.

A few minutes later, Zach stepped out of the medicine lodge. He raised a hand to shade his eyes against the brightness of the sun, to which he had become unaccustomed during his sojourn in the lodge. Whirlwind and Blue Elk were nowhere to be seen. Only a handful of warriors lingered. They watched him, as they would a rabid dog, and none ventured near.

Bushrod was standing off to one side, arms folded across his barrel chest. He stared at Zach in wonderment, shaking his head.

"Beats all I ever seen," he said. "Zach Hannah, you got more lives than a cat."

XVI

The Blackfeet wasted no time in bringing Zach a horse, a good-looking dappled gray. Bushrod's mount was near at hand, so he was quickly in the saddle and ready to go.

"We're not leaving yet," said Zach.

"Why the hell not?"

"I won't leave without my Hawken."

"God A'mighty," breathed Bushrod, exasperated. "You're pressin' yore luck, Hannah. And mine too, come to think on it."

"I want my rifle back." Zach was adamant.

"You're more stubborn than an ol' knobhead mule."

Zach told the young brave who had delivered the horse to go to Whirlwind and inform the chief that

Longshot wasn't going anywhere without his rifle. The Blackfoot was clearly afraid of him and took off at a run as soon as Zach had finished giving him the instructions.

With a sigh, Bushrod dismounted. He hunkered down in the shade cast by the horses and cut a chew off a plug of tobacco.

"I wonder if Moon Singer is all right," mused Zach.

"Now don't tell me you're gonna demand to see her next!"

"There's a plague in this village, Bushrod. And I care what happens to her. She stuck by me while I was laid up."

"Yeah. She took mighty good care of you. And she had that look in her eye all the time she was watchin' over you. You know, the look that would send a smart man runnin' for tall timber."

"It doesn't feel right, leaving her here."

Bushrod rose and came over to stand real close to Zach, face to face, his expression very solemn.

"They wouldn't let you take her, Zach," he said earnestly. "So you just get that notion out of yore head this minute, 'cause iffen you keep talkin' like that I'll have no choice but to knock you out cold, throw you on the back of that cayuse, and take you out of here."

The brave returned with Zach's plains rifle. But he did not have powder horn or shot pouch—an omission Zach was quick to point out.

"You can share mine," said Bushrod, crossly, as he

mounted up for a second time. "I got plenty of shot and powder. Now let's git."

Zach handed the Hawken up to Bushrod, then swung aboard the gray. Bushrod tossed the rifle back to him once he was mounted.

They rode out of the Blackfoot village keeping their mounts to a walk. Though many watched them go, no one made a move to detain them.

Once clear of the village, Zach kicked the gray into a gallop. To feel the wind in his hair and on his face, to know he was free and on his way back to Morning Sky was a wonderful feeling.

And yet . . .

He paused at the top of a grassy rise to look back at the village, down in the valley in a blue wood-smoke haze.

Bushrod rode up with a whoop of exuberance.

"Hoss, you ought to be the happiest pilgrim on God's good green earth," declared the frontiersman. "I know for damn sure you're the luckiest."

Zach did not reply. The expression on his face made Bushrod's grin melt like snow in August.

"Mebbe she'll pull through," said Bushrod.

"If not, it's one more thing Devlin will have to pay for."

"Well, not to take up for that two-legged snake, but he didn't know them blankets had the plague."

"But it seems like everywhere he goes he brings grief with him."

"For all we know he might have the sickness himself by now."

"Which is why I've got to get to Morning Sky before he does."

"Then let's go, hoss. We're burnin' daylight."

They rode on.

Not long after, four warriors left the village, following the trail of the two frontiersmen, pushing their ponies hard. One was Scar. Another was Long Runner.

And they were painted for war.

For once, Zach's guard was down.

He didn't think any of the Blackfeet would disobey Whirlwind. Indians were a superstitious bunch—the notion that the sickness was a curse and the only way to remove that curse was to let him go free would make perfect sense to them, and he didn't figure even Scar, with all his hate, would take the chance of killing him now.

Another reason for his lack of vigilance was the fact that his thoughts had turned to Morning Sky and Devlin, to the exclusion of all else. It did not even occur to him to check his backtrail.

So Scar and his three companions got within rifle range undetected.

In fact, neither Bushrod or Zach was aware of their presence until Scar's shot killed Jones's horse outright.

The two frontiersmen were caught out in the open. Scar had led his war party into a strip of timber which flanked the long meadow down which Zach and Bushrod traveled. The warriors hoped to get abreast, if not ahead, of their prey while under cover. But the forest slowed the Blackfoot stalkers, and Scar had realized that another three hundred yards would bring the two white men into a stand of trees marking the course of a steep, rocky ravine—a place with plenty of cover, perfect as a defensive position. So he had raised his rifle, intentionally killing Bushrod's mount.

Bushrod cursed a blue streak as he went down. A heartbeat later, the four Blackfeet burst out of the trees, screaming like banshees. An agile roll brought Bushrod back on his feet. Zach urged the gray forward, leaning to extend a hand.

"Jump on!" he yelled.

Bushrod grasped the proffered hand. Zach pulled, Bushrod jumped. He landed on the gray behind Zach. The horse balked, less than happy to be carrying two riders. But Zach worked the braided horsehair reins and got the animal under control before kicking it into a gallop.

He headed for the trees and the ravine. But the Blackfeet gained ground; the gray was straining under its double burden. Several shots were fired, but that didn't worry Zach. It was almost impossible to hit an intended target when shooting from the back of a galloping horse.

But then there was always the lucky shot.

The bullet struck the gray in the haunch. It wasn't a mortal wound, but it was enough to cause the animal to break stride and stumble. As the gray went down, Zach swung a leg over the high pommel of the

Indian saddle and landed on his feet, running. Bushrod's dismount wasn't nearly as graceful. He fell hard and lay still, momentarily stunned. The gray got up and crow-hopped off, twisting as it tried to bite at its wound.

A quick look back alerted Zach to Bushrod's dilemma. Without hesitation he returned to the fallen frontiersman.

"Anything broke?" he asked.

"Don't think so," wheezed Bushrod. He tried to get up, reeled, fell down again.

Zach checked the progress of the Blackfeet bearing down on them. A hundred yards. It was at least that far to the ravine. They would never make it—it was here that they would have to make their stand.

He raised the Hawken and drew a bead on the foremost Indian.

Then he recognized the warrior.

It was Long Runner.

Zach made a split-second decision, swung the Hawken slightly, and fired.

The Blackfoot to one side and half a length behind Long Runner somersaulted backwards off his horse, struck in the chest by Zach's bullet.

Zach reached instinctively for his powder horn. Then he remembered it had not been returned to him.

"Zach!"

Bushrod was holding aloft his own rifle.

"Give me yourn," said Bushrod. "I cain't see straight enough to shoot, but I kin load blind."

Zach traded rifles.

His next target was Scar. He drew a bead. But Scar knew what was coming. The warrior slid sideways off his Indian saddle and clung to the side of his galloping pony, one leg hooked over the saddle, holding on to the pommel with one hand. The pony began to veer away, no longer guided by its rider. Zach lowered the rifle a fraction and squeezed the trigger. The bullet caught the horse in the neck, snapping the spine. The animal died instantly, as Zach had intended. It collapsed in midstride, cartwheeling. Scar was thrown twenty feet.

Zach didn't have time to watch and see if he got back up. Long Runner was almost on him. Yelling at the top of his lungs, the reins gripped in his left hand, Long Runner leveled his rifle one-handed, as a knight of old would have leveled his lance in a joust.

"Stay down!" Zach shouted to Bushrod, and moved just as Long Runner fired, at almost point-blank range.

The bullet grazed Zach's arm near the shoulder joint, laying a deep, blood groove in the flesh. Zach was diving to one side; he rolled, came up to spin around with Bushrod's rifle grasped now by the barrel with both hands. He swung the rifle for all he was worth as Long Runner galloped by. The stock shattered as it struck the Blackfoot across the chest. The pony kept running. Long Runner reeled in the saddle but managed to hold on, pulling hard on the reins. Zach dropped what was left of the rifle. He drew the knife he had taken in his duel with Long Runner back in the Blackfoot village.

It was time to finish that fight.

Zach made a running leap and swept Long Runner clear off his pony.

He landed on top of the warrior, rolled on one shoulder, came up in a crouch. Long Runner powered to his feet, brandishing a tomahawk, and charged at him. Zach parried the downward stroke of the tomahawk with his knife, and drove a rock-hard fist into Long Runner's face. The blow sent the Blackfoot sprawling. But he was back up in an instant.

This time he hurled the tomahawk. Zach dodged the throw. Long Runner drew his knife and lunged. He lashed out at Zach, a lateral sweep at the midsection which would have ripped Zach open, except that he managed, barely, to dance out of the way. The warrior slashed next at the head of his adversary, but Zach ducked under and drove his own knife to the hilt in Long Runner's belly.

The knife slipping from his hand, Long Runner clutched at the bone handle of Zach's blade. Zach let go and stepped away. He was overcome with sudden remorse. He thought about Moon Singer. He had killed her brother. Unreasoning anger, focused on Long Runner, possessed him. He grabbed the warrior by the front of his buckskin shirt and shook him.

"Why?" he rasped. "Why'd you have to come after me?"

Long Runner's features were twisted into a hideous mask of agony and hate. He spat a mouthful of blood into Zach's face and then breathed his last and sagged against the mountain man.

Zach let him fall.

"Hannah! Look out!"

It was Bushrod shouting the warning.

Empty-handed, Zach whirled.

The fourth Blackfoot was coming straight at him on a hard-running war pony, bent on riding him down. The Indian was leaning out of the saddle, swinging a war club.

Zach heard the Hawken speak. He knew the voice of his own rifle. The Blackfoot pitched sideways off his horse. As the pony thundered past, Zach leaped onto its back. Gathering up the reins, he checked the animal and rode back to Bushrod. Jones was standing now. He had finished reloading the Hawken, and he tossed the rifle to its owner.

"Go check on Scar, hoss," he advised, pulling his flintlock pistol from under his belt. "I don't trust that skunk. Make shore he's gone beaver."

Zach rode over to the spot where Scar and his horse had fallen. His mount snorted and shied away as they neared the carcass of Scar's war pony. Zach saw the Blackfoot in the grass some distance from the dead horse. He rode closer for a better look.

Scar was dead. His sightless eyes stared at the blue summer sky. His head lay at an odd angle. The fall had snapped his neck.

Returning to Bushrod, Zach said, "He's dead. You take scalps, Bushrod?"

"I ain't much for that, Zach."

"Good. I think maybe I misjudged you."

"Like I give a good goddamn how you feel about me," said Bushrod.

But he was grinning when he said it.

"I owe you a rifle."

"Yeah, I noticed. How about that Hawken of yourn? That's a damn fine piece."

"Sorry."

"I didn't think so, seein' as how you was willin' to take on the whole Blackfoot Nation to git it back. How come you figure those four came after us? I didn't figure a single one of them mangy redskins was gonna chance goin' against Whirlwind."

"I don't know."

"Well, I reckon they just had a strong hankerin' to lift yore hair."

"I'm sorry about Long Runner."

" 'Cause of that lil punkin back there—Moon Singer." Bushrod nodded. "You did the only thing you could do, Zach. He was just bound and determined to kill you, or die tryin'."

"Reckon so. Can you ride?"

" 'Course I kin ride! Just had my gourd rattled." Bushrod threw a quick look around. "Hell, we were tough on the horses today, weren't we?" He glanced skyward. The first buzzard had already appeared, riding the wind currents directly overhead.

Zach spotted Long Runner's pony grazing over near the ravine.

"I'll see if I can catch that one up," he said.

"You do that. Meanwhile, I'll see which one of these rascals' rifles suits me best. Just in case any more of 'em try to tamper with us 'fore we git across the Missouri."

Zach started to rein the horse around, then thought of something and turned back to Bushrod.

"Thanks for sticking by me."

"My pleasure. You're so lucky, I reckon if I stick with you, I'll live forever."

But Bushrod Jones would soon be dead.

XVII

At first Zach thought Bushrod had hurt himself worse than he knew in the fall—had busted something inside. The bearded frontiersman kept bending over the pommel of his saddle. His face, twisted in a constant grimace of pain, was buried in the mane of the Indian pony. Zach would bring his own horse alongside Bushrod's and ask Jones if he was all right. The first half-dozen times Zach did this, Bushrod straightened up, though the effort obviously cost him dearly, forced a wan grin, and nodded that he was. But as the day grew old he worsened, so that eventually he could not straighten up, and did not even respond to Zach's worried voice. At that point Zach took the reins out of Bushrod's hands and led his mount.

They camped that night in a stand of scrub cedar. Bushrod was by now delirious and perspiring heavily, his buckskins soaked with sweat, his face flushed, his skin hot to the touch one minute and clammy-cold the next, as the fever was interspersed with chills.

He had switched his saddle and gear from his dead horse to the Indian pony, so he had a blanket, and Zach stayed up all night making sure he stayed covered. Bushrod thrashed and tossed, mumbling incoherently. Zach dared not risk a fire, though the night was cold. They were still in Blackfoot country, and while Zach figured it was unlikely that any more warriors from Whirlwind's village would defy their chief, there were other villages, and other warriors not bound by Whirlwind's decision.

By now Zach could no long deny the truth about Bushrod's illness. The man had the plague. That scared Zach clean through. Grizzly bears and Blackfoot Indians could not scare him the way this sickness did. A man had a fighting chance against bears and Blackfeet. But you couldn't fight the plague. There was no defense against it.

His first reaction was a purely natural one—to get as far away from Bushrod as he could. But he forced himself to remain at the man's side. He would not abandon Bushrod, no matter what the cost. Not even if it killed him.

To make matters worse, Bushrod's ailment opened the gates to a flood of unpleasant memories for Zach. Of that time, many years past, when cholera had struck Copper Creek, Tennessee. Zach's mother, always the good samaritan, had tended sick neighbors, against her husband's advice. And she had brought the sickness home. Zach had lost both parents. But he hadn't gotten sick at all. Not even a stomachache. Though at the time, torn by grief, he had wished the plague *had* gotten him. He had railed against God Himself, as he stood over the graves of his family, for letting him live while taking his folks away from him.

In the early-morning hours Zach dozed off, sitting cross-legged near Bushrod with his Hawken rifle across his lap.

The next morning Bushrod regained consciousness. Zach fetched him some water from a nearby creek. But Bushrod couldn't keep the water down. He tried to put on a brave face, but he was scared clean through.

"I'm done for, ain't I, hoss?" he asked, his voice weak and reedy thin. "I got the plague."

Zach shook his head. "You don't know that."

"The hell I don't. I'm finished."

"I thought you were a fighter. A man who never quit. Sounds to me like you're quitting now."

"You cain't fight this, Zach."

"You can try. Give up, and you're gone for certain."

"You're the one needs to git gone. What the blue blazes is wrong with you? Are you plumb crazy? Git away from me, or you'll catch the sickness too. Iffen you haven't already."

"I won't leave you."

"I want to die alone, dammit. I don't want nobody sittin' around watchin' me die, like some damned vulture. Now git!"

"No. You took your chances sticking by me."

"That was different."

"Not at all."

Bushrod lapsed into unconsciousness a moment later. In two hours he was awake again, and coherent, and Zach thought he looked a lot better.

"Burnin' daylight," muttered Bushrod, sitting up. He winced. "God, every bone in this ol' body hurts. I feel like I got trampled by a herd of buffalo."

"Just rest."

"Rest?" Bushrod snorted. "I'll rest when I'm dead, hoss. But I ain't never been one to lie around all day long, so let's go."

"Sure you can ride?"

"Just fetch me my horse."

Zach did just that, daring to hope that by some miracle the worst was over for his companion.

But they only made a few miles. On the bank of a minor river which fed into the Missouri a half-day to the south, Bushrod suddenly pitched sideways off his horse.

Zach covered him with the blanket where he lay.

Having had nothing to eat for days, aside from a couple of strips of jerked venison Bushrod had amongst his possibles, Zach spent the day fishing. He whittled one end of a long stick to a sharp point. With this makeshift spear he waded out into the river shallows. The mountain-fed river was crystal-clear, and Zach could see fat and sassy rainbow trout. Catching them wasn't easy, but he finally speared one. He cleaned it and cooked it over a small fire started by striking flint against the blade of his knife to get a spark with which to ignite the moss and twigs that were his kindling. He used aspen wood, and the fire was smokeless.

He spent a sleepless night, angry and upset, because he knew Bushrod was dying, and there was nothing he could do about it. The man had stuck by him, in his own way, and Zach felt bad about having judged him so harshly upon their first meeting.

Early the next morning, Bushrod started coughing up black blood. His fevered eyes were sunk deep in their sockets. His skin was alabaster-white, dry, and hot to the touch. Zach couldn't believe a disease could suck the life out of a man so quickly.

Bushrod's lips were drawn back. His teeth were clenched. He was in constant agony.

"I don't want to die like this," he said.

Zach shook his head, and started to say what people always said in such situations—that he wasn't going to die. But he didn't say it. What was the point of lying? He knew Bushrod was as good as dead, and Bushrod knew it too.

Bushrod dragged the flintlock pistol out of his belt and offered it, butt first, to Zach.

"Do me a favor, Zach."

"No."

"You'd kill a horse that was sufferin' and beyond saving, wouldn't you?"

"I reckon."

"I'm gone beaver." Bushrod's tone was one of desperation. "Mebbe I'll get through the day. But I don't want to. Not like this. I don't want another day of this pain. Not another damned hour. Make it quick for me, Hannah. I'm askin' you."

"I just can't."

Bushrod sighed. He coughed up some more blood. When he was able to speak, he said, "Don't feel bad about it. I didn't figure you could. I ain't sure I could either, was I in your moccasins. It warn't fair of me to ask it of you. My pa allus said never ask another to do sumpin' you wouldn't do yoreself." He tried to smile. "Reckon I'll see you on the other side, hoss."

He turned the pistol on himself.

Zach grabbed the barrel and yanked the weapon out of Bushrod's grasp.

"What the hell are you doing?" gasped Bushrod, close to tears.

"Damn it," muttered Zach.

"Do it, or give me the pistol."

Zach stood up. He stood there for a long time, the pistol in hand, dangling at his side. He tried to think it through. Bushrod was right. He was going to die. It was merely a question of when—and of how much pain he would have to endure before death released him. Shooting him would be mercy, pure and simple.

It all made perfect sense. But Zach just couldn't do the deed, and he thought he was weak and lacked courage. He realized that shooting Bushrod was something he didn't want to have to live with, and that was just downright selfish, because Bushrod was depending on him for help and he was letting the man down.

"I can't," he said finally, and surrendered the pistol to Bushrod. "I'm truly sorry."

"Forget it, Zach. I got one request. Don't stick me in a damned hole in the ground. Just put me in that river yonder. Will you do that for me?"

Zach nodded miserably. Unable to say anything else, he turned and walked away.

The report of the pistol made him jump, even though he had tried to prepare himself for the sound.

He didn't turn around. Just kept walking, and walked quite a ways, wondering why he felt as though he had lost a longtime friend, when he had really scarcely even known Bushrod Jones. And not only did he feel as though he had lost a friend, but also as though he had betrayed that friend as well.

Eventually he composed himself sufficiently—and steeled himself too—to return to Bushrod. Wrapping the corpse in the blanket, he dragged it down to the river. He waded out into the shallows, and beyond, until the water was up to his armpits, and then he let the blanket open up. The body slipped away, carried by the current. It rolled over once, and an arm broke the surface, almost as though Bushrod was waving good-bye, and then it was gone.

Zach let Bushrod's Indian pony loose. He wondered if it would make its way back to the Blackfoot village, and if Moon Singer was still alive to see it, and then to know that her brother was dead.

He mounted his own horse and headed south.

Late afternoon found him at the Missouri. The

river had gone down some since his last crossing, as a prisoner of the Blackfeet. But it was still an angry, turbulent, dangerous son-of-a-gun.

He swam across, clinging to the pommel of the Indian saddle. Safely on the other side, he paused and stared at the opposite bank.

Seemed as though everything which had transpired on the other side of this river had been a bad dream. How many times had he reconciled himself to dying, to never seeing Morning Sky and his precious little Jacob again? In a way he *had* died, a number of times, and then been resurrected. And, in a way, he was not at all the same man who, weeks before, had crossed this river on the end of a rope, his hands bound, his future bleak. He was profoundly changed.

For one thing, he knew now that when he and Morning Sky were reunited this time, they would be together forever. Nothing—absolutely nothing—would separate them again. He would see to that.

Which meant Sean Michael Devlin had to die.

He rode south, making for the Yellowstone country.

Chapter 5

The Reunion

I

The day after he crossed the Missouri, Zach got caught in a snowstorm.

It had snowed heavily up in the high country weeks earlier, but this was the first real blue norther to sweep down out of the mountains and roar across the high plains, and Zach almost froze to death that night.

He managed to build a fire in a hole dug out of the frozen ground with his knife, and when he had a nice bed of glowing coals, he covered it with dirt. He sat cross-legged directly over this, his back to the howling wind, a blanket over him. The heat from the coals came up through the dirt and provided some warmth. Not much, but enough to keep him from freezing.

The next morning when the sun climbed into a

crystal-blue sky, its light revealed a world of blue ice and white snow.

Zach came across a single bison that afternoon. The creature was floundering in deep snowdrifts on the north side of a hogback ridge. A pack of wolves were after it. They had chased the buffalo for more than two miles, and now, sensing that the end was near, they were closing in.

The pack's leader was a big silver-white male.

When he reached the rim of the bare, rocky ridge and looked down at the drama of nature unfolding below him, Zach felt a cold chill run right down his spine.

He realized he had seen that silver-white male wolf before.

It had been the winter he'd busted his leg, the winter of '23–'24, miles from the Rocky Mountain Fur Company stronghold on the Yellowstone, when he and Devlin had struggled to survive the trek across a frozen wasteland. And then a pack of wolves, led by this very same silvermane—or one that looked just like him—had appeared to kill one of their horses. The horsemeat had given the men strength enough to go a little further, and when that strength had been spent the wolves had come calling again, and that time Devlin had shot and killed one of them, and the wolf meat had sustained them long enough for them to reach the fort.

On that same occasion, a big silver wolf had visited Morning Sky. Her spirit-wolf.

After that, his first winter alone in the high country, when he had turned his back on humankind following the disappearance of Devlin and Morning Sky, he had shared a lonesome snowbound valley with a pack of wolves. That winter it had seemed as though he and the wolves had been the only living creatures in the Shining Mountains.

Again last winter, a pack had haunted the valley where he and the brigade had waited on green-up. The day of his fight with Long Runner in the Blackfoot village, wolves had struck the horse herd, and the Blackfeet had taken it as an omen.

Now this.

The wolves down yonder were after a buffalo—had chased the creature to this spot—right in his path. And what he needed more than anything else at this moment was the pelt of that bison. A buffalo robe might be the difference between life and death for him, now that he was about to climb into the mountains, where the cold would be so severe that it could crack full-grown trees right in two, and the creeks would freeze clear down to the bottom, and the icy crystals would hang in the air like a diamond haze, and if a man spit, his saliva would turn to ice before it hit the ground.

Was this just a happy coincidence?

Had all those past events involving wolves been mere chance? Or some supernatural design?

Zach was not a superstitious man. Yet he could not help but wonder.

Why was that silvermane—if it was the same one

he had crossed paths with before—always showing up in times of crisis?

It seemed ludicrous. But Morning Sky would have made something of it. Maybe there was some mystic connection between a man who loved this land and the land itself and the creatures nurtured by the land. The Indians thought so. Every person had his totem—something of special significance to him or her, and from which he or she usually acquired a name. Maybe the wolf was his totem.

He unsheathed the Hawken, aimed, and fired.

The bison fell to lie still in blood-splattered snow.

At the sound of the rifle the wolves retreated, but they didn't go far before settling down to watch and wait.

Zach reloaded the Hawken, and kicked his horse into motion, guiding it down the slope. The horse balked as it drew near the carcass of the buffalo. Zach wasn't sure if it was the dead animal or the nearby wolves that most bothered the pony. Finally he dismounted and tied the reins around a rock. With his plains rifle shoulder-racked, he proceeded to the base of the ridge, waded through snow that at times was waist high, and reached his kill.

He skinned the carcass, cut out some choice hump meat, and then worked his way back up the slope of the ridge. Retrieving his horse, he continued to the rim. Again he ground-hitched the horse. Moving off a little ways so that the blood spoor would not agitate his horse, he settled down to scrape clean the buffalo skin.

As he worked he glanced downslope now and again to watch the wolves. They had waited, silent and patient, while he skinned the carcass. Now they had closed in again and started to feast. Only the big silver male stood apart, sometimes watching the pack as the other wolves would quarrel over a chunk of meat, sometimes checking the top of the ridge where Zach was sitting, and sometimes scanning the horizon, alert for danger.

Scraping the skin took quite a while. It needed to be rubbed with a mixture of fat and brains and then smoked and sun-cured, but Zach couldn't do all that. So he settled for cutting two slits in the skin, through which he could put his arms, and cutting off a long strip, which he used to belt the makeshift robe together.

His pony did not care for the smell of the bison blood that covered Zach, but Zach managed to get mounted and stay aboard, even though the cross pony crow-hopped a little.

Once he had the horse under control, Zach checked the base of the ridge again. The pack had gorged itself on buffalo meat. The big silver had eaten last. Now, as the rest of the wolves, as though on a silent signal, moved off, loping across the snow, the big silver, its muzzle scarlet with blood, lingered a moment to look again at the mounted frontiersman up on the ridge before following the pack.

Zach watched them until they had vanished from sight in a distant dark line of conifers.

He rode on, then, making a few more miles before

sunset, and camping in the shelter of some trees, he built a fire so that he could spit chunks of the hump meat and roast it. He ate snow to quench his thirst. His belly full for once, he hollowed out a hole in the snow and lay down to sleep, the buffalo robe and blanket pulled tight around him. He was almost warm, and he slept well.

At dawn he was on his way again.

The mountains, gray and snow-clad, looking bleak and forbidding, lay before him. He longed to be back up in the high country. The plains were not for him. He knew he would live out his days in the *pays d'en haut,* as the Canadians called it.

His sense of direction was infallible. The Shoshone Range was his destination. He figured Sky and little Jacob were holed up in the Yellowstone country for the winter. At least he hoped so. And if that were the case, they would be snowed in, for he knew of no way out of that place in the winter. But they would have plenty of game, and good shelter, and the sulfur springs to keep them warm. He wished there was a way to reach them before green-up.

But since there was none, as far as he knew, he had decided to return instead to the valley where Devlin and his Blackfoot allies had killed Fletcher and interrupted the brigade's trapping. He was hoping that Devlin, and probably some other American Fur Company men, would be there. Devlin had mentioned that they planned to harvest a lot more brown gold out of that valley to augment the haul of plews they had stolen from Zach's brigade.

Zach's purpose was twofold. First he was going to get the stolen plews back. Then he was going to hunt Devlin down and kill him.

This was going to be Coyote's last winter.

II

Devlin wondered every day if he would last through the winter.

He couldn't stand being stuck in this godforsaken valley, snowed in with nowhere to go and precious little to do. Oh, he could get out through one of the southern passes, but for what reason? Vanderburg expected him to stick with his brigade. The other men gambled or hunted or just lazed around their fires and smoked and told tall tales.

But Devlin didn't feel too sociable most days. In fact, he was perfectly miserable. All he could think about was Morning Sky.

Where was she?

Wherever she was, it wasn't where she belonged, which was by his side, sharing one of these wretched, vermin-infested lean-tos. He cursed Zach Hannah daily for taking the secret of her whereabouts to his grave.

There were six other men in the winter camp, and one woman. The woman was Baptiste's squaw, Flower. The French-Canadian and Keller had found their way back after a harrowing horse-stealing excursion into Shoshone country.

"Those Shoshones were riled up," Keller had told him. "A nest of red hornets, hoss. Seems a bunch of Absaroka Crows had just hit the village and made off with some ponies. So they were in an ornery mood, and not too happy to see a couple of horse-stealers like us come along."

Devlin's smile was ironic. "Yeah. I met those Absarokas. And rode one of those stolen ponies for a while, too."

"How's that?"

He told them of his encounter with Red Claw's bunch. How he had been their prisoner for a spell, destined for a bad death—until Zach Hannah had intervened and saved his bacon.

"It's a small world, sure enough," remarked Keller, shaking his head.

"Not small enough," muttered Devlin, wondering how he was going to find Morning Sky and his son in this big country.

Keller did not question this enigmatic remark, and Devlin realized he really didn't want to talk about it anyway, so he changed the subject.

"You got your horses, at least."

"Almost lost our hair doing it, though."

"Had to kill a couple of Shoshone," added Baptiste, in a matter-of-fact way. Killing Indians wasn't something that bothered the French-Canadian.

"Flower's Shoshone, isn't she?"

"*Oui.*"

"How did that sit with her?"

Baptiste shrugged. "You know how she is, Devlin. She will not say much. But it doesn't matter. I am her man. I do what I have to do. If it bothers her, she will just have to get over it."

"It was them or us," said Keller.

"What about your woman, Devlin?" asked Baptiste.

Devlin grimaced. "I haven't found her. Yet."

After he and Bledsoe had said so long to Scar and his Blackfoot war party, Devlin had tried to track the rest of Hannah's brigade. One day out and he had lost their sign. It was Shadmore's fault. He was a crafty old codger, that one.

"But I'll find her," he vowed. "Come green-up, I'll keep looking."

"So Zach Hannah's dead," mused Keller. "Can't hardly believe it."

"Believe it," snapped Devlin. "The Blackfeet put him under."

"Did you see him die?" asked Baptiste. "I mean, with your own eyes?"

"No."

Baptiste was frowning.

"But he's dead," insisted Devlin, exasperated. "No question."

Baptiste just grunted.

"You find that hard to buy, don't you?" observed Devlin, caustically.

"I just know he is hard to kill, that one."

"Well, the Blackfeet done it. And, if you ask me, it's good riddance."

Still, Devlin couldn't help but feel miserable, and he knew it wasn't entirely on account of his failure to find Morning Sky and Jacob. Some of it had to do with Zach Hannah. In spite of everything that had passed between them, Devlin experienced a keen sense of loss. He didn't understand why, and it came as complete surprise to him, but there it was. He was sorry Zach was dead.

He had admired Hannah at first, and then the admiration had turned to envy, as Zach excelled in the ways of the mountain man, and when he had met and married Morning Sky. The envy had caused Devlin to do some despicable things, but he realized he had never actually hated Zach, even though Zach had exemplified the kind of man Devlin could never be.

Devlin blamed the fact that he wasn't like Hannah on circumstances. It wasn't his fault that his folks had died when he was a child and fate had thrown him in with the wrong crowd of rivermen, and he had learned that it was easier to steal what he wanted than to work hard to get it. He failed to comprehend that it was his lack of inner strength and moral conviction that was the source of his problems.

All he knew was that Zack Hannah's death had left an emptiness in him.

Unlike Baptiste, he knew Zach was dead, even if

he hadn't seen it with his own eyes. He could have remained in the Blackfoot village long enough to make certain—in fact, he had gone there with the intention of doing so—but at the last moment he had pulled up stakes, not wanting to bear witness to Hannah's demise.

He'd been wrong, all the way down the line. He could see that now. He'd been wrong in stealing Morning Sky years ago, and wrong for bringing the Blackfeet to this valley, and wrong for not lifting a finger to save Zach from those redskins. To have Morning Sky again was Devlin's sole aim, for he knew there was no turning back the clock. He was well down the road to hell and there was nothing he could do about it, not a damned thing. Except feel bad, and wish things had turned out differently, and curse his fate, and know, with that awful feeling in the pit of his stomach, that he was going to pay— and pay dearly—for his sins.

III

Morning Sky, too, felt miserable. It seemed as though everything inside her had died. She was a listless, empty shell. The world held no allure for her. All was colorless and cheerless. She scarcely felt the cold. She hardly ever thought of food. Shadmore had to make her eat. He did so by pestering her until she tried something just to buy some peace and quiet.

She knew Zach was dead. She told Shadmore as much.

"You don't know that for a fact," argued the old leatherstocking, stubbornly shaking his head.

"Yes I do. So do you."

"I don't!" said Shadmore. It was a lie, and his protest was too strong, and she saw right through it.

"I won't believe it," he insisted angrily. "Not till I see his scalp, or his body."

"He would be here now if he was alive."

Shadmore cast about for some argument that would stand against her reasoning, but he could find nothing that would hold water.

"I dunno," he muttered. "but I do know that twice before, I wrote Zach Hannah off. And I was wrong both times."

Of course, this conversation, and several more in the same vein, were never conducted in the presence of little Jacob. At first, Sky agonized over how to tell her son the truth. But the boy was sharp as a tack; he could tell something was terribly amiss. Sometimes he caught her crying, though she tried not to cry unless she was alone. And sometimes he would ask her where his father was—because the other truth she had kept from him was that Zach Hannah was not his true sire—and she would answer evasively that he had had to go away. But she couldn't fool the boy; she shouldn't have tried. Her eyes and expression and the tone of her voice all conspired to betray her. Then one day, after he asked her the question again and she provided the stock reply, he observed, with an astuteness one would not expect from a four-year-old child, that she never said Zach was coming back. Only that he had gone away.

"Did the Blackfeet kill him?" he asked.

Morning Sky knelt down and took little Jacob by the shoulders. Tears welled up in her eyes, but she fought them back. It was time, she decided, to be strong for her son.

"Yes, Jacob," she replied. "They killed him. He won't be coming back. Ever."

The boy was silent for a moment. She felt a shudder pass through his little body, but he stood there, rigid, his lips pressed tightly together, and a silent tear on his cheek.

"When I grow up I'm going to kill every Blackfoot in the world," he declared.

"Don't say that."

"I'm gonna. And nobody can stop me."

They fared well that winter in the Yellowstone country. As Zach had promised, there was an abundance of game, and a lake that steamed in the frosty air, never had a bit of ice in it, and was full of fish besides. The geysers and the sulfur springs and the mudholes were wondrous sights. Sky believed the place to be filled with magic. It scared her a little, and she thought it no wonder that Indians did not linger here if they came at all.

Not a sign of Indians could they find, and Shadmore concluded that the brigade was as safe here as anywhere in the world. As far as he could tell, there were only a couple of ways into the valley. One was by a narrow pass, now completely snowed in. The other was through the canyon where the river raged. To attempt that passage would be suicide, because the only means was an ice-glazed ledge high above the canyon floor, and no horse, in Shad's considered opinion—and probably no man—could negotiate that trail. He would not have put money on a mountain goat having any success.

"Come green-up," he told Montez and MacGregor and Jubal Wilkes, "we'll go back to the Shoshone Range."

"What for?" asked MacGregor. He had a hunch, but he wanted to hear Shad say it.

"You know what fer," said Shadmore, scowling. "I reckon Devlin and them American Fur Company hooligans will be there, usin' our traps and skinnin' our beaver. I aim to get our plews back. And teach them boys a lesson, too, while I'm at it."

The others were enthusiastic.

"I only wish we could pay them a wee visit right now," sighed the Scotsman.

"We'll just have to wait."

"Maybe not," said Jubal. "Maybe there's a way out of this valley we don't know about."

"Well, you're welcome to try and find it, boy."

"Good. I'll try."

Shadmore merely shook his head and smiled a tolerant smile. Young Wilkes reminded him a lot of Zach Hannah when Zach had been wet behind the ears. Like Zach, Jubal was smart, and quick to learn, and chock-full of "can-do" enthusiasm.

So Jubal spent a lot of time away from camp, just as Zach had always done, exploring every nook and cranny of the valley, while Shad and Montez and the Scotsman whiled away the winter days, occupying themselves with thoughts of next spring, and vengeance. Sometimes MacGregor would unlimber his bagpipes. Even after all the years the Scotsman had been with the brigade, Shadmore still couldn't bear the god-awful screeching sounds that the infernal instrument produced.

Shad kept an eye on MacGregor, knowing how he felt about Morning Sky. He figured MacGregor might see his way clear to make advances, now that Zach was gone. But MacGregor did nothing untoward. Shadmore finally decided to have it out with him.

"Aye, I love her," MacGregor said, pensive. "I've made no secret of the way I feel about Sky. But I'll not broach the subject with her, now or ever."

"Why not?" growled Shadmore. "That plumb makes no sense to me."

The Scotsman laughed. "I'm not surprised, you old wolverine. She loves one man. Always has, always will. Her heart belongs to Zach Hannah, and it matters not if he's alive or no, because she'll never love another. I'm her friend, and she's come to trust me as such, and I want to keep that friendship, as it's all I'll ever have with her. I wouldna do anything to risk it. So you can stop watching me like a flamin' turkey buzzard. I'll not make any advances towards her. You'll have to find another excuse for shooting me."

Shadmore stared. Then he chuckled. "I've got all the excuse I need already. Iffen you blow into that goldurned bagpipe agin I'll pull the trigger, sure as rain."

MacGregor was pretty certain ol' Shad was joking—that this was an idle threat. He figured he would have to prove that theory. But the Scotsman never got the chance to take his life in his hands, for the next day Jubal came tearing into camp on a lathered pony, his boyish features all lit up with excitement.

"I found a passage!" he exclaimed.

"You shore?" queried the skeptical Shadmore.

"Sure I'm sure. Gather up your plunder and let's go get our plews back."

Shadmore had to smile. "I like yore spirit, younker."

Someone had to stay behind to watch over Sky and little Jacob. Shadmore's first inclination was to assign Jubal that task. The boy was young, and no where near as experienced as MacGregor and the Spaniard when it came to a ruckus.

And Shad knew there would be a fight. They talked mostly about retrieving those stolen plews but all of them knew they were going for more than that. Like as not, Zach and Fletch were gone under, and their deaths had to be avenged. That was unwritten law.

Besides that, there wouldn't be any trouble here—at least none that Jubal couldn't handle.

Problem was, the lad had found the way out, and it didn't strike Shad as fair to leave him behind. That was a poor reward for his accomplishment.

So he chose MacGregor instead.

The Scotsman was surprised, to say the least.

"You trust me?" he asked, incredulous. "You'll leave me here along with Sky?"

"Yeah," said Shadmore. "I trust you. At least as far as I can throw you. Besides, Sky can take care of herself. She's a hand with a pistol. And she likes yore dangblasted bagpipes. If I leave you here, at least I won't have to hear 'em."

"Aye, she has good taste."

"And why," said Shadmore, "should I worry about a feller who wears a skirt over his leggins making advances on a woman, anyroad?"

"It's a kilt, you bloody fool."

"Furthermore, it's clear the Spaniard is a durned sight better shot than you."

MacGregor threw back his head and laughed.

"You're full of it, old codger."

Shadmore said his good-byes to Sky and little Jacob.

"I know you're afeared of Coyote," he told her. "But you won't have to be no more, once I git done."

"Just come back safe."

"It's sartin."

And so Shad and Montez and Jubal Wilkes embarked on their mission of vengeance.

IV

Aside from Devlin, Keller, Baptiste, and Bledsoe, there were three other American Fur Company men in the winter camp. Their names were Roberts, Hogan, and Dutch William.

Zach didn't know them, but he knew they were veteran mountain men—he could tell that much after a day or two of stalking them. He figured he would spend as many days as it took to become thoroughly familiar with the routine of the brigade. The problem was that in winter a mountain man didn't have much to do. Occasionally a pair of them—they were savvy enough never to leave camp solo—would go out to hunt. Half the time it wasn't so much for dire want of fresh meat as it was an excuse to get away from camp. About the only other chores were chopping firewood or fetching water, and that didn't take a man far from camp—not if the camp had been set up in the right location, with plenty of timber and a creek near at hand.

As a result, the American Fur Company trappers spent much of their time lingering around the winter camp. And the plews Zach was after were in the camp, too. So his task was to find a way to whittle down the odds, improving his chances of absconding with the brown gold which rightfully belonged to his brigade.

His other reason for being there was to kill Sean Michael Devlin.

The deed could be done at long range—Zach

knew he could drop Devlin right there in the middle of camp. He had found several vantage points from which such a shot could be made.

But if he killed Devlin outright he would have the other six after him. Even if he managed to elude them—and there was no certainty of that—he would never get anywhere close to the plews once they knew he was near.

Besides, he wanted Devlin to know—he wanted to look in Coyote's eyes as he killed him.

The men he was up against were not novices. This was manifest by the way they conducted themselves when they ventured out of camp. Ever alert, always checking for sign, never relaxing their vigil. It was no easy matter for Zach to keep an eye on them, to shadow them, without being detected. He had to be careful where he left a trail—and it was virtually impossible not to leave one with snow covering most of the ground. A light snowfall during two of the nights worked to his advantage, covering his tracks. But the days were consistently fine. For the first time in his life Zach found himself wishing for an honest-to-God blizzard.

Eventually he formulated two plans.

One was to scatter the brigade's horses. If he could get to them. It would have to be under cover of darkness, and at night there was always a guard posted. Conceivably he could slip up on the guard and render him unconscious and then spook the cavallard.

It was likely that the American Fur Company men

would split up in an effort to retrieve their mounts. Maybe one or two would stay behind to watch over their plews and possibles.

But he couldn't execute this plan without leaving tracks in the snow. That was the one drawback. His only hope for carrying out the scheme would be if and when a fairly heavy snow was falling.

The second plan was to wait until one man ventured out alone. If that man failed to return to camp the others would go out in search of him. Then Zach might have a chance at a couple more of them. Whittling down the odds.

Zach preferred the first plan. He had come all this way to kill one man, not seven, and he figured the first plan would work with a minimum of bloodletting. The same could probably not be said for the second. Still, he was reconciled to accepting whatever was offered.

Both plans depended on an event beyond Zach's control: a change in the weather or one of the American Fur Company men making a mistake. All he could do was wait for one or the other to occur. But he couldn't wait forever. Sooner or later they would discover he was there.

So he was relieved when, on his sixth day in the valley, clouds rolled in from the north—a heavy gray overcast. The wind whipped up, so cold that it cut to the bone. A heavy snow was coming, and at about dark the first flakes fell, gently at first, swirling in the wind, and then more heavily. Before long a full-fledged storm had kicked up.

Zach was already in position, and wasted no time making his move.

V

Devlin's brigade had built the corral in a stand of aspen. Cutting down young trees, they had stripped the trunks of all their branches and then used the trunks as horizontal poles, secured to trees with lengths of rawhide. The corral was spacious and secure, and the aspen provided good shelter for the horses. A makeshift rawhide hinge tied one end of the gate pole to a tree, and the other end rested in the fork of a split tree.

The cavallard was sizable. There were nineteen horses in all. Every man had his favorite mount, and Flower had an Indian pony. Some of the trappers had brought along a pack horse, and thanks in part to the horse-stealing exploits of Keller and Baptiste, there were seven more Shoshone ponies available for packing out the plews.

Zach approached the corral through the trees, secure in the knowledge that all but one of the American Fur Company boys were huddled in their lean-tos. The one who wasn't was the man called Dutch William. Zach knew where he was: as soon as the storm hit, Dutch had moved nearer the corral.

He was a large man, a head taller than Zach, with a hefty build. He wore a buffalo robe over his buckskins to keep out the biting cold. His flop-brimmed

Kossuth hat was pulled low over his eyes, while a ragged woolen muffler covered the lower part of his heavy-jowled face. A lumbering bear of a man, he was respected for his prodigious strength. The others thought him a little slow because he didn't talk much and kept to himself. When he did speak it was with such a thick accent, and such a tenuous grasp of the English language, that he was misunderstood half the time.

It was experience which motivated Dutch William to move closer to the corral as the snowstorm increased in intensity. The chances of an enemy approaching the camp under such adverse conditions were remote, but the storm increased the chances that the horse herd might attempt to break out of the corral. The driving snow and the howling gale whipping up the trees agitated some of the ponies, while others huddled together.

Zach located Dutch William, but he had to move in close to do it. Visibility was reduced to twenty or thirty feet. At a glance Zach realized he would have to deal with the frontiersman before he could take the horses. He hoped he wouldn't have to kill him. And he hoped to avoid any shots being fired. No one could see the corral from the camp, a hundred feet through the trees, on an overcast night and through the dense curtain of swirling snow. But a shot would probably be heard.

Others would have slipped up on a giant of a man like Dutch William and slit his throat, preferring not to take any chances. Zach slipped up on him, but he could not bring himself to act the role of assassin. Instead, he drew the flintlock pistol out of his buffalo-skin belt. Holding it by the barrel, and with the Hawken plains rifle in the other hand, he crept forward.

He was halfway there when a loud *crack!* overhead gave him pause. A limb fell almost at his feet. Dutch William heard the noise too and whirled around. Zach jumped behind the trunk of the tree. With his bulky buffalo robe on, he wasn't completely concealed. But he remained perfectly still, and in the stormy gloom Dutch William failed to spot him. He turned back to the corral, wondering how the noise had affected the horses. Several were milling around, unnerved by the wind and noise.

Zach belted the pistol, picked up the limb, and closed in.

Dutch William was blissfully unaware he was being stalked. His attention was riveted on the horses in the corral. So Zach succeeded in slipping up behind him and clubbing him with the limb.

It was a hard blow, with limber green wood as thick as a man's arm, but it was measured—Zach just wanted to render Dutch William unconscious, not crack his skull open.

The American Fur Company man crumpled without making a sound. Heartened, Zach dropped the limb, stepped over Dutch William's body, and moved to the corral's gate pole.

His plan was going to work, and without a hitch! He would scatter the brigade's horses, and the storm would cover his tracks. Everyone would figure the limb had fallen on Dutch William and knocked him cold. What other explanation could they arrive at, if they could find no sign of an interloper?

But Zach's elation was premature.

Dutch William had only been stunned by the blow. He hadn't blacked out, and he was quick to recover. At first he didn't know what had happened to him. Then he sat up, looked around, and saw Zach at the corral gate, and the mystery was solved.

With a growl low in his throat, Dutch William got to his feet, plucked his rifle out of the snow, and checked the priming. The rifle was a flintlock, and what gunpowder remained in the pan was wet. He didn't waste time re-priming, but lumbered towards Zach.

Now the situation was reversed. Zach had his back turned, with no idea that Dutch William was closing in on him—not until the huge man hammered him between the shoulder blades with the stock of his rifle.

The blow slammed Zach into the gate pole, knocking the breath out of him. He lost his grip on the Hawken, and it fell into the snow at his feet. He groped for the pistol in his belt with one hand, grabbing the gate pole with the other to hold himself upright.

But before he could bring the pistol to bear, Dutch William had tossed aside his own rifle. A ham-sized fist came down in Zach's forearm, jarring the pistol out of his grasp. Dutch William straight-armed him and sent him sprawling.

Zach got up, staggering. Dutch William wrapped his huge arms around him, lifted him off the ground, and propelled him face first into the nearest tree trunk. Then he hurled Zach to the ground and raised a foot to do a little stomping.

Zach had taken just about all the abuse he was willing to take for one day.

He rolled over, grabbed Dutch William's moccasin-clad foot with both hands, and twisted for all he was worth. Dutch William grunted and fell on his face in the snow.

Zach jumped up. Dutch William was getting to his feet, too, but moving slower. Zach didn't think he could stop this man without using a weapon of some kind. Yet he still hoped to avoid firing a shot. So he kicked Dutch William in the ribs to keep him down for a few precious seconds. Dutch William took a swipe at him with one bearlike arm. Zach danced out of his reach and ran for the corral. Roaring like a bull moose, Dutch William powered to his feet and went after him. Zach figured he had the frontier goliath plenty riled up now; if Dutch William got his hands on him, the buckskin-clad giant would likely tear him limb from limb. Literally.

Fueled by rage, Dutch William was moving faster than he had ever moved in his life, and he almost caught Zach. His clawing fingers brushed the back of Zach's buffalo robe. Zach went into a tightly tucked roll, head over heels, and came up with the limb he had used a moment before, with less-than-sterling success. Spinning, he swung the limb in a double-fisted grasp for all he was worth. The limb connected with Dutch William's skull. It staggered the man, but did not drop him. Dutch William just stood there, arms limp at his sides, staring at Zach like a man who did not remember where he was, much less what he was doing there.

Zach was starting to get worried. It was beginning to look as though only a bullet would stop this man. And he wasn't absolutely convinced that even a bullet would do the job.

Dutch William shook his head to clear the cobwebs. Then he raised his arms and with a growl charged at Zach.

Zach mustered all the strength he had left and drove the limb into Dutch William's midsection. The man doubled over. Zach raised the limb overhead and brought it down on the back of his adversary's neck. Dutch William dropped to his knees.

It was all Zach could do to raise the limb again. His arms ached, and the limb felt as heavy as an anvil. Again the limb came down on Dutch William's neck. The goliath sprawled face down in the snow.

Zach just stood there a moment, sucking air into his lungs, watching Dutch William for the least sign of movement. He prodded the giant frontiersman with the limb. The man was out cold. Vastly relieved, Zach dropped the limb and turned to the corral, wiping blood off his face. There was a nasty gash in his cheek, inflicted when Dutch William had driven him into the tree. Zach reckoned it would leave a nice scar. Well, one more, to go with all the other scars his body carried as mementos of his captivity at the hands of the Blackfeet, would scarcely matter.

He was lifting the gate pole, which felt like it weighed a ton, when a bullet smacked into the forked tree just to his right. An instant later he heard the crack of a rifle's report.

He didn't waste time looking over his shoulder to find out who was shooting at him. Instead, he let the pole fall to the ground, scooped up his pistol and the Hawken, and plunged into the cavallard, yelling like a madman.

VI

The horses bolted.

Zach stuffed the pistol in his buffalo-skin belt, tossed the Hawken from left hand to right, and lunged for a sorrel horse as it thundered past. He got a handful of mane and swung aboard.

Another rifle spoke. He saw the muzzle-flash, off in the trees, but could make out little else. All he could do was bend low and try to guide the sorrel by pulling on the mane. This didn't work very well. The horses were stampeding, and without bit or bridle reins, Zach could exert precious little influence over the direction the horse was taking.

Through the trees they thundered. Some of the ponies split off on their own. The sorrel stuck with the balance of the horse herd—ten or twelve horses running together. Zach didn't know where they were going until they broke out of the trees. Then, quick to get his bearings, he realized he wasn't far from the spot where he had left his own horse. He executed a running dismount, deftly dodged a couple of the other ponies, and made it clear without getting trampled.

He threw a sharp look back at the dark line of trees, checking for pursuit. Two shots had been fired at him, but in the darkness and confusion he hadn't seen the men who had fired those shots. Apparently his donnybrook with Dutch William had been heard in the brigade's winter camp. Mountain men were notoriously light sleepers. He wondered if they had managed to snare any of the loose ponies.

But no one, mounted or afoot, emerged from the trees. While he waited, letting his nerves settle, Zach checked the Hawken, making certain that the percussion cap was in place and the charge secure in the barrel.

Satisfied that there weren't any American Fur Company man hot on his heels, Zach headed for the place where he had left his horse.

His mood was grim. He had succeeded in scattering the horses of Devlin's brigade. But they knew now that he was here. Probably didn't have a clue to his identity, yet that didn't matter. They would start tracking him as soon as they had retrieved their ponies. And they would protect the plews like a wolf bitch would guard her litter.

But he wasn't going to give up. Discretion might be the better part of valor, and a smart man interested in his own welfare would probably cut his losses and quit the valley while he was still able. Zach didn't much like his chances against seven riled-up mountain men. It looked like the war he had predicted long ago—the war between the Rocky Mountain and American fur companies—had started. Vanderburg had lighted the fuse, letting loose his Blackfoot dogs on the Rocky Mountain brigades.

Zach had never wanted to participate in this war, but he was in it now up to his hairline, whether he liked it or not. There was going to be some killing if he stayed—a lot more killing than he wanted or had a taste for—but there was no alternative. Not anymore. It had gone too far. His back was to the wall now. Those plews belonged to his brigade, and as booshway he had the responsibility of getting them back. Apart from that, he and Sky and little Jacob could never live in peace as long as Coyote walked the earth, and what Zach wanted most of all was peace.

He figured it was worth fighting for.

Dying for, too. Which seemed pretty likely, for one man against seven.

Once committed to war, Zach went about it with coldblooded efficiency.

The American Fur Company men managed to catch only a couple of wayward ponies that night.

The rest had scattered. It was decided that two men on horseback would venture away from camp and attempt to round up the horses. The others would stick close to the precious packs of hairy bank notes—seeing as how there was at least one hostile presence in the valley.

Zach hung back the following day to see how Devlin and his companions handled the situation. When he saw two men ride out—one of them Baptiste, the other man he could not recognize—and the rest remain in camp, he realized he had only one recourse. He was going to get to Devlin, and he was going to recover those plews, if it was the last thing he did. Apparently that meant he was going to have to deal with these men one at a time.

He figured he would start with the pair going out to round up the horses.

But the first day, Baptiste and his companion returned with four horses. As a result, on the following day, two teams departed from camp, going in opposite directions. Keller and Baptiste rode out together. Bledsoe and the man who had gone out with Baptiste the day before took the other direction.

Zach decided to start with them. Of all the American Fur Company trappers, he had the most respect for the prowess of Baptiste and Keller.

There was an easy way to do it—he was an accomplished marksman, and could plug them, one by one, at long range. They would never even see him. But that method smacked of cowardice. Every mountain man deserved a fair fight. He recalled that

Bushrod Jones had often made that point, and Zach believed it to be true. No matter how low-down a man was, he didn't deserve to be bushwhacked.

Zach had reconciled himself to spilling blood. That was what you did when you waged war. He didn't indulge in second thoughts. Yet there were still a few rules he would live by.

He stalked Bledsoe and his partner that morning. The storm had passed the day before, and the morning was clear and bitter cold. The sunlight reflecting on the blanket of snow covering the ground was so bright that it was almost blinding. He wished he had some tobacco to mix with saliva and dab under his eyes to prevent snow blindness. He also wished he had a good set of buckskins and a better-made buffalo robe. The Indian leggins and breechclout beneath his uncured buffalo skin just didn't do the job. He was cold right down to the bone marrow. Bledsoe and his fellow frontiersmen were vigilant. They were looking for horses, but they were keeping an eye peeled for him. Their alertness made Zach's task that much harder. All he could do was hang back and wait for his chance. He had an advantage in that he knew every square foot of this valley from his exploring the previous summer. He knew it better, he figured, than any of Devlin's brigade, who had enjoyed only a fortnight of trapping before winter had set in and pretty much confined them to their camp.

As it happened, one of the stray ponies gave him the opportunity he was looking for.

The valley floor on the southern end was an undu-

lating plain, fine graze in the summer, now covered
by a blanket of snow. When Bledsoe and his partner
came to the top of a gentle rise they spotted one of
the Indian ponies Baptiste and Keller had pilfered
from the Shoshones down in a hollow, a hundred
yards away.

Bledsoe let out an ill-advised whoop and kicked
his horse into a gallop. The other frontiersman followed. The stray plunged into trees that lined the
creek. The two American Fur Company men went in
after it.

Zach urged his horse forward at a quicker pace,
knowing that the attention of the two men he was
stalking would be focused on the stray.

The stray fled into a ravine and headed south.
Here the banks abruptly became steeper, and the
pony found itself trapped. Bledsoe and the other
trapper also rode down into the ravine. Coming up
fast from behind, Zach stuck to the bank. He knew
the ravine made a jackleg bend and then petered out
suddenly. There would be deep snow at the end of it,
too.

Making the bend in the ravine, the stray hit the
deep snow, foundered, escaped, and turned at bay.

Bledsoe and the other trapper turned the bend
and saw that their prey was cornered. The banks
were twenty feet high here, and almost perpendicu-
lar. The two riders checked their horses, blocking the
stray's only avenue of escape. The stray reared up on
its hind legs. Bledsoe shook out a rope of braided
hide.

Unbeknownst to Bledsoe and his companion, Zach reached the rim of the embankment above them and executed a running dismount. Leaving his Hawken on the rim, he drew the pistol from his belt and without hesitation launched himself in a flying leap.

That's when Bledsoe saw him for the first time.

With his gashed, bearded face and ragged garb, Zach Hannah looked like an unholy apparition to the startled Bledsoe.

For the first time in he couldn't remember when, Bledsoe was downright scared.

The last time he had seen Hannah, the man had been belly-down over a Blackfoot pony, a prisoner of the warrior named Scar, and destined to die.

Bledsoe let out an incoherent yell, half utterance of fear and surprise, half warning shout to his partner.

The warning came too late.

Zach slammed into the other trapper and knocked him off his horse.

VII

The mountain man's name was Roberts.

He had worked for the now-defunct Missouri Fur Company and after that, taken up with a Yankton Sioux woman and lived among the Indians for a spell. He had callously wagered his squaw on a horse race, thinking he couldn't lose. But of course he *had* lost. Consumed by jealousy, he had cut the woman bad and tried to kill the buck who had won her. He'd only managed to wound the warrior, but the act had aroused the entire village against him, and he had lit a shuck for parts unknown. Redcoat Kenneth MacKenzie had signed him up with the American Fur Company.

Roberts was a pretty good shot with a rifle, but his weapon of choice was the tomahawk. He carried one, Sioux-made and -decorated, in his belt. Since he lost his grip on his percussion rifle in the fall, he groped for the tomahawk as he got to his feet.

When Zach stood up and turned and saw Roberts yanking the tomahawk out of his belt, he leveled the pistol and pulled the trigger. The powder in the pan flashed, but the gun misfired—the charge had been jarred loose somewhere along the way during his leap, his collision with Roberts, and his fall to the ground.

Roberts uttered a savage yell and ran at Zach, brandishing the tomahawk. He struck, and Zach flipped the pistol in his hand and swept it upward to block the tomahawk. A second later he threw a fist that connected with Roberts's jaw and sent him reeling. Zach closed in and clubbed the man with the pistol. This time Roberts went down on one knee. He lashed out with the tomahawk again. Zach danced out of the way, then slipped in to drive a knee into Roberts's face. The American Fur Company man sprawled in the snow, blood gushing from his damaged mouth. Tossing aside the pistol, Zach stepped on the trapper's wrist, bent down, and wrenched the tomahawk from his grasp.

Maybe thirty seconds had passed since he'd jumped off the bank of the ravine and carried Roberts off his horse, and Zach knew he was going to have to deal with Bledsoe. Bledsoe had a rifle, and though Zach hadn't spared his other adversary a glance, he figured Bledsoe was bound to be lining up a shot. He had to assume so. He was spending too much time on Roberts. He had to finish the man off, and do it quick.

But Roberts wasn't all out of fight. He grabbed Zach's ankle and yanked his leg out from under him. Zach fell, rolled, kicked, trying to get free, but Roberts was clawing at him, trying to keep him down. And now Zach did spare Bledsoe an apprehensive glance, and saw that he was right. Bledsoe *was* lining up a shot.

Zach leaned forward and buried the tomahawk in Roberts's back, between the shoulder blades.

Roberts screamed; his body arched, went rigid. Blood from his ruined mouth sprayed Zach.

Zach pulled the tomahawk free and kicked clear of the dying man. He rolled, came up on one knee, and reared back to hurl the tomahawk at Bledsoe.

But Bledsoe fired his rifle before Zach could throw the war hatchet.

The bullet slammed into Zach and knocked him backwards.

Bledsoe kicked his horse forward with a triumphant yell. He dropped the empty rifle and pulled a pistol from his belt. Checking the pony alongside Zach's motionless form, he pointed the pistol at Zach's head.

Hannah looked dead.

But, then, Bledsoe had thought this man was dead—or close enough to dead to qualify—once before.

This time he wouldn't take any chances.

He thumbed back the hammer of the pistol and aimed at a spot between Zach's eyes.

Zach surged upward and buried the tomahawk in Bledsoe's thigh.

Bledsoe howled. His horse reared. At the same time, Zach tried to pull himself upright, using the hatchet planted in Bledsoe's leg as a man scaling a steep slope of glacial ice might use a pick to haul himself up a few more feet.

He clawed at Bledsoe's woolen coat, then found himself lifted clean off the ground as Bledsoe's pony stood on its hind legs. Zach threw a leg over the pony's haunches. Bledsoe came out of the saddle and Zach slipped off the back of the horse, dragging Bledsoe with him. The pistol in Bledsoe's hand went off, but the ball it discharged plowed harmlessly into the snow.

The deep snow cushioned their fall; Bledsoe escaped Zach's clutches and scrambled away, the tomahawk still buried in his leg. Snarling like a wild animal, he grabbed the handle of the Sioux war hatchet with both hands and pulled. His roar of pain and rage seemed, thought Zach, to fill the entire valley and rise up to bounce off the grim gray peaks frowning down on them.

Bloody tomahawk in hand, Bledsoe somehow managed to get to his feet and lurch towards Zach.

Zach was slow in getting up. The bullet had hit him high on the right side. He felt numb, cold and weak. He'd been shot before—he knew the feeling was shock, and he knew he had to resist succumbing to its effects. He fumbled for the knife in his belt, praying it was there, aware that if it wasn't he was a dead man. He was suddenly very much afraid of Bledsoe, as anyone in his right mind would be of a man who had extracted a tomahawk from his own flesh and was on his feet waving the damned weapon around.

The knife was there. Bledsoe was there, too, bringing the hatchet down, screaming gutturally, his features a horrible twisted mask of pain and hate.

Zach fell backwards in the face of this onslaught. Bledsoe stumbled and came down on top of him. Zach drove the knife into Bledsoe's chest, turning the blade sideways so that it slipped neatly between the ribs. The tomahawk missed Zach's head by a scant inch, clipping some of his long flax-colored hair. Bledsoe spasmed; then his body went limp. The knife had pierced his heart, killing him instantly. Zach used all the strength he had left to push the corpse aside.

He lay there, trying to muster enough get-up-and-go just to get up, but all he wanted was to lie there in the blood-splattered snow and sleep for a while. By sheer force of indomitable will he rolled over, made it first to hands and knees, finally to his feet.

Standing there, swaying slightly, he surveyed the carnage. All the horses were gone. At least Bledsoe's and the other trapper's, and the stray they had been after. He checked the rim of the ravine and saw with relief that his pony was still around.

Impassive, he stripped the corpses, taking leggins and buckskin shirts and buffalo robe and woolen coat, leather belts, a pair of moccasins, knives, a pistol, rifles. He put some of the clothes on, discarding his makeshift buffalo robe and Indian breechclout. The rest he bundled up in a blanket, retrieved his Hawken, and struggled up the steep embankment. Achieving the rim, he looked down once more at the naked, bloody bodies of Bledsoe and Roberts. He felt no remorse.

They had brought it on themselves, he thought, by being party to the bloodthirsty scheme hatched by Major Vanderburg and his American Fur Company cronies. They had suffered the consequences.

There were five more who had to pay.

He mounted up and rode deeper into the trees.

VIII

Bledsoe's horse returned to the brigade's winter camp that evening.

Keller and Baptiste had just gotten back from their

horse-hunting foray. Their outing had been success-ful, and now the brigade had six more horses. So the next morning Devlin picked a horse and joined them to ride out in search of Bledsoe and Roberts, leaving Dutch William—still not fully recovered from his en-counter with the unknown assailant three nights earlier—Hogan, and Flower behind.

They had no problems backtracking the horse all the way to the ravine.

What he saw there made Devlin's stomach do a slow roll.

"Jesus Christ," he muttered.

Keller was already checking the ground. Devlin didn't know how a man could make much sense of sign in this churned-up snow. But Keller perused the ravine for a while. He picked up something Devlin couldn't identify at this distance. Then he rode off a little ways. Meanwhile Baptiste and Devlin sat their horses, rifles ready, eyes peeled. Neither man spoke, each keeping his thoughts to himself.

Devlin was thinking it was time to quit this valley, dead of winter notwithstanding.

He had pretty much made up his mind on that score by the time Keller came back.

"How many?" asked Baptiste.

He meant how many hostiles had been involved in killing Bledsoe and Roberts.

"One man."

Devlin's blood ran cold.

"One man did this?" he protested.

The impassive Keller nodded.

"One man," murmured Devlin. "One man took Dutch William on hand to hand, and won. And one man killed Bledsoe and Roberts, and that close work, too, with knife and tomahawk, by the look of it."

"Tall job for one man," remarked Keller.

And Devlin was thinking there was only one man he knew of who could do it.

But Zach Hannah was dead.

Wasn't he?

"By the way," said Keller. "I found this down yonder."

He produced the breechclout.

"It's Blackfoot-made," he added.

"God," said Devlin.

"Warn't a Blackfoot, though," opined Keller.

"How do you know?" asked Baptiste.

"A few things. Most of all, though, no Blackfoot would've left their hair on their heads. Besides, the man Dutch fought warn't an Injun. That man, and the one who done this, are the same. I'd bet my possibles on all."

Devlin nodded. "Yes, it's the same man."

The others looked at him. The way he said it sounded like he knew exactly who that man was.

"It's Zach Hannah," said Devlin.

"*Sacre bleu!*" exclaimed Baptiste.

"You swore he was dead," said Keller.

"Well, he's not," replied Devlin, with conviction. "Somehow he got away from the Blackfeet. I wasn't sure when Dutch William tried to describe the man he tangled with, 'cause it was clear Dutch never got a good look at him. But Dutch did say the man had yellow hair."

"Hannah ain't the only yeller-haired pilgrim west of the Big Muddy," said Keller.

"I know. But now, this Blackfoot breechclout. When I last set eyes on Zach he was wearing Blackfoot gear. It's him. I just know it."

Baptiste was warily scanning the surrounding woods, a tight grip on his rifle.

"He's come back," continued Devlin flatly, "for the plews we stole from his brigade."

"That all?" asked Keller.

Devlin fired a sharp glance at him. "Probably not. I reckon he's come back to kill us, too, on account of what we done. We killed one of his men."

"You mean the Blackfeet did."

"Same thing. I brought Scar's bunch here. We as much as killed him. At least, that's the way Zach will see it. And since he's a booshway, he's responsible for evening the score."

"Mebbe it's you he wants to kill most," said Baptiste.

"Whatever he wants," said Keller, "it don't much matter. He's here, and he's declared war. So what do we do?"

"Track him down and kill him," said Baptiste.

"You won't find Hannah if he don't want to be found," said Keller. "I say if it's the plews he's after, maybe we can use them hairy bank notes to lure him into a trap."

Baptiste shook his head emphatically.

"No, that will not work. Hannah will not walk into a trap."

"We'll ride out," said Devlin.

"What?" It was Keller's turn to shake his head. "In the middle of winter? Pack out? No."

"We don't have enough horses, for one thing," said Baptiste. "You would have us leave our plews?"

"No," said Devlin. "We'll use all the horses we have for packing out the plews. All of us will walk back to Fort Union, if that's what it takes. I'll be damned if I'll just give them up to Hannah. But I won't play his game, either. He'll wait out there, damn his eyes, for as long as it takes—until we get careless and he can get one or two of us at a time. We can't find him, and we can't just sit and wait for him to kill us. So we'll leave. Take all we can and destroy the rest."

"Destroy?" echoed Keller.

"Yeah. Cut the plews up. Burn 'em. I don't care. But he won't get a single pelt back. And he won't get us, either, if we stick together and move out quick. We can make it to Fort Union. Might not be easy, in this snow, but we can do it."

Keller and Baptiste exchanged glances. Neither one of them was particularly eager to tackle Zach Hannah. But they both felt as though Devlin's plan was akin to tucking their tails between their legs and skulking away like yellow dogs, and their mountain man pride rebelled against that.

"Look," said Devlin, knowing exactly how their minds worked, "we've got a fortune in brown gold back in camp. More plews than any brigade I've ever been a part of has hauled in from one season's work. I say to hell with Zach Hannah. Let's take those furs back to Fort Union, and every last one of us will be richer than we've ever been before."

Greed was a great motivator, and Devlin knew it. It was the only thing that could conquer pride.

Baptiste caved in first. "I think you are right, Devlin."

"I dunno," said Keller. "Hannah's got it in for all of us, and I ain't in the habit of leaving a man above snakes who wants my scalp. Reckon 'cause I don't hanker to have to keep lookin' over my shoulder all the time."

"Stay if you want," said Devlin. "The rest of us are leaving." He was confident Hogan and Dutch William would follow his lead. Bledsoe might have stayed behind along with Keller, being the type who liked nothing better than a fight. But Bledsoe was dead. "We'll take the plews, and set aside your share of the profits, in case you manage to make it back."

By his tone of voice, it was obvious that Devlin didn't think there was even a remote possibility that Keller would survive a showdown with Zach Hannah in the snowbound valley.

Keller mulled it over for a moment. Then he shook his head. "No. It ain't that I wouldn't trust you boys with my share, but I'll go along with you."

Devlin suppressed a cold, self-satisfied smile. Of

course, that was exactly why Keller was going along, because he didn't trust his partners.

And Devlin didn't blame him one bit.

IX

The previous summer, Zach had found a shallow cave sheltered by a jutting brow of rock, up on the shoulder of a mountain, a thousand feet above the valley's floor. He had realized then what a good spot it would be for a man who needed a place to hide. Where the Blackfeet roamed, a wise man always took note of such places.

There was water conveniently close by, a creek fed by the snowfields thousands of feet higher. The creek just cascaded straight down the mountain, falling over the ledge within spitting distance of the cave.

Long ago a rockslide had cleared out the trees directly below the cave, providing an open field of fire and a splendid view of the valley below. Aspen and conifers on either side of the clearing provided abundant firewood as well as a perfect place to keep a horse—or a whole cavallard, for that matter, out of sight.

This had been Zach's base of operations since his return to the valley, and here he repaired followed the fight with Bledsoe and Roberts.

He built a fire with smokeless aspen wood, heated a knife, and got to work on the bullet in him, trying to extract the half-ounce ball of Galena lead from his flesh. When the bullet finally came out, he slapped on an already-prepared poultice of tree moss and frozen mud. Then he lay his aching body down, pulled a blanket and buffalo robe over him, and passed out.

Late in the afternoon he regained consciousness. He felt light-headed and nauseated from loss of blood. Though he didn't feel like eating—or even moving, for that matter—he spitted what was left of a snowshoe rabbit he had snared the day before, cooked it over the stirred-up fire, and ate. He felt considerably better after eating and went back to sleep. His body was crying out for more rest.

He slept the night through and woke at daybreak. At first the floor of the valley was completely obscured by a frost haze. He wondered if Devlin and the others had found Bledsoe and Roberts. If so, what had been their response? He figured Devlin would vote for sitting tight at the winter camp. Keller and Baptiste, by their very natures, would be inclined to go out and hunt him down. He knew he was in no condition to fight again anytime soon. At least a couple of days to recupcrate was what his battered body required. Later today, he decided, he would venture down to see what the American Fur Company boys were up to. But he would be careful to avoid a confrontation. There was no hurry. They weren't going anywhere until green-up.

So when he saw them—when the haze dissipated finally and he could see the valley floor, and the single-file line far below, scarcely more than black specks moving across the snow—he was more than surprised.

It had to be Devlin and his brigade. No question about that. They were heading for the southern passes, the only exits from the valley this time of year.

Zach knew what he had to do. It didn't require a conscious decision.

He wasn't going to let those plews—and Devlin— slip through his fingers.

He armed himself. Two flintlock pistols, primed and loaded, went under his belt. Bledsoe's rifle, and the one which had belonged to Roberts, were slung on his back. He carried the Hawken in its beaded leather sheath. The beadwork brought Morning Sky to mind. Not that she was ever far from his thoughts. She had made the fringed rifle sheath for him. He didn't think much about seeing her again. He figured he wouldn't, probably. *Not now.* But that was acceptable, as long as he killed Coyote today before he died. Then he would know—and perhaps it would be his last thought –that Sky and little Jacob would never be terrorized by Sean Michael Devlin again.

Leaving the cave, he made his way down into the trees where his horse was waiting. He tried to grit his teeth against the pain from his wound. Walking was bad enough. Riding was worse. But he stayed with it, and rode down through the forest, setting a course to intercept the American Fur Company brigade.

* * *

Devlin couldn't wait to get out of the valley.

They didn't seem to be making enough progress—at least not enough to suit him—but none of them were riding. Not even Flower. She was leading one horse and each of the five men was leading two. Every pony was laden with packs of plews. It was the biggest haul Devlin had ever seen. All they had to do was get out of the valley alive and deliver the furs to Fort Union and they would be sitting pretty.

Devlin had already decided that he would take his share in hard money. The bosses of the American Fur Company didn't like paying off in coin. They preferred trading whiskey and tobacco and lead and shot for the furs their trappers brought in. That way they made the profits twice. But they could not refuse to pay in gold if a trapper insisted. And Devlin was going to insist—because as of earlier today, when he realized Zach Hannah was still alive, Devlin had made up his mind to leave the high country.

He had it all planned out. He would go back to the river, and maybe parlay the stake he got for his share of these plews into bigger money by way of the gaming table. Then he would hire his own men, and they would have one mission: to find Morning Sky and his son. If he was lucky, one of them would kill Hannah in the process.

That was why though sometimes he wanted to run, he couldn't. It had nothing to do with pride. But he had to have these plews. They were the key to his future. His ticket out of the mountains. He would be safe from Hannah on the river. Zach would never leave the mountains. No matter what.

"Look!" shouted Keller.

The sharply spoken word dragged Devlin back to the present. He had been thinking about wearing hand-tailored broadcloth and brand new nankeen trousers and footwear that someone else could polish to a high sheen, and silk cravats; he would drink champagne and smoke expensive cigars and eat rich food and people would call him *Mister* Devlin. They would respect him, and fear him too. All he had to do was let them know he was the man who had killed Mike Fink. Everybody had known that Mike Fink, King of the Keelboat Men, had been a tough customer. They would walk a long way around Devlin once they knew he was Fink's killer.

But when he looked in the direction Keller was pointing, Devlin forgot all his plans.

His future looked bleak, suddenly.

A lone rider, directly in their path, an arrow's flight away.

"Where'd he come from?" asked Hogan.

"One minute he wasn't there," said Keller. "Next minute he was. Like he just rose up out of the ground."

"It is Hannah," said Baptiste.

Devlin knew it was, too.

For a moment no one spoke.

Then Keller turned sharply, knife in hand, and cut the ropes which secured the packs to one of the horses in his keeping. He vaulted onto the pony and unsheathed his rifle.

"Hannah's made a mistake," he said grimly. "He's come out into the open. One man alone, and there's five of us. I say we go kill him and be done with it."

Baptiste was already clearing the packs from one of his horses. Hogan followed suit. Dutch William did likewise.

"Well, Devlin?" asked Keller.

Devlin drew his knife and cut the packs off one of his ponies.

Baptiste told Flower to stay put and hold the rest of the horses.

Then the five of them rode forward to do battle.

X

Zach did not have a plan of action. He figured to let what his adversaries did determine what he did. Expecting them to take a defensive stand once they saw him, perhaps dismounting and seeking cover behind their horses, he was surprised to see them attacking. Surprised, but not dismayed. He had three rifles—with any luck he could pick three of them off before they got close.

He resolved to start with Devlin.

But Devlin refused to play his game.

When Keller, Baptiste, Hogan, and Dutch William rode straight at Zach, Devlin pulled back, then swung his horse around and returned to the spot where Flower was holding the other horses.

Zach knew right then and there that Coyote was going to run.

Which meant he had to change his plan. He wasn't going to let Devlin get away from him this time.

Devlin reached Flower and tried to jerk the lead ropes out of her hands. The Shoshone woman resisted, not knowing exactly why. Devlin's actions perplexed her, but she sensed he was up to no good.

Cursing bitterly, Devlin kicked her in the face.

Flower sprawled in the snow, stunned but not unconscious. Devlin reached out and hauled in two lead ropes. He didn't care which two. He had already decided that two pack horses were all he could handle. That was his fair share, anyway. The others could take Zach Hannah on if they were foolish enough to try. Not him. He only hoped the other American Fur Company men would occupy Zach long enough for him to get a good head start.

Once he had the lead ropes, Devlin turned for the nearest line of trees. While the others fought it out in the open, he would circle around in the cover of the forest and make tracks for the southern passes.

Unfortunately for Devlin, Baptiste happened to look around for him and noticed he wasn't participating in the charge.

It had suddenly occurred to the French-Canadian that Devlin might try to hang back out of harm's way;

Baptiste had suspected Coyote of a yellow streak all along, his fearsome reputation notwithstanding.

The timing was very bad for Devlin, because Baptiste checked over his shoulder just when Devlin kicked Flower in the face.

Something snapped inside Baptiste. While he had always pretended that the Shoshone woman meant nothing to him—at least nothing more than someone to mend his clothes and cook his food and warm his blankets—Baptiste could no longer imagine life without Flower. He whipped his pony around, let out a guttural cry, and forgot all about Zach Hannah.

He was going to kill Coyote.

Baptiste's actions left Zach with only three American Fur Company men to deal with. He had already unslung Bledsoe's rifle, which he had in his left hand. The Hawken was in his right. He rode straight at the three, reins in his teeth.

Hogan fired at him from a hundred yards away, and missed. Zach waited until that distance was halved—a matter of seconds—before returning fire. Hogan somersaulted off his pony, shot in the chest.

Dutch William and Keller both fired their rifles at Zach, and both men missed, but Keller's bullet struck Zach's horse. The pony stumbled and fell, plowing into the snow on its side, legs thrashing. Zach let go of the empty rifle but held onto the Hawken for dear life. He hit the ground, the fall cushioned by the snow, got up on one knee, drew a bead on Dutch William as the frontier giant galloped past, a stone's throw away. Dutch William was pulling a pistol from his belt. Zach killed him before he could use it, instinctively going for a head shot. With a man so huge, a head shot was the best bet. Dutch William was dead before he hit the ground.

Zach whirled to confront Keller, who had turned his horse and was coming straight at him. Keller didn't waste time trying to reload his rifle; he discarded the long gun and brandished a pistol. Zach dropped the Hawken and pulled both of his pistols.

Meanwhile, Baptiste was going after Devlin, angling his horse to intercept Coyote, who was already making for the woods. Devlin saw him and knew immediately that the French-Canadian wasn't coming to pass the time of day. He also knew that Baptiste would catch him before he made it to the trees—the two pack horses labored in the snow just to maintain a loping gait.

So he checked his horse and dismounted. Bracing the rifle across the saddle, he aimed and fired.

Baptiste was already so close that Devlin saw the puff of dust off the man's buffalo robe as the bullet struck. To Devlin's great fear and astonishment, the bullet seemed to have no visible effect. Devlin's knees went rubbery. He wanted to run for his life, and to hell with the plews, but he couldn't. He just stood there, rooted to the ground, waiting to die.

The French-Canadian was almost upon him when he suddenly slipped sideways off his horse.

Numb with relief, Devlin jumped on his horse, kicked it into motion, and plunged into the woods, dragging the pack horses along.

Zach had a pair of pistols, Keller had one. All three were discharged almost at once, at a range of thirty feet. Keller was hit once, in the shoulder. Zach, too, was hit, in the leg. Keller hurled himself off his horse and bore Zach to the ground. Zach hardly felt the leg wound, but the pain from his other wound, which was bleeding again, was worse than ever. He almost blacked out. Keller drew his knife, intent on plunging it into Zach's heart. Zach clutched Keller's arm, but Keller was strong—too strong. Zach knew he'd met his match. Somehow he had known all along that of the American Fur Company men, Keller was the one to watch out for.

The knife came down . . .

Zach dimly heard the rifle shot.

The impact of the bullet knocked Keller sideways off of him. Keller squirmed briefly in the snow before lying forever still.

Zach drifted into unconsciousness . . .

When he came to, Shadmore was leaning over him. He was still on the ground, but they had put him on a buffalo robe to get him out of the snow.

"Devlin," he said, trying to get up.

Shadmore held him down. It wasn't hard to do. Zach was weak as a lamb.

"Never saw Coyote. Was he here?"

"Got to catch him . . ."

"I'll send Montez out after him. You ain't goin' nowhere, hoss. You're more than half kilt. Thanks to young Jubal's long shot, you're still above snakes, but not by much."

"Can't let him get away."

"His day'll come. I swear, Zach, ever' time I figure you fer dead you show up agin. We got here yesterday, found their camp, figured to hit it this morning. But when the fog lifted they were gone. Got here fast as we could, but . . ."

Sky . . . is she safe?"

"Safe and sound. Soon as I get you patched up and fit to ride, I'll take you to her."

The thought of seeing Morning Sky again gave Zach new strength.

"I can ride," he breathed, but then he drifted away again.

This time he had a smile on his face.

Here's a preview of the final part
of the *High Country* trilogy,
Battle of the Teton Basin,
coming from Signet
in February 1994.

Josey Lane was a trapper. For almost a year he had
been employed by the American Fur Company. Having come west the previous summer, he had survived
his first winter in the high country and was there-
fore, by most standards, justified in calling himself a
mountain man.

Oh, and what a winter it had been! Lane had
never seen the likes back home in the red hills of
northern Georgia. It had been so cold that the creeks
froze clear to the bottom and bank to bank. Trees
cracked in two. Critters floundered in deep snow-
banks and died. So cold that the spittle froze on a
man's whiskers, and his fingers would freeze to the
barrel of his rifle or the blade of his knife were he so
greenhorn-careless as to allow that to happen. So
cold that at times Lane could have sworn the blood
was frozen solid in his veins.

Doc Letcher, the brigade's booshway, had told him
something about an "invincible summer in the
heart." Quoting some Greek poet. Or was it Roman?

Lane couldn't rightly remember which. How had Letcher put it? Something like how in the bleakest winter of life a man had to find that invincible summer down deep inside himself if he wanted to survive.

Letcher was a puzzlement, mused Josey Lane, as he sat on his heels, rifle cradled in his arms, at the rim of a cutbank, above a purling creek that danced down the heavily wooded slope of a mountain in the Absaroka Range. Letcher talked like a schoolteacher or a politician. Real educated. Used fancy words and was always quoting poets and such. Read books—which, in Lane's opinion, since he could neither read nor write a lick, was really something.

Yet in spite of all that fancy talk and book-larnin', Doc Letcher was as tough as they came. He'd been in the mountains for years. He knew it all. They called him Doc not because he was a medical man but because one day, having taken a Crow arrow in the thigh, he had calmly used balsam sap and a poultice of beaver skin to close up the wound. He still carried the arrowhead in him. That was the thing about mountain men. Minor wounds—in other words, any that were not fatal—were treated in a cursory manner, if not ignored altogether.

Yes, Letcher knew his way around the *pays d'en haut,* as the French-Canadian *voyageurs* called the high country. He had tangled with grizzlies. Had tangled with Indians too. That was one thing Josey Lane had not done—not yet, anyway. He figured he would, though, sooner or later. It was just bound to happen, did a man stay out here long enough. Lane dreaded the day and looked forward to it at the same time. To be an Indian fighter—now, that was really something. Lane's pa had fought the Creed Red Sticks with Andy Jackson. His pa had also declared him to be a lazy, no-account shirker because Josey Lane hated farm drudgery with a holy passion. It was in large measure this difference of opinion concerning Josey's worth that had compelled the youngster to head west and engage in the glamorous adventure of fur trapping.

Of course he had found out that there wasn't that much glamor in the business after all. Proof was his partner, Doc Letcher's brother, Hampton, wading up to his waist in the creek yonder. The sky was clear blue and the spring day sultry, but this creek was glacier-fed, and the water was bone-biting cold. Hampton was checking their traps. Mountain men always worked in pairs. All sorts of disasters could befall a trapper, and his chances were made a little better if he had company. One man watched while the other toiled. Lane and Hampton took turns, and Lane always preferred keeping an eye peeled to getting his feet wet in some icy stream.

Lane looked off up-creek, where the water came gamboling down the mountain through the towering conifers, cascading over jumbles of smooth rock. A magpie was winging from tree to tree, and the flash of black and white had captured Lane's attention. He yawned. The song of the creek and the soughing of the wind in the boughs of the evergreens, the air in his lungs as clean and sweet as wine, and the sun warm on his back, made him drowsy.

"Wagh!"

Lane turned his attention back to Hampton. The latter had found brown gold. He was hauling drowned beaver, trap and all, to the opposite bank, a stone's throw downstream. A full-grown beaver could weigh sixty pounds, and this one looked every bit of that. But Hampton was a burly character. On dry land, he commenced to skinning the beaver.

The pelt, bait gland, and tail was all he would retain. The skinned and mutilated carcass would be returned to the creek. The pelt would be scraped by one of the camp-tenders—in this brigade's case, two Flathead squaws—then stretched on a willow hoop and set in the sun for a day or two before being folded fur side in. Once eighty or so "hairy banknotes" were collected, a pack was made up utilizing a scissor-press of wood and rawhide. The castoreum would be extracted from the bait gland, and the rancorous orange-brown fluid stored in a horn vial until needed to bait a trap. The tail would be charred over a fire and then boiled—or basted with wild goose oil, if such was available—for good eating. It was the only part of the beaver worth eating unless you were starving. Old timers would tell you beaver meat had to be soaked in water for a short forever and then heavily seasoned with gunpowder just to render it barely edible.

Lane stood and stretched the kinks out of his legs. He figured to wander across the creek to see what kind of pelt they had harvested. If it was especially fine—a "plew"—it might bring six or eight dollars, assuming the market this year was anything like last year's. Of course, the company realized the lion's share of the take. A mountain man's percentage of the pelts he brought in was enough to pay for powder and shot, some whiskey and tobacco, and maybe some trinkets for his squaw (if he had himself one to warm his blankets and mend his buckskins).

So Lane figured he had a vested interest in the condition of the beaver skin—enough of one, anyway, to warrant wading that ice-cold creek. He was especially interested in acquiring some trinkets, and with such fofarraw enticing some young Indian maiden into becoming his squaw. Being young himself, not yet quite eighteen, Josey Lane had never known a woman, and he was ready for the experience.

Then he stopped dead in his tracks, paralyzed with fear. An Indian had burst out of the woods behind Hampton and was running towards the trapper with tomahawk raised.

Lane tried to yell a warning. It came out an incoherent yelp. Hampton looked up at him, a querulous look on his bearded face. But then he heard the Indian behind him and whirled. He had set his rifle aside to skin the beaver—all he had in his hand was the bloody skinning knife. This he raised, dropping into a crouch. He dodged the down-swing of the tomahawk, ducking under it and planting a shoulder in the redskin's breadbasket. Then he straightened up and heaved the warrior over his shoulder. The brave splashing into the creek. Hampton turned to finish him off. A rifle spoke from the trees. Hampton went rigid, then crumpled, shot in the back.

More Indians emerged from the cover of the woods. The warm, clear spring air rang with their bloodcurdling war cries.

Josey Lane turned and ran.

Josey Lane and Hampton Letcher had tethered their horses a hundred yards upstream, having decided to work their way down the creek to check the seven traps set in this particular stretch. The horses were Lane's destination.

He did not even consider using his rifle, or the pistol in his belt. Flight alone occupied his thoughts. His skin crawled, as though a thousand invisible graybacks were swarming all over his body. Letcher was dead—wasn't he? Lane threw one wild look back. He immediately wished he hadn't because he looked in time to see one of the Indians bend down and, with a few deft strokes of a knife, lift Hampton's scalp. The brave held his bloody trophy aloft and uttered a horrible, guttural scream of triumph that chilled Lane to the bone marrow. The young trapper made a strangled sound. Completely unnerved, he stumbled on.

Two warriors broke cover upstream, on the same side of the creek. They blocked his escape.

Lane fetched up. The pair of Indians started for him. They were yelping like wolves on the heels of a wounded elk. So were the ones behind him. Lane looked back again. A few of the braves were crossing the creek to get to his side. Most, though, were coming up the other side at a loping run, and were about to draw abreast of him. Several more, apparently, were rustling around in the brush to his right. He couldn't see the latter, but he heard them yelping. All he could do was take to the creek. He jumped off the cutbank.

It was his hope to land on his feet, but the current was too swift and swept his legs out from under him. He went under and lost his grip on the rifle. He was slammed against a submerged rock. The impact knocked the breath out of him. He choked down some water. He was drowning! In a panic he flailed to the surface, gasped for air, but gagged on the water in his gullet. Vision blurred, heart racing, he stumbled forward, fighting the current. He kept thinking about the horses. Once mounted he could escape these fiends. Letting the current sweep him downstream did not even occur to him. My God, how many of them were there? Some lookout he was, letting a whole war party sneak up on him and poor Hampton.

The waist-high water worked against him, and he cursed it, struggling to maintain his footing, striving to make some headway. Suddenly he was out of the main channel. Now the water was only knee-high. Now he could make better progress. They were all around him, those screaming savages. Why didn't they shoot? Lane thought suddenly about the red clay hills of Georgia and sobbed.

Ahead loomed a daunting obstacle—something he had been aware of before the attack, but had since forgotten all about. A line of boulders that the creek flowed over and between blocked his path. Lane tried to clamber up these water-smoothed rocks. He clawed at the slippery granite to no avail. He couldn't make it. Wheezing, he turned at bay, his back to one of the boulders. It was deeper here at the foot of the falls. The water came up to his chest. As an afterthought, he dragged the pistol out of his belt. Of course, it was perfectly useless now. The powder was wet. With sickening despair, Lane knew he was doomed.

Why didn't they just kill him and be done with it? But the Indians were still on the banks of the creek. They were taunting him. Laughing at him.

Josey Lane got mad then. It was bad enough that he had to die. But by God, they didn't have to laugh at him while they killed him!

The fear left him. In its place came a cold and defiant hatred for those red devils. He waded out of the creek. As he approached the bank, the Indians stopped laughing. They watched him warily, weapons raised. Most of them had rifles. Why didn't they use them?

"Go on and shoot!" he yelled, so angry he choked on the words.

Not one of them fired. They weren't sure what to make of him, realized Lane. It was his turn to laugh.

Not a very good laugh, but it made him feel a little better. Sloshing out of the creek, he headed for the nearest warrior. Five paces away he stopped and raised the pistol, aiming at the Indian's head.

The warrior, and several others, fired simultaneously. One of the bullets pierced Lane's heart. He was dead before he hit the ground.

Josey Lane died better than he had done anything else in his tragically brief life.

Through the morning mist they came, on mountain mustangs barely half-tame. There were three of them. Doc Letcher was in the lead, as usual. Leading was something Letcher was accustomed to. He had that self-confidence others looked for in their leaders. He made quick decisions, and they were usually the right ones.

He was a tall, lean man, with eyes as blue as glacier ice, and hair as black as the ace of spades. Unlike most mountain men, he kept himself clean-shaven. With his sun-darkened complexion and longish raven-black hair and his grime-blackened buckskins, he looked more Indian than white. Except for those keen blue eyes, which saw everything, and moreover understood the true meaning behind what they saw.

Letcher's burnished bronze face was set in grim lines as he reached the creek where the water fell over the row of boulders. His horse snorted, the smell of death invading its flaring nostrils, and performed a nervous dance. With firm hand Letcher brought the animal under control.

"Jaysus," breathed one of his companions, both of whom had checked their ponies alongside Letcher's.

The man who spoke was named McLeary. A red-headed, red-faced Irishman who, in Letcher's opinion, drank too much, swore too much, and talked too much. He wasn't very bright, either. Letcher came across few men out here who were his equal in intellect, and he made an effort not to appear condescending when dealing with his colleagues.

"It's young Lane," said McLeary, staring at the body across the creek.

"Yes," said Letcher curtly. He wanted to tell McLeary he had been blessed with the gift of good eyesight and could tell for himself that it was Joseph Lane. Anger and grief were a violent rising tide within him, but he endeavored to keep his emotions in check. Because he knew at this moment that what he had been dreading since last night, when Hampton and Lane had failed to return to the brigade's camp, was true.

If Lane was dead, his brother was bound to be, as well.

"Injuns," muttered the third trapper, a man named Elias Turner. "They took his topknot."

But they didn't hack him to pieces, mused Letcher, trying to think in a detached, clinical way. They hadn't stripped the corpse and opened it up and scattered the guts all over the place. They hadn't cut off the private parts, or cut off all his fingers, or carved out his eyes with the tip of a knife.

Indians often mutilated corpses in that way, when consumed by blood-craze. But, save for his scalp, Lane had been left untouched. Why? The boy obviously had impressed his foes with his courage. It wasn't easy to earn the respect of Indians. They mutilated what they despised. Lane had earned preferential treatment, then, by dying well. For that, at least, Letcher silently congratulated the lad.

"Where's Hampton?" wondered McLeary. "You figure he's gone beaver? He must—"

He stopped abruptly because Letcher's cold blue eyes were boring holes right through him. The Irishman realized sheepishly—and with a strong dose of fear—that, as was so often the case, he had spoken without thinking. A bad habit that would one day get him killed.

"Come on," rasped Letcher, and took the lead.

He paused a little further along the creek, dismounting to kneel and study the ground. McLeary and Tucker kept to their saddles. Mounted so, they could see the moccasin prints in the dirt. Indians— but of what variety? Letcher would know. The man knew it all. He could smell an Indian a mile off and tell you what tribe the red devil belonged to.

Letcher stood. "Blackfoot," he said bleakly, looking around, scanning the woods.

The other trappers looked around too, their faces twin testaments to the fear which Letcher's grim-spoken word had lanced into their hearts.

"Maybe Hampton got away, Doc," offered Turner, but the others could tell by his tone of voice that he didn't believe it possible.

"My brother's dead," said Letcher bluntly.

"The Blackfeet used to be our allies," McLeary said plaintively. "Hell, Doc, we work for the American Fur Company, don't we? Don't that count for nothin' anymore? Don't we give them guns and firewater and such?"

"It doesn't cut us any slack with the Blackfeet. Not anymore. Not since Sean Devlin delivered the plague to Whirlwind's village up on the Judith River, winter before last."

"You sayin' Devlin's to blame for this?" asked Turner.

"He is, damn his soul," said Letcher through clenched teeth. " 'Murderous, bloody, full of blame.' " As Shakespeare's words left his lips, a cancer of vengeance clawed at his guts. "And he's going to pay for what happened here. Credit where credit is due."

"But he's long gone out of the high country," said Turner.

"No matter. Wherever he is, I'll find him." Letcher climbed back into his saddle. He flexed broad shoulders and took a deep breath. What was done was done. The dead were dead, and the living kept on living. In Devlin's case, for just a little while longer. "Come on," he told the others, "let's find my brother's mortal remains."

By the year 2000, 2 out of 3 Americans could be illiterate.

It's true.

Today, 75 million adults...about one American in three, can't read adequately. And by the year 2000, U.S. News & World Report envisions an America with a literacy rate of only 30%.

Before that America comes to be, you can stop it...by joining the fight against illiteracy today.

Call the Coalition for Literacy at toll-free **1-800-228-8813** and volunteer.

Volunteer Against Illiteracy. The only degree you need is a degree of caring.